C000214268

Elissa's Castle
Juliet Greenwood

Other titles published by transita

Forgotten Dreams by Doris Leadbetter
Scuba Dancing by Nicola Slade
The Waiting Time by Sara Banerji
Turning Point by Bowering Sivers
Uphill All the Way by Sue Moorcroft

transita

Transita books reflect the lives of mature women.
Contemporary women with rich and interesting stories to
tell, stories that explore the truths and desires that colour
their lives.

The books are about women who *want* to change, or *have* to
change – and who find courage, strength, humour and love
in the process.

To find out more about transita, our books and our authors
visit **www.transita.co.uk**

Elissa's Castle

Juliet Greenwood

transita

Published by Transita
3 Newtec Place, Magdalen Road,
Oxford OX4 1RE. United Kingdom.
Tel: (01865) 204393. Fax: (01865) 248780.
email: info@transita.co.uk
www.transita.co.uk

British Library Cataloguing in Publication Data
A catalogue record for this book is available from the British Library

Cover design by Baseline Arts Ltd, Oxford
Produced for Transita by Deer Park Productions, Tavistock
Typeset by PDQ Typesetting, Newcastle-under-Lyme
Printed and bound by Bookmarque, Croydon

ABOUT THE AUTHOR

Juliet Greenwood grew up near Birmingham, where she received an 'alternative education' at a Rudolph Steiner School. Although she always dreamed of becoming a writer, she only began to seriously work at her writing when she was 'retired' on health grounds at the age of 35 suffering from ME.

The turning-point for Juilet as a novelist came when she joined the Romantic Novelist's Association and their New Writer's Scheme. Writing as 'Heather Pardoe', she has short stories regularly published in magazines, as well as five novelettes accepted for the 'My Weeky Story Collection'.

Juliet has always had family living in North Wales and has visited the area frequently since she was six month's old. For almost twenty years, she has lived in Snowdonia in a traditional cottage on the outskirts of a village halfway between Conwy Castle and Snowdon. Elissa's Castle is her first full-length novel, and is loosely based on a real incident that demonstrated to Juliet the universally acknowledged truth that (with apologies to Jane Austen) 'a single woman of middle years, being in possession of property and a reasonable income, *must* be in want of a husband'.

ACKNOWLEDGEMENTS

Thank you to everyone at 'Transita' for their enthusiasm and support, and in particular my Editor, Marina Oliver. Thank you also to the RNA and its wonderful New Writer's Scheme, to which I owe more than I can ever fully express.

Thank you to all my friends for cheering me on.

To Sally Hanson, Frances Cox and Ruth Bitowski for good food, red wine and great conversations.

To Annette Morris for being brave enough to help me collect the short story awards and make sure I didn't run away.

To Miranda Griffith, Owen Glynne, and Anita Anderson for all their help and advice.

To Dave, Nerys, Delyth and Catrin Haynes for looking after the assorted menagerie when I'm away.

And to my family, for their love and understanding.

WELSH VOCABULARY

Ach a fi	Ugh, yuck – expression of disgust
Arglwydd Mawr!	Good Lord!
Bechod	How sweet/what a shame ('Bless')
Cariad	Term of endearment – darling
Cyw	Literally 'chick'. Like 'chuck', or 'ducks'
Diawl	Literally 'Devil'. Bugger!
Duw	Literally 'God' – Heavens! Lord!
Mochyn	Pig
Panad	Cup of tea
Uffern dân	Literally 'Hell fire' – bloody hell!
Ysbyty	Hospital

CHAPTER 1

O K, SO I DIDN'T INTEND TO BUY A CASTLE.
It was the row of quarrymen's cottages, the last remainders of the slate quarries that still scar the hillsides grey, right up into the horseshoe curve of Snowdon itself, that caught my eye on that clear, sharp winter's morning of my fifty-second birthday.

Now, a chick I am not. I am too old to be sentimental; too mature to be fluffy. It was my businesswoman's head that eyed those cottages, without the faintest thought passing through of preserving or restoring anything.

The cottages stood in the photograph in the window of Griffiths and Jones, Estate Agents, on the sunny side of Llanestyn High Street. They were shown to be perched on a picturesque hillside you would never guess – from a casual glance, at least – was marooned by ice in the winter, with gales howling in from the Menai Straits, straight from crossing the sea from Ireland all the rest of the year round.

They were tumbledown and neglected, with small, square extensions from the Seventies at the back to house both kitchen and bathroom, and the long, narrow gardens in front were overgrown and wild. To my eyes they were perfect.

Potential. That was always my strength, so Robin, my most trusted surveyor, always told me: the spotting of potential, however obscure and unlikely. 'The Miss Marple of Snowdonia', he called me, in the years when I lived in Kingston-upon-Thames: looks harmless, with the long hair and the Indian-print skirts, but hiding the mind of a razor, is what he said he

1

meant. Since I had not yet spotted a grey hair amongst the brown (or 'rich chestnut', as my sister Cadi calls our mutual colouring), and had never been near a hat in my life, I was not entirely sure this was intended as a compliment.

But we go way back, Robin Lloyd Jones and I: way back to Llanestyn Primary, and many a bleak year in between, and I could forgive him almost anything. So I'd phone, and he would come down and give his professional opinion of my purchases with a detached, faintly amused, eye.

Not that I minded: detached amusement is a male defence mechanism when it comes to a female who unexpectedly shows brains, I've often found. Besides, it saved me from ever feeling obliged to sleep with him. Never sleep with a business partner: they never respect you afterwards, however smart your trouser suit and however sensible your heels the next day. Believe me, I know.

It was Potential that had saved us, the children and me, thirty years ago when Terry, (husband, erstwhile business partner) discovered a belated whiff of the Sixties and went off to Find Himself.

'But I'm leaving you the house, Elissa,' he said, his large, soft eyes darker than ever with the hurt of my irrational fury.

'The mortgage and the bills, you mean.'

'You've got your job. And your parents will help out, they're very good like that.'

Which they had been when the business somehow went belly-up amongst the flurry of a baby, who then became a toddler to occupy the day while his new little sister disturbed the night. But that was excruciatingly embarrassing, however nice they were about it, and not really the point. Mam and

2

Dad were not by any means rich, and they had their own lives to lead, and their own futures to think of. Besides, weren't we meant to be the grown-ups by now?

'You always manage, Elissa. It's what I admire about you. You were always so much stronger than me.'

Of course, nowadays experience has wrinkled the corners of my eyes and sharpened my vision no end. Nowadays, I'd tell him where to stick his admiration. Back then I was twenty-two. I thought I was so grown up and knowledgeable. I look at twenty-two-year-olds now and see they are still children: faces soft and unformed. Great flesh tones, but still clinging to their mother's milk for all their air of unassailable sophistication, egos fragile in the cold wind blowing outside the pampered warmth of the nest.

'And it isn't as if I've left you for another woman.'

Even then, that statement made me wonder what on earth I had ever seen in him. If he'd left me for another woman he'd have at least been a cad, a sod, a bastard. Leaving me in order to find a Higher Truth left me amongst the ignoble dross of humanity who can't think beyond where their next meal is coming from, and are content to chew the cud of ordinary existence.

Being twenty-two and swamped in the bewilderment of life, motherhood, and being grown up at all, I squashed the thought as that of an unfeeling cow, and therefore unworthy of me, and lapsed into feelings of inadequacy. My children screamed in public, spilled chocolate down their clothes and mine, and I couldn't even keep a husband for more than a couple of years: I cringe at the humiliation of it all, even now.

t, with only a rucksack and a change of clothes, d Himself. I've no doubt this also led to finding young women without stretch marks on their bellies, milk oozing from their nipples, and no sign of interest in sex or philosophy or the heavy trials of his day, and overcome by an overwhelming desire for sleep.

I tried not to think about that. But I couldn't avoid the postcards to the children from Paris, the Swiss Alps, a Greek island or so, Pisa, Pompeii, and Dubrovnik: all the places he and I had been, with rucksacks on our backs, in those brief years we were together before Merion and Katie had been born. Later, these progressed to game reserves in Africa, the mountains of the Andes, and an aerial view of New York. I couldn't compete with those. He had outstripped me in knowledge of the world; in daring and self-fulfilment. There was no doubt about it: here were the pictures to prove it.

And, meanwhile, I plodded on. I paid the mortgage, kept the old banger on the road, and helped the children with their first day at school, then the first day at secondary school, and homework. I had coffee with friends, and visited my mother in Llanestyn as often as I could afford the petrol. The usual kind of things.

Then Katie followed her brother into secondary school, and I discovered Potential. I'd decided to sell the house, and take the mortgage to a smaller one, where I could pay it off quicker and be free from peddling Life Assurance so that someone else could make a lot of money, and I could make a very little, so very much of which was swallowed up in child-care.

I looked around. Did the sums. Then, watching Merion and Katie playing with the tent in the garden one day, I had a blinding brainwave. One of those moments that can change your life for ever.

I read everything I could find on mortgages, interest, tenancy agreements and property management – no Internet in those days, of course – and then phoned Robin back in Llanestyn. We moved to a smaller house, all right, but I didn't sell a thing. Instead, I got tenants to pay the mortgage. You see, I had spotted that our new little house needed a bit of attention, but not that much. Then I could let it out, too, and move on. Onwards and upwards.

'Property is always a wise investment,' Robin remarked, approvingly, when I came back to visit Mam for a weekend, and she tried to set the two of us up. Well, we were both single, now, weren't we? I was still all hedgehog prickles as far as romance was concerned. But Robin and I had a closer bond than my mother could ever have imagined. Scarlett O'Hara had always been my favourite heroine: like her, I had discovered the hard way that money is the key to survival in an uncertain world. And the Eighties was a very uncertain world, I can tell you.

I used my eye for Potential to the full. I was going to make damn sure that the kids and I never had to ask for help again, and I would never, ever, wake in that darkest hour before dawn (3 am, summer and winter), and imagine the electricity cut off, the bailiffs at the door, and the urine-drenched arches under Hungerford bridge beckoning us into their cardboard boxes as home.

I always did have a vivid imagination; always did imagine the worst. Nothing like a vivid imagination for the worst to sharpen the mind. But then I was a Fifties child, born in the shadow of the nuclear blast that would obliterate us all. And it would happen, it could. From the moment I could listen with a conscious ear to the adults around me I heard them talking about war, bombs falling. The war they never thought would really happen, not even when Uncle Wynn saw the barrage balloons rise above London as the first sirens went.

Uncle Wynn had been in the East End when the bombs fell. Uncle Gareth had been a fireman in Birmingham. He was on leave, he used to tell us, visiting friends one night, in the peace of the Worcestershire countryside, when they saw the red glow in the sky that was Coventry burning. Imagine that: an entire city burning.

That was real. Uncle Gareth had seen it, so it must have been. He would talk about it sometimes to Mr Ernst, from down the road, who had been in Hamburg when the British bombers went over and left a firestorm of their own in their wake. The fire that grew, and grew, he said, and sucked everything into itself as it howled and raged through the streets, and out into my dreams.

Neither of them ever talked about such things with Miss Rosenstern who, like Mr Ernst, had somehow drifted to Llanestyn, and the wild reaches of the Snowdonia foothills, after the war. I would pass her as she sat on the park bench, her bags all around her, permanently packed and ready to go. Mam said Miss Rosenstern had come from a place called

Auschwitz, where the unthinkable happened. Which made the atomic bomb, and the end of life-as-we-know-it, thinkable with every plane that cruised low overhead.

Which, living within easy distance of at least one RAF base, made for a highly nervous childhood.

I have no intention of having a nervous old age, if I can help it. Hence the cottages. My properties had all gone up in value over the years. I'd put first Merion, and then Katie, through University and into jobs, and their first houses, and set aside enough for at least one marriage apiece. This was my time now.

So I'd sold up in Kingston-upon-Thames – where we had only gone to further Terry's career prospects, between that unfortunate business venture of ours and Terry going off to Find Himself – and come home to Llanestyn. The proceeds were going into properties up here. Some to rent out, and the rest for the lucrative tourist market. Plus a nice little cottage with a garden for me to potter around in for my old age.

Which was when the fateful cottages made their appearance in the window of Griffiths and Jones, Estate Agents, and lured me inside.

'Tanybwlch Cottages?' said the young man who, according to the friendly and informative label on his desk, was Mr Jones. Mr Aled Jones. A very young Mr Jones, with the pale, rather pickled complexion of too many hours under fluorescent lights, interspersed with too many business lunches, topped off by too many evenings in the Snowdon Arms. He looked just like his dad did at that age.

Even at school, we'd all known Gareth Jones would end up rich. He was a tedious, plodding sort of a child, dwelling in the safe anonymity of being neither noticeably bright, nor noticeably naughty. But Gareth's dad was Mr Aneurin Jones of Griffiths, Williams and Jones, as it was then, before that unfortunate business of Mr Williams and Mrs Aneurin Jones, which had never been lived down by anyone.

Gareth Jones had always been heading for riches and his smart, custom-built mansion on a hillside below Snowdon, complete with tennis courts and a swimming pool, and an enormous garage to house his collection of four-by-fours, a Volvo, an Aston Martin and several BMWs. Young Aled Jones was clearly heading the same way.

Now, I considered, was probably not the time to let slip that his father had invited me on several occasions to become the third Mrs Gareth Jones, before he discovered that young wives were less troublesome – at least for as long as the glamour of the swimming pool and the holidays in Spain, and as many lavender-coloured leather sofas as the heart could desire, held out. I could so easily have been Aled's wicked stepmother. *Bechod.* I smiled at him sweetly.

'That's right. Tanybwlch Cottages. I'd like to see the details, please.' I saw his eyes slide past towards the young couple who had come in after me. Double income, no kids, first-time buyers, no chain. Anxious to get on the property ladder, and new to the game. I could see he was safely pocketing the commission already. 'If you don't mind,' I added, somewhat louder.

'Ah, yes.'

I was, I thought, just a little sadly, an old woman to him. I'd passed him several times in the streets when I came back to visit Mam over the years, but he clearly had no idea his eyes had ever passed over me at all. To his youth, I fell into the amorphous mass of middle-aged and elderly females who pass invisible. We take no leading role in films or poster campaigns – not unless we are sanitised, digitally smoothed out, and smiling benignly on the youth around us. Aha! But what they forget is that the best secret agents are the ones nobody notices. Besides, years ago I resolved to give up anxiously seeking approval from everyone I met, and have never looked back since (well, almost).

'I'm afraid they are not being sold singly, madam. It's the entire row.'

'I am aware of that. I'd like to see the details, please.' His eyes travelled briefly over my un-ironed trousers, my comfortable old fleece and walking boots, and my still-long hair, with the roots showing, tucked hastily into an old velvet scrunchy. And no, he did not notice that I still have some pretty decent curves on me ('voluptuous' has been the enthusiastic verdict from more than one discerning male of my, um, acquaintance), and that my skin is really not that bad at all, considering. Ah, well.

Aled's father had always flaunted even more money than he had got, and it was clearly beyond Aled himself that anyone with the kind of cash that could buy a row of even the most derelict of cottages would not be encased in an Armani suit and pearls. But the quickest way to get rid of me was to hand over the details and bear down upon the young couple before they had a chance to escape.

'Of course, madam.' He turned to the filing cabinet at the back of the office. My eyes followed him, unthinkingly, as you do.

And there it was. I was bowled over. Breathless. My heart pounding in my chest, and shivers going up and down my spine. This was love: deep, wonderful, perfect love.

And I just knew I was never going to recover, not for as long as I lived.

CHAPTER 2

'MADAM?' ALED WAS STILL THERE, holding out the details of the cottages, impatient to move on towards a dead-cert commission.

'Thank you.' I took them, blindly, still stunned by what had just happened to me. 'And I'd like some other details, please.' He couldn't quite hide his irritation. If I'd told him this beforehand he could have avoided a second trip to the filing cabinet, and more precious minutes lost! I could see his point, but, hey, that was his problem.

'Which ones, madam?' he enquired, politely enough.

'Those,' I breathed, far too overcome to voice its name.

'Bryn Glas Castle?'

'Yes.' Now he was incredulous. I was clearly a house-viewing junkie, the kind who trails around properties for sale as a cheap version of the Ideal Home Exhibition.

'It's in a rather sad state of repair, I'm afraid,' he muttered. Mm. Well, perhaps Aled wasn't ever going to have a swimming pool all of his own: Gareth would never have passed up such a chance, however unlikely.

'I'd still like to see the details.' He sighed, and delved into the filing cabinet once more. It took rather longer, this time. I blinked at him innocently as he straightened, red faced and puffing, with a dog-eared leaflet in his hand.

Old Miss Tudur had died over eighteen months ago. I remembered it clearly; I came up for the funeral. She had left me a treasure in her will: an ammonite, dark and tightly coiled, the stone polished from years of handling. She had found it during her exploring days, in the 1920s, when aeroplanes were new, and there was still an Empire, and rocket science and nuclear bombs had not been thought of.

At least, that's what she told me, after she caught me and Cadi playing explorers in her shrubbery and invited us in for tea. Mam always said I led Cadi – who is four years younger than me – astray, so I took to doing my best. Old Miss Elinor never seemed to mind. She lived on her own in Bryn Glas, and her own relatives never did emerge from the woodwork until there were the proceeds of her castle to fight over.

Bryn Glas Castle should have had prime space in the window, not tucked away, yellowing, next to the filing cabinet, and no one appeared to have asked for the details for months. I smiled.

'Here you are, madam.'

'And I'd like to make an appointment to view.'

'To view?' His smooth, still faintly spotty, brow furrowed. Was this to be yet another property? A nice little modern bungalow, perhaps?

'Yes. To view the castle.'

'The castle?' I could see as well as him that the young couple had picked up a couple of details and now appeared in imminent danger of escaping to Applefords, just across the road.

'Yes. Two o'clock OK?'

'I'm afraid I'm all booked up – ' I saw him slide me a sideways glance, torn between the young couple and the possibility that I could always be in possession of a rich husband. Or a rich son, come to that. Griffiths and Jones must have been gleefully certain that castle would be snapped up instantly for a hotel, or a nursing home, or even by a minor celebrity after a nice bit of Victorian mock-gothic as a pad in the Snowdonian highlands. No doubt the family had thought so too. Desperation must be setting in on all sides, that was my reckoning. 'Two-thirty OK?'

'Fine. Two-thirty, it is.'

'You'll find a map and instructions on how to get there on the back.'

'Oh, I'll find it,' I murmured, with my most innocent of smiles.

Robin clearly thought I had gone mad.

'But what about Tanybwlch cottages? I was going to tell you about those. I could have got you a really good deal on them, Lissa.'

'I am sick of doing up houses,' I replied. 'And I'm tired of buy-to-let.'

'Elissa Deryn!' One elegant eyebrow was raised above that long, straight Lloyd Jones nose of his. 'Those were your pension! Your reward for all those years of hard graft. *Arlgwydd Mawr*! What happened to the clued-up business-woman who was determined never to be poor again?'

'She grew up. No, I tell a lie: she became single. Don't you see, Robin? I could never take a risk while I had the children. I had to play it safe and make sure there was a roof over their heads and food on the table, and I could give them the best possible start in life. I could never have lived with myself otherwise. I couldn't create life, of my own free will, and then just abandon it. But now it's just me. I can risk me. When you come down to it it's the only thing I have. And no one has any right to tell me what to do with it.'

'But what about all those plans to travel, see the world? Lissa, that's what you've talked about for the past ten years, at least. I thought you couldn't wait until the first Saga brochure fell through your door?'

'I couldn't. And I love them, and I'm certainly not giving up the idea. I'm still going to travel. But I can't just travel from place to place for the next fifty years until I drop down dead. I'll always have to have something to come back to.'

There was method in my madness, you see. It was the thought that had been there, niggling in the back of all my grand plans for when the children left home and my life was my own again. You know the kind of niggle? The sort you can't quite fish out and identify, but is there going nip, nip, nip, nip, nip, round the edges of your thoughts, like a caterpillar munching holes through nasturtium leaves: they might not have teeth, but you know the little blighters will get their way and leave more holes than leaf, in the end.

That was what had happened to me, in that blinding light when I saw Bryn Glas Castle and all those vague anxieties had suddenly fallen into place. Whether they would turn out to be moths or butterflies, only time would tell.

Robin was frowning at me. I might not have slept with him, but he still felt a need to protect me. It was the only thing that truly irritated me: in my mind it indicated that he still thought I might. While I am of the opinion that, past a certain age, it is a woman's prerogative not to change her mind.

'You really should think this through, Lissa.'

I sighed. Robin is only five years older than me, and, with his dapper white suits and good genes in the balding department (and a possible discreet dose of hair colouring for men), could pass for five years younger. But there were times he still acted as if he were my father.

'I have thought it through.'

'In half an hour?'

'Yes. Oh, not all the details, of course, and if the survey is vile I'll give this castle a miss and look for another one. Although I would like it to be this one,' I added, sounding wistful even in my own ears.

I had been fond of Miss Elinor Tudur, and I believe she had been fond of me. I liked the thought of living in her home, seeing the sights she had seen each day, hearing the sounds, catching the elusive scents of wet grass and lavender. It would be like living with an old friend. And then there had been all those stories she had begun to tell me about the place, and never quite finished.

'Lissa – '

'Bed and Breakfast.'

'I beg your pardon?'

'Bed and Breakfast. And I could turn the cottage and the stables into self-contained holiday lets for extra income.'

'But Lissa, for that kind of enterprise you need to research the market! Business plans – '

'Don't be so pedantic, Robin. I may not have lived here for a while, but I've kept in touch, and this is my home turf. Snowdonia. Castle. Tourists. American tourists. Japanese. Australians, New Zealanders. Londoners. Which of them *wouldn't* want to stay in a castle?'

'Not everyone wants to stay in castles. Lots of visitors are climbers and cyclists. Not to mention those damn motor bikers trying to squash their middle-aged spread into Hell's Angel-type leathers and clogging up the roads as soon as the sun comes out.'

'I'm not talking about stockbrokers. I'm talking about history freaks. Painters. Twitchers. Americans in search of genuine old history. Oh, and don't you worry, I'll research the market all right. I'll make sure I know what the most successful B&Bs are up to, and I'll have every room en suite, and as Olde Worlde as the best in Snowdonia. You know, four-poster beds. Medieval banquets. That kind of thing.'

Robin groaned. 'Lissa, it's *not* a medieval castle, it's a Victorian folly. Some nineteenth-century Posh and Becks threw it up in a misguidedly vulgar attempt to join the local aristocracy.'

'Isn't all history a fantasy?' I countered, crossly. I'd just had my road to Damascus: couldn't he see? Bloody men! All facts, figures, lists, and so-called rational explanations! As if emotions never got involved at all – and could be rational enough, in their own way. 'In particular a male fantasy,' I snapped. 'All kings and battles, and women never did anything at all. Apart from getting trussed up in corsets and fainting, of course.'

'Don't exaggerate.' He was growing irritated, which I thought, on reflection, was probably for the best. I had particular reasons for not wanting to go into too much detail as to why exactly I thought Bryn Glas Castle might turn out to be quite a bargain, even if the roof did turn out to be a trifle dodgy.

If my hunch was right, then we were talking Mega-Potential, and the most rip-roaringly, gut-wrenchingly exhilarating journey of my life. I trust Robin, of course I do. Up to a point. But all's fair in love and war and where money is concerned. And if half those things Miss Elinor Tudor once told me were true...

'If the place is raddled with dry rot, Lissa – '

'Then I'll bow to your expertise.' And get a good second opinion. There's dry rot and there's dry rot, I've discovered over the years, to my cost. And at times it can depend on the – shall we say – interests of the particular expert involved. And Robin regularly invested in property, and might not be above a little social climbing and a castle of his own, if he had any inkling there might just be a national treasure sleeping beneath the rotting cover of dog roses and montbretia.

'Good.'

'So you'll come with me?'

'Of course. But remember, I can only give you a general opinion. No details.'

'That's all I want. The details can come later. I want to know if it's sound enough to put an offer in, or whether I should forget it and move on.'

'To another castle.'

'Yes. The idea is sound. I know it is. I can feel it in my bones.'

'Hrmph,' he grunted, wincing at this apparition of female intuition. 'We'll see.'

We walked to Bryn Glas Castle that afternoon. It was only just outside the village, along a twisting narrow lane with hedges on either side, and branches hanging overhead. Dark green and mysterious, was how I remembered it; and so it still must be in summer. The walls appeared out of the undergrowth; huge grey stones, strangled under ivy and the tendrils of honeysuckle. They went right around the grounds, sealing the castle and its gardens into its own private world.

I'm sure it had been the general idea of its Victorian builders to emulate the medieval town walls of Conwy, just along the coast. Mind you, these walls might have the look of keeping the local peasantry at bay, but I had a feeling the enemies of Bryn Glas were more likely to be rabbits heading for the vegetable patch. Not to mention harsh winds screeching down the valley from Snowdon, and salt-tinged gales belting in from the sea, that could shrivel delicate blooms without trying.

Inside the walls, I remembered, the remains of all kinds of exotic plants had once bloomed. This was not as crazy as it might seem: the mountain tops may be bleak, but near this coast we are close enough to the Gulf Stream to avoid the worst frosts. It's no surprise to see palm trees growing quite happily in the gardens of houses quite high up on the lower hillsides. Along the shores, and over the Menai Straits in Anglesey, they are almost *de rigueur*.

I could never get over it as a child: watching the sub-tropics fly by on Christmas day, as we drove visiting relatives along the winding road to Beaumaris – forever bathed in sunshine, whatever the weather – to view the round-bellied towers of its perfect, fairy-tale castle, and have a good view of the thick snow lying low on the mountains of the mainland.

Surprising what you can grow here, particularly with the benefit of a walled garden. Not that I was about to tell Robin that: I was quite sure he would not approve of the garden being a major reason for buying a house. Or, even worse, a castle.

For all my bravado about cutting free and travelling, I had spent thirty years of my life in primary nurturing. Even though Mam was gone, and the kids had flown, I couldn't just switch it off like that. Feeding and growing: watching the changes year-by-year, season-by-season. And roots. *Duw*, I needed roots.

The gate was open. Fresh tyre tracks skidded through the weed-speckled gravel making its way up towards the castle. I'd never been through the front gate. Cadi and I had found a smaller entrance, a Secret Garden entrance a retreating handyman had forgotten – or not cared enough – to lock, years ago. I hesitated. It still didn't seem quite right, somehow, to boldly go in the front door. It seemed like an imposition. A sacrilege, even, to the hidden tranquillity of the place.

'Changed your mind?' asked Robin, prepared, by his tone, to generously forgive me the waste of an afternoon.

'No,' I said, firmly. 'Not at all.'

A peacock strutted leisurely across the drive in front of us, gilded feathers trailing.

'I'd forgotten those bloody birds were still here,' said Robin, with glimmerings of distaste. 'Noisy little blighters.'

'I rather like them,' I remarked. A shiver went up my spine; whether of anxiety or delight, I was not quite sure. Memories came back of frosty autumn mornings, with rampant masses of dying goldenrod sprawled amongst the borders, punctuated by the seed-heads of oriental poppies: all brittle with ice, ready to shatter at a touch.

Mist would ooze from the grass, and from between the sharon roses, until I would drift in a mythical landscape, where King Arthur watched between the laurels and the Lady of the Lake might raise her arm from between the irises that clogged the fishpond, while the harsh cries of peacocks echoed amidst the frozen breath of the air.

We make our own stories, I thought, suddenly. We might understand them a little better – or even escape them for a while – in tales of knights and space-captains, and the harmless-looking, tireless sniffers-out of evil – but we still tread the one-way track of our own epic, right until the very end.

In front of us the driveway was opening up to glimpses of towers and turrets, bay windows, and the mildewed glass of an imitation-of-Kew-Gardens conservatory.

'Well?' asked Robin, giving me my final opt-out. But, of course, he knew damn well I wouldn't.

'No time like the present,' I replied.

CHAPTER 3

B RYN GLAS CASTLE WAS VERY MUCH as I remembered it. Much smaller, of course: I've seen a wider world since then, and all my childhood prairies have shrunk to modest-sized lawns. It might look like a castle on the outside, but inside it was more manageable and ordinary, with bedrooms; sitting rooms; even the remains of a library.

It wasn't a grand castle, like Penrhyn, or a ruined one, like Conwy, Caernarfon, or Beaumaris. The embarrassing truth remains that it was an overgrown house masquerading as something it was not and never could be. Mind you, saying that, it still had seven bedrooms, and that was quite enough for me.

Aled Jones was waiting for us by his brand new and spotless BMW. He was paler than ever, and looked decidedly out of place away from his natural habitat of desks and flickering computer screens. He didn't spot us at first, being far too preoccupied with the parade of six or seven peacocks strutting slowly round the intruder and his vehicle, crowns at the alert, feathers trailing, eyes ever-so watchful, after the manner of Indians circling the wagon train in one of those old John Wayne films.

'Beautiful creatures, aren't they?' Aled remarked, brightly, as we approached.

'Spectacular,' I replied.

'Quite a feature of the place. Have been for years.' The lead bird stayed just a little too close to the BMW's immaculate doors, causing the remaining blood to drain from Aled's features. He waved, without conviction, in the offending creature's direction. 'Although they don't necessarily have to come with Bryn Glas.'

'Really?' Several of the birds had, by now, lost interest in Aled, and were viewing Robin and me with clear intent. I watched them back, severely. Elinor's peacocks had always possessed an eye for the main chance, in my experience, and I had no intention of spending the rest of my life being stalked for morsels of cake, and any other feathered equivalent of a fast trip to McDonald's, the moment I stepped outside my front door.

'Oh no. No, indeed. One of my previous clients has already opened negotiations with the Tudur family to purchase them.' Aled was removing something greenish and slimy from the bottom of his polished shoes with a pained expression, but he still managed a smile. 'One of the new houses beneath the Orme at Llandudno. Footballer. Very high profile,' he added, lowering his voice. 'Very keen to take possession as soon as arrangements can be made. Very keen.'

'Certainly not.' I frowned at him, indignantly. What a come-down for any bird, to swap the faded grandeur of Bryn Glas for the red-bricked, fake lead-paned multi-million-pound weekend retreat of some here-today-gone-tomorrow C-lister, who was probably already banging on the jungle drums of *I'm a Celebrity, Get Me Out of Here*. 'This castle wouldn't be the same without its peacocks.'

'You think so?' Aled blinked in astonishment: I was clearly even more barking than he'd thought. I couldn't help but note the calculating gleam that appeared in his eyes as he scribbled a quick memo to himself. One footballer still in search of second-hand ornamentation for his brand-new terrace with hot-tub, then. *Bechod.*

'Definitely,' I said, in my best the-customer-is-always-right tones. 'Now move it.' This to the peacocks, not Aled, I hasten to add. They obliged, slowly, one by one, sweeping away in trails of gilded feathers, shrieking loud indignation at this unceremonious treatment as they vanished into the shrub-bery. 'Shall we make a start?' I smiled, sweetly.

'Most of the rooms have been shut up for a number of years,' said Aled, ushering us through. Well, he couldn't exactly draw a polite veil over the cobwebs and the encroaching dust, along with the faded wallpapers half hanging off the walls and the panes of windows rapidly turning into a black deathbed of flies. Aled appeared to be somewhat reassured by the presence of Robin, although he hadn't quite been able to mask the astounded look in his eyes when he recognised my 'friend' as the proprietor of one of the canniest surveying practices in town. However, it had also signalled to him that I was, after all, serious. Funny how he'd stopped glancing at his watch from that moment on. 'Miss Elinor Tudur, the last member of the family to live here, was a little infirm during the final years of her life, and tended to use just a few downstairs rooms.'

'I see,' I murmured, casually.

'I believe she was quite an eccentric,' put in Robin.

'Yes, she was a little. A remarkable lady. She lived to be over a hundred, you know. She flew aeroplanes in – oh, must have been the early part of the twentieth century, or thereabouts. Ran her own charter business, taking passengers all over the place. She must have had guts to fly in those old Tiger Moths. They say she even worked with Amy Johnson, for a while.'

'Really?' said Robin, with a quick glance at me. 'Fascinating.'

'Oh, indeed.' Aled was warming to this piece of local colour. Good selling point, local colour. I can't say I blamed him. 'The Tudur family are an interesting bunch. They're supposed to have been here since Tudor times. Old Vernon Tudur, Miss Elinor's father, apparently used to claim that they were cousins of Elizabeth the First. She had Welsh blood in her, you see. He was convinced she had stayed here on several occasions. Not in the castle, of course. Before its time.'

'I don't remember any mention of Elizabeth the First visiting this part of Wales,' said Robin, with a smile.

'Oh that didn't stop old Mr Vernon. He wrote a book on the subject,' said Aled. 'Self-published, I believe. I'm told he had an enormous collection of papers, but I expect they have all been destroyed. Pity. Not often you get a bit of real history surfacing around here.'

I was quite sure there was history surfacing all over the place, but I knew what he meant: not kings and queens, and international intrigue, kind of history.

'Fascinating,' I mumbled, for want of anything else to say. I did my best to look innocent.

'He was quite adamant about Elizabeth the First. He used to swear it was for trysts with a secret lover.'

'Rather spoils the "Virgin Queen" bit,' remarked Robin, dryly.

'Hence the "secret", I presume,' I put in. I could see Robin was noticing that I was unusually quiet, so I thought I'd better act more in character. He might begin asking awkward questions, otherwise.

'I expect so,' he replied. Aled was already leading the way up a narrow flight of stairs.

'And up here are the attics. They would have been the servants' quarters when the castle was first built, of course. But they have plenty of potential. And great views over the surrounding countryside.'

I'd never been up this far. When I first visited Miss Tudur I had just read *Jane Eyre,* and I knew just what was kept in attics. Even now I found myself looking around a little nervously as if a mad wife with a candle in one hand and a torn wedding veil in the other was waiting behind the door to slit my throat as I went in.

There was, of course, nothing but charmingly sloping roofs and, as Aled said, a spectacular view of the mountains on one side and the sea on the other. A window opened onto a small balcony at the front of the house, overlooking the garden between the mock battlements and a few vacant-looking gargoyles, who appeared to have grown bored with their place in the guttering several years ago and had given up on the encroaching ivy.

'Beautiful,' I murmured, as I looked down into the tangled expanse of garden below.

'This is the best location from which to view the grounds,' said Aled, stepping up hastily to join me. 'There is an excellent collection of mature shrubs, and some quite exotic plants, I believe. I'm not an expert on these kinds of things, but I have heard it was quite a noted garden in its day. It would need some work to bring it back under control. But it's not often you find a property like this with all its grounds complete. At least, not ones outside those belonging to the National Trust.'

'I'm sure.'

'Are you a keen gardener, then, Mrs Deryn?'

'Miss.'

'I beg your pardon?'

'Miss. It's Miss Deryn.' I'd gone back to my maiden name the moment Terry left, and I didn't see why I should be anything else now. And besides, I didn't really want to answer his question: it might lead on to other things and get Robin's brain-cells moving in unfortunate directions.

'Oh. I see.' Aled looked faintly embarrassed. For me rather than himself, I suddenly realised: an ancient spinster forced to own up to her state – and to a virile young male of the species, to boot. He probably thought I'd once been kissed, and mourned for a repeat of the experience ever since. Probably since the time before Bryn Glas was built, I muttered inwardly to myself.

I mean, it's not even as if I'm old. I may be halfway through my life, but I'm not at the end of it, thank you very much. Had he no idea about the realities of modern life? Hadn't he heard that women have babies in their thirties and forties? Several of my London friends are still picking up their kids from primary school, for heaven's sake! And I wasn't going to enlighten him and own up to being an abandoned wife for even more of his pity, either, thank you.

Elinor had once loved and lost: I'd seen his photograph in faded sepia tones, a young man in leather flying jacket, goggles swinging jauntily from one hand. She'd mourned him. I remembered the sadness still in her tone when she would speak about him. But I also remember there were other – later – photographs, as well.

Aled was probably under the impression I was working hard on Robin to marry me, as my very last hope in life. But now was not the time to give a rundown of my post-Terry swinging from the chandeliers with a rather gorgeous –

'Shall we go down?' I said.

We descended the staircase once more, and after a quick inspection of the kitchen, were ushered out into the conservatory. It smelt of damp and moss. Sticky slug trails were slung over the paintwork of the bricks, and all that was left of Miss Tudur's plants were a few cracked pots and bits of dead twig in a corner.

Elinor Tudur had loved her plants. I'd often found her sitting there, even in the depths of winter, with only the faintest of warmth creeping though the glasswork, huddled over a small radiator but still queen of a slightly frost-bitten tropical rain forest. Suddenly I missed her. Strange, after all these years, to miss a woman I had scarcely known, with a pain that felt as if my innards had been half torn away. I stepped out into the garden.

'Well?' I demanded, seeing Robin making his way towards me, so that we were just out of earshot of Aled Jones, who tactfully took to a deep inspection of his personal organiser.

'This is just a rough impression, Lissa.'

'Robin!'

'OK, OK. On first impressions, I'd say it seems pretty sound, considering. You'll still have your work cut out, and a considerable investment to make. Considerable,' he added, for emphasis.

'Good.'

'I did note several problems – '

'Great. You can go over them with him on the way back, when I make my offer.'

'You are sure about this?'

'Never been surer.' He eyed me with raised eyebrows. 'You do know you'll be burning your boats, Lissa. There will be no going back from this – and especially not to the London area.'

'This is where I want to be,' I replied, firmly. 'I'm not a young thing any more, Robin. I'm going into this with my eyes wide open. I know exactly what I'm doing.'

Which, at the time, I did. I was perfectly clear about the potential of Bryn Glas Castle. I was perfectly clear that I no longer wanted to be a landlady, but that I wanted a project – a big, real, satisfying project – instead.

And then there was the matter of the garden. All those plans Miss Tudur had told me she had for the garden. She had seemed old to me as a child but, I suddenly realised with a shock, she had probably not been much older than I was now, at the time. And she'd lived on for over forty years after that. That would have been an entire lifetime, not so very long ago. It felt like a lifetime now, all of a sudden, standing there at the beginning of it.

Old, indeed!

I wondered about those ideas Elinor had about the garden: about a real secret garden lying sleeping and forgotten beneath the Victorian lawn and shrubbery. It was something very special, she had said. Something quite unique. And something very, very secret I should never tell anyone, in case the rest of the family got wind of it and manoeuvred her out of there, greedy lot that they were. Not that they would have taken any notice of my childish prattling, of course.

Had she ever found what she was looking for? Or had she been distracted? Or maybe she had, after all, never dared, in case it wasn't there at all. Lavender and patterns, was all I could remember. And something about Queen Elizabeth. The first one or the second I was not entirely sure, but I had a feeling it was the first. Or maybe that was Aled, talking just now.

'Ready?' said Robin. We were playing this cool. I glanced towards Aled, who was blissfully unaware that Robin and I were old hands in this matter of buying property – or that Robin was not just a friend, and was being paid in hard cash for his services on this visit, just in case he got the wrong idea – and nodded.

'Let's get the ball rolling,' I said.

These past years, I have come to think that you only get through youth due to its state of blind ignorance. How else would anyone even contemplate bearing children and raising them, of making a home and forging a career, let alone the entangled web of relationships along the way, unless you simply had no idea what it all entailed? These past years, I'd thought I'd grown beyond that. I was all knowing, all cynical. I went into everything with my eyes open, and nothing could surprise me.

Ha!

If that were true, then I was not entering upon middle age that day I bought the castle, but rushing headlong into a second youth. Oh, I'd a good idea about the mess, the delays, the inevitable overbudget, and the stress. I'd been through that all before. I'd owned property before. Been prosperous, in my own modest way. Just not visibly. Not in-your-face, to the naked eye, so to speak.

I've never been one for challenging hairstyles and flash cars. Ever since I've worked from home my clothes have been for comfort, not effect – apart from a few party pieces that lurk in the back of the wardrobe until the need arises.

Since hitting forty-five, I've never felt the need to be perked up, sucked in, pulled, stretched or botoxed. I've never had the time. And I've gloried in the post-forty bliss of just being me, and to hell with what anyone else thinks. And if the young want to judge me, let them judge away: their time will come, and sooner than they think. I never thought it would happen to me, either.

Mmm. I thought I knew everything, that day I was fifty-two; that I had nothing else to learn, and nothing would ever again arise to shock me. But there was just one little fact of life that I had never come across before, and had never been fully explained to me.

That day I bought Bryn Glas Castle, I was looking forward to a life of single, middle-aged, purple-wearing, self-indulgent bliss, with natters with my friends and flying visits from my children, as the headiest excitement of my future existence. Apart from the appearance of grandchildren, of course. Ah, well, ignorance is bliss. But someone could have warned me.

For it is a truth universally acknowledged – amongst middle-aged men, at least – that a woman of middle years, being in possession of property and a reasonable income, must be in want of a husband.

And I, brave in my blissful innocence: I bought a castle.

CHAPTER 4

I SHOULD HAVE SEEN ENOUGH OF LIFE BY NOW to know that, along with the proverbial lunch, there is no such thing as a free castle.

When I was young, of course, I had quite different ideas. Between my sixth birthday and my thirteenth I was quite convinced it was all a mistake: my fairy godmother had simply missed the nearest Royal Palace and tossed me, head first, down the chimney of Tyn-y-Coed cottage, Llanestyn, instead.

She'd be back soon, along with a tiara, pink slippers, and the floatiest tutu you could imagine, and then Cadi, and all those horse-riding girls at school with the paddocks and the holiday homes in Spain, would have to curtsey as I passed.

Or possibly some handsome prince would be dispatched to search me out, cutting all that tiresome business with the mattresses and the pea and getting straight down to the – well I wasn't quite sure what, except that it was what a prince expected once he'd serenaded you into his castle; and it was supposed to be nice. Scary, but nice.

During my teenage years – hell, I was too off the planet on hormones and angst to know what I thought during my teenage years. But things settled down again as I hit my twenties. And he was still there, my prince, somewhere in the background behind the lanky spottiness around me. He was always there, ready to appear and whip me off to his castle where his sole aim in life would be to love me, adore me, and never let me worry my pretty head about anything ever again.

Mmm. As I drove up to Bryn Glas Castle, with all my worldly processions that had not been put in storage stashed in the back of my Skoda, I finally understood why he never turned up through all those years. I mean, any prince worth anything would have had to fight for right to rule his kingdom, right? And here I was having fought tooth and nail all the best years of my life to get to where I could buy my castle – and wasn't about to give it up to anyone who asked, however sweet their smile, and whatever promise lay waiting to be unleashed in their pouch. No way, José!

I smiled at Robin, who was waiting for me at the door, looking rather thoughtful.

'You sure about this, Lissa?' he murmured. Concerned. In a fatherly way, of course. 'The Mabinogion has a room free; I checked with Alyce Jones this morning. They do a good breakfast there, you know.'

'I'll be fine.'

'Or I do have a spare – '

'No! Thank you,' I added, quickly, as a look of hurt crossed his face. Once installed in Robin's elegant spare room, it would all be, well, a little too domestic, if you see what I mean. Come into my parlour, said the spider to the fly. Not that Robin was deliberately spinning any webs for me. At least, giving him a sideways look, I didn't think so. But, given good food and a good bottle of wine and no given reasons as to why not – well I am only human, after all. And I wasn't about to allow history (i.e. my history with Terry) to repeat itself: at least not until my castle was shipshape and sorted, and in no more need of the best Project Manager I'd ever worked with.

Afterwards I could afford to think again. I might consider it my prerogative not to change my mind, but flexibility is a sign of eternal youth, so they say, and never say absolutely and finally never, is always the best policy. You never know what you might be missing.

Robin heaved a deep sigh. 'At least the phone's working. And you have your mobile, I take it?'

'All present and correct.' I fished it out to demonstrate.

'The bathroom on the first floor is the one that's finished. I'd take the double room with the en suite next door to it, if I was you. At least you'll know all the plumbing works in that one, too. Just keep the lights on, and don't wander around in the dark, for heaven's sake, there are all sorts of things left in the corridors, and we don't want you with a broken leg, now, do we?'

'No, Robin. I promise I'll be very careful.'

'And if there's anything, anything at all – '

I smiled. 'I'll phone you.'

'Mm.' He sounded a little happier. Not much, but just enough to help me unload my sleeping bag, blow-up mattress, a rucksack full of clothes and two cardboard boxes of necessities, and take them inside.

You know when you do something that seems like a really good idea at the time, and then when you get it out and look at it, it seems like a really bad idea instead? Well, that was me and Bryn Glas, the moment I stepped through the door.

'Oh,' I said. All these months since it had legally become mine, I had held in my mind's eye Bryn Glas as it had been when I last saw it: musty; faded; cobwebs trailing from the ceilings and light dancing in the dust. A moody, atmospheric castle, ready to welcome the high-flyers from Hollywood as the set for a costume drama or some subtly chilling Gothic fantasy. The Bryn Glas Castle that had memories of Elinor Tudur oozing from its unwashed pores.

'Progress, eh?' said Robin, clearly mistaking my momentary dismay for sheer awe at his efficiency in carrying out our mutually agreed orders.

'Er – yes.' Katie was going to kill me, if she turned up next weekend as she had threatened. I may not know the intimate details of her private life, but I know my daughter well enough to be quite clear that when I said 'castle' she would be envisaging exposed beams, four-poster beds, Medieval tapestries in a long dining hall and reclaimed furniture in the hallways. A building site was not on order.

I could see what Robin meant about leaving the lights on if I ventured out of my quarters. I pushed my way past bags of concrete, ladders, wheelbarrows, spades, hammers and various other tools crouched amidst the white dust of major renovations, and up the uncarpeted staircase.

'I'm afraid everything has been left inside,' said Robin, apologetically, eyeing the amalgamated clutter as we passed. 'Ideally, it should all have been left outside. We can move it all if it really gets in your way.'

'Of course not, Robin. I remember what the kids of Llanestyn are like.' How could I forget? Little buggers. Have anything they could shift without too much effort, they would; especially these last weeks of the summer holidays when freedom had became seriously boring. Irritating: but it could be worse.

At least the major part of thievery in the area was destined for the local stream, or, for the more enterprising, kamikaze dives from the headland onto the sands below, much to the irritation of the coastguard who had to clean it all up again and check if the now ex-Ford Fiestas and Vauxhall Cavaliers had anyone trapped inside them as the next tide rose.

There was no real concerted effort of a crime wave in Llanestyn, even now. Nothing really professional, beyond a few hanging baskets, and the more promising contents of garden sheds, heading off on Saturday night for the local Sunday car-boots the next day. There were more organised gangs sweeping down through the countryside from the more sophisticated city lights of Liverpool and Manchester, cleaning up on the antiques and the credit cards and the odd DVD player. There were more druggies feeding their habits, now, so Cadi had informed me, but they tended to smash an entire car park of car windows after closing time, and head off for the sunset with any souped-up Ford GI or X thingy whatever.

Good job I gave up driving anything with street cred years ago. I mean, a car is just wheels, when you come down to it. Reliable, A to B, preferably without electric windows (my imagination for severed necks and being trapped inside in blazing sun with all electrics buggered and no signal on the mobile, tends to work overtime – and hey, it happens. Not often, but it happens), and with the kind of label that no teenager would be seen dead inside, let alone driving. That's my kind of car. And sorry, Herr Doktor Freud; I've never yet felt the urgent desire for gas-guzzling, computer-dictated, raving maniac of a penis extension. Should I ever find it (the desire, I mean), you'll be the first to know.

But I digress.

One of the downsides of owning a castle – so Cadi had also informed me, just a little gleefully – was that I was likely to throw myself into the notice of thieves and general purveyors of evil and skulduggery.

Oh well, I comforted myself, as I made my way up the staircase, treads creaking, footsteps echoing off into the far distance, at least the grapevine would have informed the population of Llanestyn – if not the entire length of the North Wales coast – that there was nothing inside Bryn Glas apart from a few radiators and that batty old bag Mr Robin Lloyd Jones was shagging in his spare time. And you don't take on a Lloyd Jones, unless you can help it.

OK, it might be a little dent in my pride to be taken by rumour as Robin's latest squeeze, but never look a gift horse in the mouth if it can keep you out of serious trouble. Robin's big brother, Iestin Lloyd Jones, had just made it to judge on the London circuits, and was a rolled-up-trouser man to boot (at least, that's how the rumours went). Now *there's* protection, for you.

By the time we arrived at the first floor landing, I was getting used to the new torn-apart and being-put-back-together version of my new home. Here the electrics had been finished and plastered over again, and the bathrooms had even arrived at the tiling stage. A faint film of dust lay on everything, half-extinguishing the ancient industrial-strength hoover stashed along the corridor, but you could begin to see the end result peering through the gloom.

'Here we are. It's got a view over the garden: I thought you'd like this one.' Robin ushered me into a large, light room with a bay window at one end. Like the rest of the rooms leading off the corridor, it had been freshly painted white all over, complemented by newly stripped and varnished floor-boards. 'Sorry about the curtains, we couldn't find any others that would fit.'

'They're lovely,' I replied. They were Elinor's curtains: soft green velvet, sun-faded and with the pile almost worn to the disintegrating-into-shreds lining. I remembered them with a stomach-clench of memory that sent shivers all over me. But they brought back with them the grubby and cobwebbed Bryn Glas of my inner mind, like old friends with a talisman to keep me safe.

'You should be OK camping here for a few days until the top floor is ready,' said Robin, becoming anxious again. 'If you're sure...'

'Oh, yes. Quite sure. I've got to face spending a night here some time or other, so it might as well be now.'

'I just wish you'd left it until the alarm was fully connected, that's all, Lissa.'

I didn't like to say it was more the ghosts and the ghoulies that were causing the irritating squelching noises in my stomach, rather than any humans who might object to my presence. Knowing Robin, he would have felt obliged to stay and keep me company, and banish all my fears. Plus worm his way into a share of my single sleeping bag, I'm quite sure.

'Oh, I'm sure it'll be OK for a couple of days: I'll leave the car in an obvious place and the lights on.' With relief, I found a source of distraction. 'And you managed to find me a microwave! Oh, Robin, that is so thoughtful!'

He blushed, right to the roots of his faintly thinning hair.

'It was the least I could do.' He fished out the more expensive kind of microwaveable meal from a cupboard, and placed it on the table, next to the microwave. 'As you wouldn't let me take you out to dinner on your first night.' He opened a small fridge – the kind you keep beers and complimentary drinks in – and brought out a bottle of Very Expensive white wine. 'For you to toast your new house with,' he added, just a little shyly.

Ah. *Bechod*. I could have hugged him, the old softie. Except that I suddenly noticed that the Very Expensive wine was around the same scary percentage in alcohol as the British sherry Cal the Caravan used to down as breakfast, sitting at the picnic table by Llanestyn falls and sending the Tourist Board into deep despair at the Wrong Impression he gave of the place. A glass or so of that could take one right over the legal limit without trying, and prevent one from driving back to one's elegant house the other side of town, no messing.

'Thank you. I'll save it till later,' I murmured. 'I'm so knackered I'll just fall asleep if I have any now.' He looked faintly crestfallen. 'I'll save it until I'm properly moved in and can cook you a real dinner.' And was all prepared with a spare room (and possibly a daughter on hand) just so the fact could be established before the first glass and there was no misunderstanding that might – at this point, at least – prove terminal to our friendship.

'Oh, no, Lissa; it's for you,' he replied, so very earnestly I was nearly unwise and changed my mind about the drink. But if a woman can change her mind about a drink, she can change it about other things, too. And since Robin comes from one of those generations of males who were taught in the cradle that no woman ever knows her own mind, and needs to be shown it – nicely, of course, but firmly – I placed the wine back in the fridge.

Robin is also of the generation convinced that ladies delicately sip at a mouthful of Croft Original before heading for the Blue Nun or the Lambrusco, finishing off with a Babycham on special occasions. I'd never liked to point out that rollicking, cheapish, Australian red was more my style, with a whisky bottle stashed under the kitchen sink for serious emergencies.

Sadly, my wild partying days are well and truly over. It used to take me a couple of gins to get going: now, just a whiff of juniper berries, and I've an instant hangover. And a real hangover knocks me out for a week. I suppose this is mother nature's gentle way of hinting I no longer need the bravado necessary for the mating game. And, hey, getting quietly mellow with friends can be just as much fun as the working-week ritual of getting rat-arsed on a Friday night.

Just don't let the youngsters in on the secret, or we'll never get rid of them to the disco or the nightclub and have a bit of houseroom to ourselves, is what I say.

I walked down with Robin to the front door to see him off and pick up my final box from the car.

'And, remember, anything. Anything at all,' he said, pressing his key-ring with a flourish, and sending his BMW into a paroxysm of squeaks and flashes as it geared up to receive him.

'Yes, Robin.'

'Well, have a good night, and I'll see you tomorrow. We could go up to Conwy, have lunch there. You've been saying you're dying to see the castle and have a stroll on the quay.'

Lunch is safe enough. And it was years since I'd had a real shufti around the ruins of Conwy Castle. And Conwy is a real castle, not like my poor old fantasy of a place.

'That would be lovely,' I replied.

Robin disappeared down the drive in a hailstorm of gravel. I lifted out my final box, and locked the car doors one by one, in the reassuring, old-fashioned way, and began to make my way back inside.

Duw, it was quiet! I should know by now, but each time I return to Llanestyn I am still stunned by the quietness. No hum of traffic, no ambulances, police sirens; no airplanes low overhead, heading for Heathrow.

Of course, there were sounds: birds chattered amongst the trees with the last of the day's urgency as the purple haze of dusk began to settle. Now and again a peacock shrieked, setting the echoes resounding through the shrubbery. A pair of squirrels swore at each other overhead – no doubt narked by their recent ejection from Bryn Glas attics – and shot off, still cursing, sending a rain of unripened beechnuts onto my head.

On my way up from London, I had merrily planned stashing everything inside and then going to investigate the garden. My garden. Now, all of a sudden, I wasn't so sure. My feet on the gravel echoed as if in a vast, empty space. There was a chill dampness to the air, and bats zinging their way, this way and that, against the first pale glimmer of stars.

Now, don't get me wrong, I like bats. Cadi and I used to go bat-watching when we were kids. Uncle Gareth – who knew about that kind of thing – would take us to the barns where they clustered, hanging upside down from the beams, shuffling in their sleep, waiting for the night's hunting to begin. It was the night bit that I suddenly wasn't so sure of: the shadows between the trees, where anything might lurk, biding time.

Bugger.

Why are lone females in lonely houses so popular in cheap and cheerful slasher movies? Especially the kind beloved of teenagers when I was working at serious weekend bonding sessions with my two before they fled off to university and a life of their own. I never liked to confess just what an out-and-out wimp I really was, and couldn't we have a nice costume drama instead?

I felt obliged to be cool, in those days. Nowadays I couldn't give a stuff, but it's too late: all those images of severed limbs and writhing entrails planted there, firmly in my mind. Oh, well. It was always young, nubile women running screaming from the phantom axe-man. And no one can accuse me of being young, or nubile. Not for a long time. So clearly of no interest to phantom axe-wielders, then.

Get a grip, Lissa! In real life the majority of murders are undertaken by someone known to the victim: so you are far safer here alone than with company. All the same, I was beginning to feel a little, well, exposed, out in the open air.

There was a tingly feeling down my spine, as if eyes were there, watching me. Although they couldn't possibly be watching my spine as that was by now firmly facing the walls of the castle. Unless walls really do have eyes, of course.

Mmm. I could see a dog becoming a necessity, rather than the last resort of a man-less, child-less woman, at this rate.

Ah, well, nothing for it. I clutched the box of private necessities for my eyes only, and braved my back exposed to the darkness of the woods as I made my way back inside.

Oh, and there was nothing rude, or illegal in that box, if that's what you're thinking. Yes, I have been to Ann Summers parties, mainly on a can't-refuse-to-help-a-friend/mustn't-be-seen-to-be-a-dried-up-old-prude basis. We had a good giggle, but if you think I'm letting one of those battery-operated, twirling, swirling, vibrating, dream-on-mate, joy-sticks anywhere near regions mainly useful for sitting upon, you've another think coming.

My nether regions have better things to do with themselves, thank you very much, and have enjoyed a cystitis-free, thrush-free existence for years. Since my last bout of untrammelled, hedonistic sex, if you must know. Now Raph – beautiful, exotic, never-to-be-domesticated Raphael – was worth it, in ways no gyrating piece of plastic with ideas above its station could ever even aim for.

And the illegal? Like alcohol, that does my head in big-time, nowadays. I'm just hoping it's legal by the time I enter the very finally decrepit stage of old age (like in fifty years' time) when the arthritis starts playing up, and the short-term memory is completely shot, anyhow.

Which means I've given it up, of course.

All the same, I didn't particularly want Robin inspecting my stash of oestrogen-boosting pumpkin and sunflower seeds tucked in besides the dried apricots, next door to my copy of *Living the Menopause without HRT,* and the bottles of multi-vitamins and cod-liver oil. Then there were those vital anti-hot-flush combatants: Evening Primrose oil, Black Cohosh, Dong Quai and Red Clover. Not forgetting cranberry juice to keep my peeing bits healthy, garlic for the heart, walnuts (good for lowering blood cholesterol), and the large bag of roasted salted cashews that must be good for something or other, salt or no salt, they are just so delicious.

Oh, and not to forget my stash of chocolate and red wine: for medicinal purposes only, naturally. Robin would never have missed the suspicious clink of glass on glass as I hauled my box up the steps and into the safety of my castle.

CHAPTER 5

I 'D JUST FINISHED MY GOURMET MICROWAVE LASAGNE, along
with a bag of wild herb salad, with sachet of lemon-grass
and wild-thyme dressing – also thoughtfully provided
by Robin, who had always liked a woman with a trim figure,
and so was a connoisseur of salads – and was just settling
down to my own contribution to the meal of a pot of tiramisu
(yum, yum), followed by seventy per cent, organic dark
chocolate, and a good slurp of my Australian Shiraz, when it
struck me.

This was Elinor's room.

I'd only been here once or twice: Miss Tudor's favourite
place had been the room opening into the conservatory
downstairs. That room – her 'library' she called it – still hung
in my memory like dust in sunlight, with a scent of musk and
old leather intertwined with the slim cigars that always rested,
half-smoked, amongst the Arabic markings of a bowl she had
brought back from Morocco in the days of biplanes and Amy
Johnson.

The library had been lined with shelves of books,
interspersed with yellowing maps mounted onto wood, and
black and white photographs of long-dead mountaineers and
cyclists, along with pilots posed by a succession of rickety-
looking aeroplanes that made me nervous just looking at them.

It was where we were always invited, Cadi and I, when we
became regular visitors. That and the conservatory, with its
fading and moulding collection of plants, also brought back
from Elinor's travels. On one of the early visits, when I didn't

know her well enough to be quite certain of the dos and don'ts in this strange place (adults, in my experience, being unpredictable like that), I blew the dust off a small fossil on the shelf next to the wine and gin bottles.

That must have been before the days of Elinor's computer, come to think of it, when it was the out-of-the-ark typewriter that snuggled up to the bottles of strange liqueurs, some labelled in alphabets I failed to recognise at all.

'You're interested in fossils, then,' said Elinor, catching me polishing the stone to peer at the delicate fronds of an ancient fern. I hadn't thought I was until then; in fact, I hadn't considered the matter at all. But I nodded, in sudden enthusiasm, and a feeling that everything old was out of bounds as far as touching was concerned, like they were in museums.

But Elinor had seemed delighted and brought us up here, to her bedroom crammed full of mementos, with stone axes, flints and fossils of every size and shape you could imagine. And pride of place, above the mantelpiece, were the ammonites in their wooden and glass cases. Her father had found those, she told us, in the days when that was what gentlemen did, and boxed them up for display as ornaments, along with stuffed foxes and bouquets of flowers cunningly crafted from shells.

It had to be this room. I remembered the bay window, with the green velvet curtains bleached at the edges by the sun, and the view out over the garden. I swallowed, the wine souring in my gullet. What was that Cadi had told me? Lucky

46

Miss Tudur, to die like that in her own bed, before her hungry relatives could whip her out like a rotten tooth and pack her off to hospital and a nursing home.

OK, I've lived and stayed in plenty of houses, some of them old where the chances are at least one life had breathed its last where I spent the hours of darkness. But that's not the same as knowing someone died there. Someone you knew, someone you even loved, in a strange sort of a way, with hardly knowing them at all. Someone who might just feel personal enough to take notice of you sitting there with an empty pot of tiramisu and a half full glass of wine, merrily scattering chocolate slivers all over the floor, with everything ripped out and changed around with not so much as by your leave.

'People expect en suites nowadays,' I found myself explaining aloud, defensively. 'And I can't afford to stay here in the long run if it doesn't pay for itself.' I downed half the glass in one gulp.

Savour? You can forget the niceties when it's a quick fix of Dutch courage and the dulling of the senses you're in need of. The alcohol obligingly hit my stomach hard, and shot up into my head. Slightly anaesthetised, I looked around once more. Where exactly had Elinor's bed been? It was dark outside by now: a dark, impenetrable wall of blackness beyond the protection of the curtains. I had no particular desire to move from my little camping ground and go wandering around in a castle where – if horror movies were anything to go by – the electrics could go at any moment. On the other hand, I had no desire to have my blow-up bed right on the spot...

'Weird,' I muttered, looking around. I blinked, and blinked, and looked again. Seriously weird. I know the room had shrunk and changed shape a little with the addition of the en suite, but I didn't think it had changed that much. It had to be the same room: the bay window was right; the view was right. The other rooms I'd looked into didn't have such an impressive view at all. I'd particularly admired it on my last look around before the contracts were signed, I remembered. Which was, of course, why Robin had bust a gut getting this room as ready as could be for my arrival when the inevitable delays meant the servants' quarters would not be finished in time.

But where was the fireplace? It had been a real fireplace. The last time I'd been up here in Elinor's time there had even been coals in the grate: the flames had warmed my legs as I peered at the ammonites on the mantelpiece. I know I'd just had central heating put in, but Robin wasn't daft enough to miss a trick like a real, *gen-u-ine* fireplace for my American customers to exclaim 'now isn't that just *dar-ling!*' over. We wouldn't ever have had to discuss it, if it had been there, that is. It had been a carved slate fireplace, full of intricate twirls and swirls. The kind that would have found a prominent place on my website, alongside the as-yet-to-be-purchased four-poster beds.

The relatives could have whipped it out, of course, and just not mentioned it on the inventory. But surely there would still have been the hole? Or at least fresh plasterboard and paint. I peered around. Not a dicky bird. The decorators had not even begun in here, so there was nothing covered up. Even in the light of a bare 100-watt bulb left by the builders in the central ceiling light, there was not a sign.

Curiouser and curiouser. Not that Elinor would have frozen, even on the chilliest nights: there were already radiators on this floor and the ground one, when I'd first viewed the place. Put in some ten years ago, Robin had guessed. Not bad condition, but best to replace them as we were doing the entire place.

Surely it couldn't have vanished inside the en suite? But that was the wrong side of the room. The chimney had to be on the outside wall, which stretched back at a right angle from the window... It must have been! I remembered light streaming in at an angle, sending the African mask and the carved crocodile placed next to my favourite ammonite into deep, and just a little unsettling, shadow. The wall had not been touched yet. Even the faded wallpaper was still there, peeling a little. I ran my fingers along its surface. Well, it felt like a wall. There was only one thing for it: I thumped hard with the end of my fist.

Oh, it was hollow, all right.

And no, I didn't get to work, there and then, wielding pickaxes, hammers and the odd chainsaw that might have been lying around. I went back to my mattress, poured myself another glass of wine, and thought about this. OK, a fireplace boarded up when the radiators went in, fair enough. But an entire wall?

I shut my eyes tight, and tried to picture the mantelpiece, once more. I mean, *dar-ling* it might be, but it wasn't that special, not like it was made of gold, or anything. And they weren't even that rare: they'd gone out of fashion at some point and been ripped out *en masse*. At Tyn-y-Coed the neighbours were always digging them up in their gardens. It couldn't be the stuff on the mantelpiece, because that was just daft, and a complete waste of energy, and, anyhow, two of the ammonite boxes *weren't* there, they had been left to me and Cadi, and no one had had to rip down a wall to get at them.

And the third one – nah, that wasn't gold, either, I'd stake my life on it. They were a set, the three of them. Elinor probably felt she couldn't leave it to me, or to Cadi. It just wouldn't be fair. So no doubt some crusty relative had their Gollum-like paws on it at this very moment and was digging around in the base in a vain attempt to strike hidden diamonds.

So what had been around the mantelpiece? I squeezed my eyes tighter. Pictures. Paintings of mountains, as far as I could remember. There had been one of Dolbadarn Castle, its single round and ruined tower overpowered by the rise of Snowdon in the background. Other, similar scenes. A large mirror above the mantelpiece. And some kind of tapestry. One on either side.

Cadi had asked Elinor once if she'd made them. Elinor had just cackled and said no, it was not her kind of thing; someone in the family had made it. Some aunt or other. I couldn't remember a name, or when. I couldn't even remember what was on the tapestries (I wasn't a tapestry sort of girl, either). A few flowers, perhaps? But no unicorns, like in those medieval things. I'm sure I'd have remembered a unicorn.

My eyes shot open as my phone – carefully in my pocket, just in case a mad axe-man appeared at the door – jumped and burred and jingled itself into life.

'Yes?' For once, I was too in a fluster to check the name.

'Hi, Mam! You OK?'

'Katie. Yes, I'm fine.' I shook myself and made an effort to sound un-fazed and stone cold sober. 'All settled in. You OK?'

'Yeah, fine, Mam. I was just calling to see if you'd got there.' She giggled. 'Not interrupting anything, am I?'

'None of your business if you are,' I retorted.

'Spoilsport. I told you ages ago, Robin fancies you.'

'He does?'

'Don't be evasive, Mam. I don't mind if you're settling down to a nice little love-nest, honest. Time you had some fun again.'

'And you don't call moving into a castle of my very own "fun"?'

'You know what I mean. Just give me the nod and I'll buzz off.'

'It's OK, really.'

'Oh.' She sounded a little disappointed. But then Katie has been trying to marry me off ever since she left home. I have a feeling she thinks I can't manage on my own. I changed the subject.

'How's Tim?'

'Fuck Tim.'

Oh-oh.

'Want to talk about it, darling?'

'No.'

'OK, then.' I waited for a moment.

'Bloody men! D'you know what he did last night?' The question was clearly rhetorical, so I made sympathetic noises, and listened to my daughter's ensuing tale of woe. I did try to be fair and see both sides. After all, I knew Tim quite well by now, and from what I could see he wasn't any more particularly self-centred than most twenty-somethings. His crimes weren't even extraordinarily wicked, even as recounted by his Wronged Woman. And Katie was rapidly heading for thirty, and was definitely a grown up with her own life, and had never yet listened to any advice I'd cared to give.

Funny that: a definite flaw in God's grand plan. Why can't we learn from someone else's mistakes? It would save a hell of a lot of time when we could be profitably doing something else. But there we go, generation after generation, learning from our own experience.

I never listened to a word my own mother said. I'd thought she'd forgotten love, and had no sense of adventure when she'd muttered darkly about Terry and Unreliable, when he turned up horrendously late – well past the cake stage – for my twenty-first birthday meal with my assorted family. Fine, it was with the family. A-1 embarrassing and tedious. But you did those sort of things.

At least, boring, conventional, ordinary people like me, did those sort of things, just to keep the peace and avoid questions when you went out for the real celebration later. Part of me had admired him for being a free spirit.

Ouch.

So I murmured sympathetically, which was all Katie really wanted at this point, I judged, having tactfully elicited that two of her girl friends were arriving within the hour, armed with Bacardi Breezers, a large tub of double-choc ice cream and a copy of *Pretty Woman*, for some serious comforting.

Having said that, Katie was still my baby, and I'd have his balls off and out of the window soon as look at him twice, the selfish, heartless, two-timing –

'Oh! That's the doorbell.' I heard Katie sniffle quickly, and begin to make her way down the stairs.

'Take care, *cariad*,' I said. 'I'm here if you need me.'

'Thanks.' Another sniff. 'I'll see you next weekend, right?'

'If you feel up to it.'

'Yeah. It'll do me good to get away. And I can't wait to see this castle of yours in the flesh.'

'Well, it'll be lovely to see you, darling, but the – ' But Katie had reached the door, and was not stopping for the tale of the late finishing of the top floor.

'Right, see you, Mam. Bye!'

I put the phone back in my pocket. Then fished it out again and put it on charge next to my bed. Never run out of battery in an empty house with a missing fireplace and a secret wall, that's my policy. Especially a secret wall.

I looked at the wine bottle. And no, I had not finished it. Not nearly. And I did not intend to: I knew from experience that nowadays a glassful more and I'd have a splitting headache all next day. And, OK, there are still times when it's still worth it. But not with a real castle to visit next morning. Not to mention lunch with Robin, who always noticed if I was 'under the weather', and would triumphantly conclude I was too chicken to sleep alone in Bryn Glas without getting pissed.

Between the drive and the unpacking, and all the new sights and sounds assailing my senses for the past few hours, not to mention Katie and her problems, I was getting beyond caring if anyone had been bricked up alive in the room, let alone died there.

I did the bare necessities. I staggered off for a pee (my bladder only just lasts the night, these days), then shuffled myself into a comfortable tracksuit, ready for action in the night if necessary, and climbed into bed.

I didn't even try to sleep. The art, I've found before, is to approach the thing in stages: lull the mind into a false sense of security. I had switched off all the lights on my way back from the en suite, leaving me with a table lamp within easy reach, and a small portable TV that appeared to be in mourning for the good old days of black and white, and never quite lost the ghost of itself, however much I swivelled the aerial away from that death-knell of any signal – radio, TV, mobile, or otherwise – that are the mountains.

I hastily checked my phone. Battery was charging; signal was on full. Phew. At that moment I knew I would never regret that my castle was near to the coast and the town, and not perched more romantically (but signal-less) amongst the Snowdonian hinterland, with the *Brenin Llwyd* – the Grey King – sweeping down in the mists to chase all strangers from his domain.

Duw, I'm not superstitious, but why take chances? So I lay there, pretending I had no intentions of sleeping, watching TV and not listening to the owls hooting to each other outside. It worked: I drifted off, and came to again. This time I switched the light off. One step nearer. Now it was just me and the TV.

This time it was the roar of a helicopter overhead that had me awake again. It was so low I could hear the turn of the blades. That was it! There was a nutcase on the loose with an axe – despite there being no mention of one on every news I could find that night – and the helicopter was the police vainly trying to catch him. Or hovering up above, watching helplessly as he climbed in through a ground-floor window and began to slowly make his way upstairs...

There was no smash of the double-glazing. No creak of the treads of the stairs. The helicopter chugged away into the distance. I switched off the TV and held my breath. In the distance, I could hear the scrunch of the sea on Llanestyn beach as the tide pulled away at the pebbles. I could hear the drunks being thrown out from the pubs and staggering home with a burst of singing and the faint echo of a police siren.

It was OK. All was well with the world. And the helicopter? Oh, I'd heard them often in my time: night manoeuvres from RAF Valley over the waters on Anglesey. Or more likely some poor bugger stuck in a gully halfway up Snowdon or the Glyders with a twisted ankle, or lost in the vastness of the Carneddi range.

I shivered. We'd got lost up there on the Carneddi ourselves, once, Dad and Cadi and me. The mist came down and we took a wrong turning: ended up missing Pen-yr-Ole-

Wen, which led to the car park, and coming down the Bethesda side, by the *Ysgolion Duon*, the Black Ladders cliff-face, instead.

We'd found ghosts there, all right. They'd loomed up at us out of the mist: the decaying carcases of planes. Bits of wing. Whole engines lodged in a stream. Twisted pieces of metal everywhere. A graveyard of planes – not modern ones, the early twentieth century kind – that didn't clear the ridge and came down on the bleakness of the hillsides.

Some pilots made their own way down, Dad said; others were helped by local villagers. But that graveyard of planes could still haunt me. It was still there; books had been written about it. But, somehow, I'd never had the guts to find my way up under the shadow of the Black Ladders again.

I snuggled down into my sleeping bag. I could feel the chill of a night spent on the mountains creeping into my bones. I hoped the poor sod up there would be found. Then I dozed off once more into an uneasy sleep.

CHAPTER 6

WHEN I WOKE UP AGAIN IT WAS ALMOST DAWN. You know; that reflected kind of a light just before the sun rises.

Well, I had survived the night. No axe-murderers, no thieves, no vandals throwing stones shouting 'piss off, rich bitch'. And no ghosts. I yawned, and tried to sink myself back into sleep. I could have done with a few hours more after the upheavals of yesterday, but my brain had decided enough was enough and there was work to be done. And was there work to be done! There was a castle to get shipshape and furnish, and a new life to begin. Which was all a bit much before the first cup of tea.

I wriggled out of bed and put the kettle on, groaning a little at my stiff back, stiff thighs, aching knees, and shoulders in urgent need of a very expensive massage. Cod liver oil did its best, but it couldn't quite keep the creaks and the cracks at bay at times like this. First thing to go on the 'to do' list for Monday morning, I noted, was to find a yoga class.

Not the virtuous, sculpture yourself to anything you choose, (or whatever was computer generated onto the inside pages of *OK!* or *Hello!* last week) lose your entire body fat in an hour, kind. I need my body fat, thank you very much, helps keep the sinking oestrogen levels from diving out of sight in the steaming crater of a hot flush. Nor do I need one of those endlessly impossible positions, limbering up for sex, kind. Per-*lease*. All those young bodies twisting and entwining themselves around each other, eyes closed, faces turned inward, absorbed utterly and entirely in themselves and their own perfections?

Yuck.

For me it's definitely a case of been there, done that; moved on into utterly unknown territory. Just don't tell the youngsters, that's what I say: let them keep on merrily gyrating, thinking they've discovered something deliciously naughty in the shed at the bottom of the garden.

We don't want them muscling in on the real action. Let them keep on thinking the over-fifties are just doddering towards their graves, rather than having the time of their lives. So, for heaven's sake, keep those Saga brochures under wraps, or there'll be a flourishing trade in instant-wrinkle, instant bits-sagging cream before you know it, and the under-thirties will be busily back-dating their passports, before you can say 'Kilimanjaro'.

Now, where was I? Ah, yes: yoga classes.

No, a nice gentle, keep those joints supple, keep the blood moving, sort of a yoga class, with plenty of deep relaxation at the end, I determined, as I dunked a tea-bag into my cup and reached for the milk. There had been several in Kingston-upon-Thames, and there must be at least one around here, especially with all the pensioners installed along the sea front from here to Llandudno, and the alternative types stashed around the hillsides growing organic lettuce and breeding goats.

I yawned again and rubbed the back of my neck, still rigid from avoiding the I'm-so-god-dammed-important-I-haven't-a-moment-to-lose, so-move-over-woman-driver, maniacs overtaking on double-blind bends all the way up from the Severn bridge before tail-gating a tractor from Beddgelert and then revving impatiently behind the tourists dawdling on the bends past Snowdon, who were actually daring to enjoy the view.

Good job I hadn't drunk any more, I reflected, as I took my first sip: I was going to have a headache as it was. I drank my tea slowly, sitting on the dubious comfort of my mattress, supporting my head against the wall. Opposite me, the hollow wall in front of the old fireplace stood and gleamed in the quietly increasing light.

Yep, it was still there. I even roused myself to go over and bang with my fist once more. Just as hollow. Just as false. Just as it was last night. Of course, if I had been a true heroine – or a hero – I'd have taken a chair-leg to the thing and had it down in a jiffy. Sod that for a lark. This was something I needed to think about. Psych myself up to – and employ some muscle-bound builder who knew what he was doing and wouldn't bring half the building down on me if there were some load-bearing joists up there.

Besides, I may be a big girl now and fight my own fights and clear up my own messes, but something like this called for a bit of moral support. After all, men have been known to wall up their faithless (or just plain inconvenient) wives from time to time. Supposing Elinor had taken the hint and carved out a career for herself as Bluebeard in drag? Elinor? My Elinor? Tiny, elegant, best-girl's-school-accented Elinor, with a head for heights and a taste for the exotic? Never! But then, I knew so little about her, and aren't there always more things in heaven and earth, Horatio?

I poured myself another cup of tea. My joints were loosening up from yesterday's excesses, but my neck was just as stiff, and the headache was definitely looming. I took the tea and myself over to the bay window to where my first-aid box was still tucked alongside the evening primrose oil and the over-fifties' vitamins.

I fished out the strongest painkillers I could find – bugger me if I was going to let Robin think I had a hangover when I hadn't got one – and downed them with a piece of last night's chocolate to line the stomach. Then I peered between the half-closed curtains.

Big mistake.

The sun was thinking about it, but hadn't quite hit the horizon yet. It was still pre-dawn: the time that is neither one thing nor the other. The time, for my Celtic ancestors, when the boundaries between the living and the dead were just a little blurred, and anything could happen.

And there, down in my garden, it just was.

Oh, there wasn't the Ku Klux Klan arranged in semi-circle, or a witch's altar with a crucified cat, or even King Arthur come charging down from his cave on Snowdon to chase out the jumped-up peasant of a woman who had dared to aspire to a castle of her own. Even my car was still there with its windscreen intact.

But the mist had rolled down from the mountains in the night and had lain itself in streaks across the lawn, between a covering of cobwebs scattered with dewdrops, shimmering lacily in the uncertain light. And between the mist and the shrubbery, someone was walking.

I froze. *Uffern dân!* I've never been that cold! My blood was a glacier with the end bits blue and luminous and crumbling into the sea sending slivers of ice into my brain. A cat? Dog? Stray piece of mist? Imagination? No, it was moving. Slowly; stealthily, even. Definitely human. Or, at least, of a human form. Man or woman it was impossible to tell, and, to be honest, at that moment I wasn't all that fussed. It appeared wrapped up in a long coat of some kind. Not necessarily twenty-first century, then.

I swallowed.

OK, I'd taken on a castle, and castles have these sort of things. I should have been more prepared. I just thought it happened in storybooks. Or turned out to be some hormonally-charged alpha-male with a fixation – bordering on stalking – for poor little down-trodden me, and an urgent need to gather me up in his arms, take charge of my castle and all those other worries clogging up my pretty little head, and give me a rollicking good seeing-to in return.

For a could-be-a-grandmother fifty-two-year-old? Ha! In my experience, self-styled alpha males just don't go for self-made-with-blood-sweat-and-tears maybe alpha-ish females. Particularly those who are not too proud to show the signs of the aforementioned blood, sweat and tears.

Hey, if wrinkles work for Sean Connery as a mega sex symbol, they ought to sure as hell be good enough for me. So there. So alpha males can take themselves off, nose in air, hand on dick, and run along to whatever alpha males get up to in their spare time.

My visitor was by now moving away from me – thank heaven for small mercies, but who was to say it wasn't about to change its mind? It made its way to the centre of the lawn, to where steps made their way down into the rough patch of garden beyond. The pond! It was stopping by the pond! By this time at least I had the sense to move to the corner of the window, where I wasn't so easily spotted should the interloper turn suddenly.

I stood there rigid. My visitor stood at the edge of the water, rigid, looking down into the water. Surely it wasn't some nut with a fixation about mistletoe and silver sickles, about to make some druidic offering in my fishpond? It bent down towards the water, enshrouded within the mist. I blinked. Maybe it would just vanish? Leave me nervously looking over my shoulder each time I made my way through the shrubbery?

All right, so I could have dashed down and gone out to investigate. But I'm the one at the back of the cinema, or behind the sofa, with my eyes closed, muttering 'get out of there, for crissake, just get out of there, you stupid cow!', or in this case, don't leave the safety of solid walls and locked doors behind.

One more minute of this and I was dialling 999. My shadow was up again. Whether having put something in, or taken anything out, or merely communed with the newts and the Koi carp, I didn't like to even guess. They turned, and began to make their way down the steps.

Ach a fi! Just as I thought it was safe to make a move for the mobile, I could have sworn they turned back for a moment. No glowing eyes, or a bladed disc spun at me to slice my head from my body. Just the faintest of pauses that could possibly have been my paranoia, but I didn't really think so, and this time it really did vanish, moving rapidly down the steps and disappearing between the rhododendrons.

Just when I thought I was doing so well. Just when I thought I had cracked this staying-in-a-castle-on-my-own malarkey.

Bugger.

And there was no one there now. Just the mist vanishing as the sun cleared the mountains.

CHAPTER 7

THE SUN WAS SHINING BRIGHT AND CHEERFUL when I reached Conwy later that morning.

'Idiot!' I muttered to myself, as I emerged from an avenue of trees to find the town walls striding there in front of me in all their medieval glory, with battlements patrolled by battalions of backpacked tourists clutching guidebooks and bottles of mineral water.

OK, you have to admit that it was a reasonable thought at the time. I mean, what the sodding hell was I doing with an overgrown Victorian folly – without a cat's chance in hell of matching up to the National Trust glories of Penrhyn Castle just down the coast – with mildew invading the walls, possibly walled-up-alive ex-lovers in the bedroom, and a haunting in the garden? When, for the money, and a fraction of the financial and emotional investment, I could have bought myself a nice little pad inside a medieval walled town, with a harbour opening out onto the Irish Sea, and a real castle standing there with its towers and turrets dominating the skyline?

I turned the car into the wide stretch of ring road alongside the walls and followed the queue between the narrow arch and into the streets of the town. I have always loved Conwy. When I was a kid, long before the A55 dual carriageway had the traffic speeding (well, most of the time) along the coast, the entire road population had to make its way through the medieval streets of the town, which had clearly found Thomas Telford's nineteenth-century road for the horse-drawn variety of transport enough of a shock to its system, and creaked nervously at the cram of cars, lorries, buses, vans and caravans squashing themselves through the bottleneck of medieval streets.

Consequently, this had left plenty of time for the passengers of these vehicles to spend long hours gazing at the ruins of Conwy Castle while the archways of the walls breathed in to allow a particularly fat caravan to inch through.

Personally, I wouldn't restore Conwy Castle, even if it was offered to me, plus the twenty million or so it would take to return to its former glory. A real fairy-tale castle, rising on a rock above the shoreline where the river Conwy met the sea with rounded keeps, battlements and towers just like those in my story-books, except that, even then, there were always a cluster of sightseers braving the heights to gaze down over the railway line and Robert Stephenson's railway bridge across the river Conwy.

I eyed the castle as I crept down the main street, pausing by the traffic lights that let the tourists pass over the road and under the arch that led out to the quay. Why, oh why, Lissa Deryn, can't you ever choose the simple, straightforward, sensible options in your life? I asked myself, with a groan. And yes, I did sound like my mother. And like the mother-me who tried to get her children to think through their life-plan, despite never having thought through mine in the least at their age.

I escaped the kids with nets and buckets and the parents with chips and ice cream, found a parking place within the shadow of the castle – how romantic can you get! – and made my way down to the quay. The call of seagulls filled the air. I could hear the rattle of masts and the whoosh of sails flapping in the wind. Brine and the seaweed scents of stale seafood drifted up towards me. Bliss. As I walked down the quayside, past the mussel-fishing museum and the boats tied up waiting for the tide, the scent of fresh chips and old candyfloss mingled with the smells of the sea.

Wouldn't life be so simple if I had just eased myself into one of the cottages tucked away beneath the walls? I could tend my courtyard garden, stroll along here every morning with my faithful retriever at my side, visit the castle every day of my life, and just sit on the benches at the seafront, watching the ships come in and out, dreaming of the places they were going to, the sights they would see, and cursing the seagulls as they hassled anyone who stood still for a moment. I looked down into the green water lapping the sides of the quay and slopping against the *Llys y Gwynt*, the *Palace of the Winds* pleasure cruiser as she swayed gently at her moorings.

'A penny for them?' I found Robin emerging from the Liverpool Arms, pint in one hand, a tonic water and ice held out for me.

'Thanks,' I said, with a smile. Lord! You'd think we were an old married couple already! Which made him that steady, thoughtful and considerate, but frankly rather boring guy living in the flat downstairs that you just *know* the heroine is going to end up with after she's had stonkingly good sex with a few love-rat contenders along the way, proving that while you kiss the rats the prince is always there, blinking from the depths of his well, croaking softly into the dusk and just waiting patiently for his charms (plus his close blood relation to the royal family and his very large castle) to become blindingly obvious.

Personally, I always feel he should get a life and take up snowboarding instead.

Mmmm. I couldn't quite see Robin with his pale linen suit – uncreased, of course – and immaculate hair, heading off on a snowboard. Any more than I could imagine any rats giving me a second look, nowadays. Ah well, you live and learn, I suppose. I seem to have done a lot of living and not enough learning, when you think about it. But hey, that's life.

'Have a good night?' Robin was asking.

'Very.' He gave me an old-fashioned look. 'Well, comfortable. You know what it's like in a new place.'

'No regrets, then?'

'Regrets?' I looked away along the quay where children were sat in a row with their buckets fishing for crabs. An idyllic scene. (Unless you were a crab, of course, and didn't know you were destined to be thrown back to the joys of the harbour mud, rather than ending up as dinner.) Suddenly, I was grinning from ear to ear like a five-year-old waiting for the party to begin.

'I know you've always enjoyed a challenge, but it's a lot to take on, Lissa,' said Robin, gently. As understanding of me as any guy in the flat downstairs, and just as ready to take on my grief for my foolishness, and guide me through to the happy ending.

Except he didn't understand me at all. Not that I blamed him: it was only the sudden bolt of vision that hit me, bang, slap in the face at his words that made me have any understanding of this part of me at all.

I hate challenges. Always have done, always will. I hate the tightness in the stomach, the waking up at three in the morning with imagination let loose on every last detail that could possibly go wrong and leave me and the kids in that cardboard box under the arches. I hate going out of the house to risk being run over by the number seven bus, come to that.

Given half a chance, I'd cocoon myself in a room of padded silk, with fantastic sunset views between the double-glazing, with a satellite dish and a DVD player to live out my fantasies – and even then only the nice ones I know have happy endings and no gratuitous blood, gunge and body-parts flying all over the shop – eating watermelons and chocolate and never stirring outside where time works its changes and no happy endings last for ever.

It's why I've always thrown myself at challenges, ever since Terry – my croaking prince who was supposed to provide me with the silk-lined room at least on a part-time basis – went off to Find Himself, and left me wanting to bury my head beneath the pillow and never come out. I set them up and throw myself at them without giving myself a moment to think. And once you are in the middle of them it's too late.

And I'm not talking about fairground rides or a blind date: signing the mortgage payments with a prayer that my careful calculations really were correct, and that tenants as a species didn't immediately vanish from the face of the earth – now that's the chill wind on the dusty streets that really gets the adrenalin going.

Not to mention launching the majority of your carefully-garnered comfortable-old-age pension investments into doing up a rickety old castle, of course.

'No regrets,' I said quietly.

'Good. I'm glad.' He still didn't sound entirely convinced.

'But you know what I'm like with doing up places: only interested in the girly, decorative things,' I added. 'I'll be glad once the building work is finished and I can get on with the four-poster beds and the ancient carved chests – ' I could see disapproval and the word 'woodworm' rising to his lips, so I hurried on: 'and get on with the garden, of course.'

'Ah, yes. I was meaning to talk you about that.'

Oh-oh. Swimming pools? Tennis courts? The whole thing turned into lawn? Or had some little whisper reached his ears at last...

'Yes?'

'I think I might have found you a gardener.'

'Oh yes?' Mmm. Tall; sexy; sunburned. Nice bum. (OK, so I might not be in the market any more, but a girl can still enjoy looking, can't she?)

'She's worked on several of my client's gardens. They've always been very pleased with what she's done.'

No nice bum, then. Well, not from my point of view, at least. I should have guessed!

'Do I know her?' More than likely, knowing Robin's tastes in women, she'd be young, blonde and could take the catwalk by storm, with 'gardening' involving twiddling a pen into a fancy design, incorporating several constructions made in steel and a twelve-foot high water feature, before wafting her mud-free arms at the hired help.

In fact, given Robin's current determination to avoid making eye contact with me at this moment, she probably *did* storm the catwalk in her spare time.

'You might do. Arwen Jenkins. She took over the gardening centre when Phil Jones retired. She set up her own gardening business a few years ago.'

Ah, so not-so-young bimbo! More like buxom bleached-blonde with a penchant for over-cropped tops and free-flowing breasts.

'I don't remember her.'

'Elsa Jenkins' granddaughter.'

'Who's Elsa Jenkins?'

'Lissa! You must remember Mrs Jenkins: Miss Tudur's housekeeper.'

'I thought she was Mrs Jones.'

'There *was* Mrs Jones. But then she retired and Elsa Jenkins took over.'

'Must have been after my time,' I murmured.

'The past fifteen years?' he retorted, just a little impatiently.

'Oh.' I blushed. OK, hands up: I hadn't noticed. She must have let me in when I came to visit Elinor, but I couldn't picture her at all. Surely I wasn't growing as bad as the Tudurs themselves, not noticing if the domestics existed or not?

'Arwen knows the gardens. She's been keeping them tidy for the past ten years.'

'Really?' I wasn't sure I entirely liked this. Ms Arwen Jenkins might have ideas of her own. Might not like change.

'Miss Tudur was talking about restoring the garden at one point. You know, take it back to the way it was in Victorian times. I know she and Arwen were discussing it. You might find she has some good ideas. She certainly knows her stuff, and she's done some work with garden archaeologists.'

'Garden archeologists?' I nearly choked on my ice. This was a new one on me. 'Are you serious?'

'Of course. Gardens have a history. Garden archaeology is doing useful work finding out about it.'

'OK, I believe you. Just as long as it doesn't involve dusting down bones with a toothbrush, I'm game for anything.'

'Well, unless you are unfortunate to find yourself situated above a graveyard, I really think bones are unlikely.'

Ach a fi! I hadn't considered the possibility of a graveyard beneath my garden. The spectre came looming up, like my figure in the mist this morning. Pagan rights. Severed heads. Walled-up wives/lovers/wicked stepmothers secretly removed and deposited beneath the pelargoniums.

Maybe I should invite Cadi to come and join me for the next few days. Just for the company of course.

'I'll talk to her,' I said, hastily, wishing to change the subject, pronto, or I'd never eat my lunch and Robin might think I'd put myself on a diet at last, and might get the seriously wrong end of the stick – like it was for his benefit, and go back to wearing that particularly stifling brand of aftershave he took to a few years ago, after my glorious Raph finally vanished from the scene. 'Have you got her number with you?'

He had the card ready. Somehow, it was not what I had expected. 'Arwen' was the lettering, in flowing, slightly old-fashioned script, above a Celtic swirl of intricate design. Just that and the usual list of garden maintenance, design, pruning. Water features. (Now that could come in useful, at least). Herb gardens a speciality. (OK, I've always fancied the idea of a herb garden.) Then a phone number, a website address and e-mail. And at least Arwen should know what Elinor's plans had been for the garden.

'Good,' said Robin, suddenly smiling broadly. 'The work I've seen of hers has been excellent. Very imaginative. I'm sure you'll get on like a house on fire. You'll not regret it.'

Ha!

Robin, *cariad*, if I'd known then what I know now...

But then fools rush in where angels fear to tread, so they say. And if I'd knocked around the planet this long and still been an angel, then I would have been in serious need of getting a life – so, really, what the hell else should I have expected?

'Fine,' said I, mutton to the slaughter.

CHAPTER 8

I PHONED CADI THE NEXT MORNING.
'Got cold feet, have you then?' was her remark. She sounded quite unnecessarily smug.

'Of course not!'

'Oh yes? I know you, Elissa Deryn: you're still a soft little thing under all that sass of yours.'

The cheek of it! My own kid sister, who used to look up to me for everything And she was quite wrong, of course.

'Fine, have it your way. I thought you might like to come and have a look around before the builders start again on Monday, that's all. But if you've got better things to do with your weekend...'

'OK, OK, *cariad*. Don't get your knickers in a twist. I'd love to come and see your castle in the air; you know I would. I'd have been over like a shot, but I didn't want to invade your space. I mean, sweetie, you could have been up to anything...'

'Well I'm not, and I'm not likely to be.'

'Really?'

'Really,' I grunted. Had Robin been sending signed memos of his intentions to all my friends and family? Didn't they know I was a clued-up, cynical old trout who'd given up men years ago and he didn't stand a smidgen of a chance, anyhow?

'OK. I'll stop off at the supermarket and bring dinner, then.'

'Great. Just remember food, Cadi. You know, that stuff you have to chew before it reaches your stomach? You might want to keep trim, but I need more sustenance than a bottle of Cabernet Sauvignon.'

'*Duw*, of course, sugar pie. So I'll bring strawberries to go with the champagne, then...'

She was winding me up, of course. Cadi was born with a naughty glint to her eye. And I have to admit it: she can run rings round me any day. I was always bull-at-a-gate, hit everything over the head, unsubtle clumsiness, as far as the niceties of social life are concerned.

Cadi just wafted through with slender elegance, leaving you quite convinced that she was far too much the lady to have realised what she had just said in those smooth and mellow tones of hers. Oh, I'd have given my eye-teeth (whatever they are) to acquire just the faintest shadow of her finesse.

So she turned up, later that afternoon, forty-nine and willowy, chestnut hair neatly trimmed, and with skin-tight jeans and an open-necked shirt, pale pink pearls and all, over sensible walking shoes. At least the boot of her smart new car was loaded with carrier bags.

I shuffled in the driveway, feeling round and dumpy in my tracksuit (no, not the one I'd slept in, a girl does have some standards, even in the most unlikely of settings), hair tied up in an old rubber band (my favourite scrunchy having wormed its way into the deepest recesses of the castle some time in the night) and not even an attempt at make-up, feeling more like the scullery maid than the lady of the castle. Cadi has this effect on people.

'Well?' I demanded, after the obligatory kissing and hugging.

'You did it!' Cadi was grinning, broadly. 'You actually did it! You bought a castle, Lissa. Only you could pull off a thing like that, out of the blue. You're a star, darling.'

'Don't be so soft. It's an investment. A business decision. Everyone's putting their savings in bricks and mortar nowadays, with the stock market being such a dead duck.'

'Yeah, yeah. And absolutely nothing to do with you being just an old romantic, after all.'

'Bugger off!' But Cadi took no notice of my irritation. She never did. No respect for my seniority in years and experience at all, that one.

'*Duw*, girl,' she was saying, 'now all we need is a nice young prince to keep you amused.'

'Young?' I raised my eyebrows.

'Of course, *cyw*. What else? Lords of the manor always go for young things. Would-be lords of the manor to boot, in my experience. So the lady of the castle has just *got* to get herself a toy-boy.'

'Don't be daft.'

'Come on, Lissa! You like a pretty face as much as the next woman. What you need is a nice, pre-menopausal male with a neat figure. And stamina, of course.'

'Oh, yeah? Like they'd be really interested in a raddled, well-past-laying, ready-for-the-pot old hen like me.'

'Plenty of men go for older women nowadays. Look at Madonna.'

'I am not Madonna.'

75

'Of course not, darling. You have even better assets.' My eyebrows were going up and down double-time by now. Probably good exercise for the crow's feet. My sister tapped one Ecco-shod foot impatiently. 'This place, Lissa: your castle. Who in their right mind would turn you down?'

'I want to be loved for me, not my "assets", thank you very much.' Cadi clicked her tongue.

'There, what did I tell you? An old romantic to the core. And this from the woman who turned down Mr Sex-On-Legs when you were penniless and he wanted to waft you over to his family's pad in Tuscany. I ask you.'

'Raph came from Cockfosters, if you must know,' I retorted, primly.

'Ah, but I bet the Italian side still had an enormous villa in Tuscany.' OK; well, close. But I was not about to go into this with my little sister who had once turned up in her breathtakingly beautiful phase and just couldn't keep her eyes off my partially-continental guitarist, with his gym-honed muscles and long black hair. Even Cadi seemed to feel she might be going just a bit too far. She cleared her throat, and turned back to my castle. 'Come on: you can help me unload, and then you can show me around.'

'OK,' I said. Much, much, safer ground.

And, in the end, it was fun showing Cadi my castle. It made me forget the dust and the bricks and the work still to be done – and my rapidly plummeting bank balance – and reminded me of exactly why I'd bought Bryn Glas in the first place.

The kitchens in the basement were still in their pre-war state. Some Tudur or other, Elinor had once told me, had ripped out the old Victorian kitchen and put in units and an

76

electric cooker. Quite a thing in those days, and probably the talk of the village, but several cookers, washing-machines and fridges later, it all just looked like the broken-down contents of a particularly greasy flea-market.

There were pantries leading off, out of action since the advent of the fridge, and still with the slate shelves in situ. My plan was to turn the entire place back to as near its original as I could go: slate worktops and slate shelving in the main part, with all modern appliances firmly banished out of sight to where joints of meat and bottles of preserves once gathered dust, waiting for the long winter months.

The library, on the other hand, just looked forlorn. All Elinor's books had been swept away – doubtless down to some posh antique bookshop on Charing Cross Road and sold for a small fortune. I'm quite certain the shelving would have gone too had it been any easier to dismantle, rather than handmade on the spot by some highly skilled Victorian craftsman. My plan was to turn it into a comfortable sitting room for my guests, but for the moment the en suites – being the most disruptive part of Bryn Glas' transformation from pretentious country retreat to working castle – were taking precedence.

'Oh, the conservatory!' exclaimed Cadi, pushing the glass doors at the far end of the room and stepping out amongst the red pattern of quarry tiles, tinged with a green growth around the edges. 'Poor thing! They might at least have left the plants, Lissa. I bet they weren't worth anything to anyone.'

'They'd probably have died by now anyhow,' I replied, trying to sound resigned, rather than ready to wallop any Tudur I might come across for being so heartless with Elinor's prized babies. For the amount of dosh they got for free, so to speak, from Bryn Glas, they might at least have employed Ms Jenkins, or someone of her ilk, to come in once a month and look after the tangled greenery. 'Anyhow, it's too late to do much this year. This is going to be my spring project.'

When the castle was all finished and spick and span, was the idea. When the Aga glowed in the bowels of the kitchen and herbs hung drying from the ceiling. When leather-bound armchairs graced the library, and four-posters wafted their muslin hangings from each spotlessly en suite bedroom. I had a feeling this was a pipe-dream, even then.

'So, come on, then,' said Cadi. 'This is the bit I've been waiting for: where's this famous flat of yours?'

'All in good time. You've got to go through everything, first.'

So, off we went, through sitting rooms, music rooms, dining rooms and libraries. All thick with dust and the mournful echoes of grand parties and evenings around the piano, with hushed flirtations swept behind the moth-eaten remains of curtains even the most dedicated Tudur had not seen fit to lay their greedy little mitts upon. Then up the grand staircase, all dark wood and banisters, to the tangled mess of half-fitted bathrooms, with baths, shower units and toilet cisterns stacked in every dark corner. Lastly, we stopped in front of a small door at the very end of a dark corridor.

'Bloody hell, Lissa! You're not telling me you're going to live in the servants' quarters, are you? A whole castle, all to yourself, and you're going to cram yourself into the smallest little corner right at the top?'

'Of course. It's private, away from the guests, and there's a view to die for.'

Robin had left me strict instructions not to venture up to this most delicately-poised work-in-progress, so the pair of us crept up the stairs like naughty schoolchildren, ready to rush off and hide at the sound of his voice at any moment. (Robin Lloyd Jones just has this effect on people without trying, I'm afraid. It's a Lloyd Jones thing.) Once up there, however, even Cadi had to admit it was worth it.

The servants' quarters had been turned into a small, self-contained flat, with a bathroom tucked under the eaves, a galley kitchen and a neat little bedroom, just about big enough to squeeze in a double bed. Robin had been worried about the smallness of the bedroom, but I'd fought for it – after all, it was none of his business – and its pokiness was in the very best of causes: a reasonable-sized sitting room, fronted by French windows that opened out onto a balcony.

The balcony was a later addition, after the Second World War, when servants grew thin on the ground, and an enterprising Tudur had set himself up as an artist, with high hopes of restoring the family fortunes. He'd made himself a very nice garret up here under the eaves, but had suffered from a distinct lack of talent. There had still been one or two of his canvases stashed around the place when we were kids: even then I could see they were vile. But they had vanished along with the rest. Probably the entire Tudur clan was badgering Sotheby's as to their unique value and several-hundred-million price tag at this very moment.

I threw open the windows, and we stepped outside. The artist Tudur had added low battlements of his own amongst the roof space to create a sheltered little suntrap. I could picture myself here, on warm afternoons, when my work was done, sitting with my pots of lavender and riotous nasturtiums, glass of wine and a bowl of olives on the table, mixed salad from my garden and a tiramisu from the local Tesco waiting for me in the fridge, watching the peacocks flaunting themselves as if there was no tomorrow.

'That's odd.' OK, I jumped. My spine had become quite cosy during the past few hours, but the shivers were back there again, sending a dribble of sweat snaking between the clasp of my bra-strap.

'What is?'

'You'd have thought they'd have sorted that out, the kind of money it must have taken to put up this place.'

'Sorted what out?' My sister was peering down onto the lawn, now streaked with the slanting light of early evening. It was one of those hot, still days of late summer when small insects hang in clouds above the dew-dampening grass. An eternal kind of a day, when time just hangs there, soaking up the fading warmth.

Gravestones. OK, it had to be gravestones. Possibly the odd gibbet I'd missed in my inspection earlier in the year. Or one that just appeared when the new owner had got themselves in so deep they couldn't possibly get themselves out again. Or maybe a past Tudur – and more than one of them had been rumoured to end their days on a gibbet, or to be damned lucky (and with equally sinful friends in high places) not to.

I peered down. Nothing. Could Cadi possibly have grown psychic in her not-so-old age?

'They must have seen it. At least from up here. I suppose you don't really notice it on the ground.'

'For heaven's sake, Cadi! Seen what?'

'The bumps in the lawn. It's uneven. See where the light catches it?'

Was that all? Phew. I followed the line of her finger. Sure enough, sent into relief by the low beams of sunlight, I could just make out a faint pattern on the grass of the lawn. I'd hired a local firm to keep the grass from running riot while I was waiting to move, so it was quite short and neat. Just the strange lines, forming a hesitant kind of a pattern amongst the greenery. Something went tick, tick, tick, in my mind, but before I could search through my vast selection of senior moments, Cadi was grabbing my arm.

'It could be the remains of a Roman Fort!'

'Here?'

'Possible. The Romans did get up this far. Not into the mountains, of course. But there's Segontium at Caernarfon, and Caerhun near me. This could have been on a route between: it's possible.'

'Wouldn't it be, well, deeper?' I objected. But Cadi was well away. My sister always did have an over-active imagination. It was the thing we shared all those years ago, when our collective over-activeness had led us through that half-open door in Bryn Glas walls and into the overgrown secrets of Elinor's domain.

Funnily enough, those imaginations of ours had led us both back from careers in the bright lights to the mountains of our birth. Mine to my castle, and Cadi's – via a slightly tortuous route – to being one of the best web-site designers in the business, working freelance from an old stone cottage in the Conwy Valley, with the odd dash to London and across the

Atlantic when she felt the need to see her clients face to face. Or a heavy dose of retail therapy, whichever was the most urgent.

There was definitely no stopping her now: she was down those twisting, winding servants' stairs before you could say 'broken ankle'. After only a moment's hesitation, I followed.

'It's probably drains,' I muttered, as we slapped away the midges – who were by now having a right old feast at our expense – in an attempt to find the lines on the ground.

'Well if it's drains this shallow, you're buggered,' replied Cadi.

'Not those sort of drains! Drainage for the garden. The Victorians were into that kind of thing.'

'OK, but that doesn't explain why there's no sign of them down here.'

'Maybe it was just the way the grass was cut.'

'Rubbish. They weren't those kind of lines. They were definitely a structure of some kind.' Cadi had a no-stopping-her-now look on her face. Her cheeks were glowing and her eyes sparkled. I knew the signs: either we followed this until she collapsed in a heap, or we'd never get onto the champagne and highly expensive-looking dips and delicacies currently awaiting us in Elinor's bedroom.

All right, I was glad Cadi had brought a blow-up mattress of her own and was clearly planning to make a night of it, but I'd rather get on with the business of demolishing the delicacies than wandering around the garden with night about to drop on us like a stone, and not so much as a mobile or a torch between us.

'Couldn't we do this in the morning?'

'Oh, come off it, Lissa. You're not spooked, are you?'

'Of course not!'

'Well then. It might be easier to spot them in the walled garden bit.'

And that was the bit I was dreading. Far from the house. Surrounded by walls. No escape. But I wasn't confessing any of this to my little sister. We passed the pond, cool in its shade beneath the laurels, and through the rhododendrons, down the steps and through the open door into the walled garden.

The tangled growth within the shelter of the high stone walls was glowing in the soft streams of light breaking between the overhanging branches as we made our way in. Fluffy parachutes of rosebay willow-herb seeds detached themselves lazily as we passed, to float amongst the final burst of dandelion clocks, and the explosions of poppy-heads.

We both stopped at the same moment, dead in our tracks. I felt Cadi fold her arm in mine, and we were both back, forty years or more, in the secret garden of our childhood. How could I possibly have memories of forty years? I wondered, still astounded by this acquisition, when all my life it had been the future I had been looking towards. Adults lived in their memories: grown-ups. I wasn't a grown-up, not yet. I couldn't be! How could I possibly have lived that long?

'Oh!' exclaimed Cadi, beside me. I heard the alarm in her voice, and the prickles were back once more, all over my scalp. 'There's someone – '

Oh, there was someone, all right. He rose up before us, out of a thicket of raspberry canes, until he seemed to stretch right up into the sky. His hair was a halo of thick yellow-gold around his head, shading the features of his face, while the light rippled softly over the sunburned muscles of his arms in the most fetching manner.

'Ooooh!' breathed Cadi, in a none-too-subtle squeak of pure delight.

But I was the lady of the castle, and I had a dignity to maintain:

'And who the bloody hell are you?' I demanded.

CHAPTER 9

'WELL?' I HAD FOLDED MY ARMS BY THIS TIME. Sickles; druids; the works: I wasn't having it. Not in my castle, I wasn't.

'Drystan,' came the reply.

Oh, yeah? And I'm Isolde. And Genevieve is snogging Lancelot over there by the Victoria plums.

'Really.' Well, what do you say when one of the Knights of the Round Table suddenly invites himself to supper?

'We did ring the bell.'

We? You mean, there were more of them?

'It's been disconnected.' Whichever of Elinor's relatives had thought that answering the door to the tinny strains of *Men of Harlech* was in any way cool, credible, or a side-splitting statement of post-modern irony, seriously needed to get out more.

I was thinking of replacing the offending tones with howling deerhounds myself. That should get the double-glazing salesmen and the Jehovah's Witnesses scampering back down the drive. Well, the double-glazing salesmen, at least. Personally speaking, I've gone some pretty good rounds with the Kingston-upon-Thames Witnesses in my time in the cause of lowering blood-pressure built up by more worldly concerns (like blocked drains and done-a-bunk tenants). And the thing about Witnesses is that they are such nice people, and they never give up. I'm quite sure they'll still be giving it one last try as I plunge my way down to the fiery furnace, and hey, who am I to deny them the pleasure?

'Oh.' At least my interloper sounded faintly embarrassed. 'I'm sorry, we didn't realise. There were cars in the drive. We thought you must be in the grounds somewhere, so we came to look for you.'

'Really?' Cadi was all attention, her best you-are-so-interesting-I-could-listen-to-you-forever smile on her lips, shoulders back, bosoms pert as she could make them – given the inevitable effects of thirty-five years or so of gravity – and sounded about to take charge of the situation, there and then. I trod on her foot, hard.

OK, I could see her point. What with the blue-grey eyes that could make the most hard-hearted female go all funny inside, thick brows frowning at us beneath a dark-gold mop of hair, and a nice clean jaw-line, even in battered tee shirt and faded jeans spattered in mud (real, not the fake kind), he was (as Katie would say) well fit.

Our visitor was looking a little bemused by now. With his Colin-Firth-in-a-wet-shirt air, I vaguely hoped this was due to being bowled over by my charm and beauty. (I mean, I'm not totally adverse to love-rats – especially not ones with such definite promise as this one.) Somehow, I didn't think so.

'I'm sorry; Mr Lloyd Jones was sure you were expecting us.'

Oh, bugger. Not the gardener, surely? I mean, I know Robin can be a sweetie, and he does try his best with the vagaries of modern life, but a gardener with a sex change? That was pushing things a little too far, surely? And it could not possibly have escaped Robin's notice that Mr Can-you-direct-me-to-the-shortest-route-to-Camelot here, was a good deal younger and prettier than himself, and Robin knows all about me and pretty guys. Terry used to turn heads every time we walked down a street (at least, I'm pretty certain it wasn't me all the girls were gawping at), and as for the show-stopping Italian(ish) love-god, Raphael...

'Who's your friend?' Cadi was demanding, the edge of her delight just a little bit soured. And I could see why: it's always a bit of a bummer when gorgeous thirty-five-ish men suddenly produce a bronzed, golden-haired, thirty-five-ish beauty from their back pocket – or from the other end of the garden in this case.

Of course, it was quite obvious who she was. Ms Arwen Jenkins strode towards us through the sun-caught grass heads and floating parachutes of seeds, and stood next to her partner-in-crime, eyeing us warily.

I liked the wary bit. Showed intelligence. A weighing up of the situation. Honesty. No 'I'll say anything to get the contract' sort of an outlook, which I understand (hey, I'm been there myself), but which, in my experience, usually ends in tears.

'Hello,' I said, rather less severely than I had intended. 'You must be Arwen.' She shook my hand: hers clean, but work-roughened. So a real gardener, then.

'I hope you don't mind, Mrs Deryn – '

'Miss,' I growled. 'And everyone calls me Lissa.'

'I hope you don't mind us making our way in like this, Miss – um, Lissa. Mr Lloyd Jones did say you were expecting us.'

'He just forgot to tell me that I was.'

'Oh.' She and Drystan exchanged glances. 'Shit!' I suspect was the expression that went between them. I saw Arwen straighten her shoulders. 'I'm sorry, it must have been a misunderstanding.'

Of course, I should have tossed the pair of them out, there and then. He couldn't quite keep his eyes off Cadi (couldn't he find some twenty-year-old to ogle?) and Arwen had the look of someone dealing with yet another hard-nosed bitch of a businesswoman, and a desire to be out of my sight as soon as possible and never darken my door again. But, in the end, I couldn't help myself.

'But then Robin always does expect me to read his mind,' I added. 'It's a man thing.'

Arwen smiled. Ah, not so thirty-five-ish, then: more like forty-ish. It was a warm, open smile, although her eyes still remained wary. Something twitched, briefly, at the back of my mind, and then vanished again before I could catch it and hold it up for inspection of danger signs.

'And I should have phoned and checked, and not just assumed that it would be all right. And you've only just moved in. We'll leave you in peace.'

'No, no, that's OK. I'm not really into the details of doing up houses, to be honest with you. It's the garden I'm interested in. Robin was right, I do want to have a chat to you. I just hadn't expected it to be quite so soon.'

'And we have lots of questions about the garden,' put in Cadi, with just the faintest flutter of the eyelashes. Not, need I add, aimed anywhere in Ms Jenkins' direction. I scowled. Drystan caught the tail end of this, and grinned. So I scowled at him, too.

I think, from his ensuing expression, he was about to tell me to get a life. I was clearly not love-ratable material then. Pity, really – but then I've been around this earth long enough to know that:

1. I'll live.
2. There are plenty more rats in the rubbish dump.
3. And it was his loss, anyhow.

But Cadi was not to be put off her stride that easily.

'Perhaps you'll be able to tell us what the lines on the lawn are,' she was murmuring. Cadi, Cadi, Cadi. Why can't you ever just stick to sex? There are times when that brain of yours is just not called for!

'Lines?' Arwen was frowning.

'Mmm,' replied Cadi, her eyes still glued firmly onto the only male in sight. 'We were watching them from the castle, weren't we, Lissa?'

'It could have been a trick of the light,' I put in, quickly.

'But it was so very definite,' smiled Cadi – who could outdo even my innocent look, any day. 'I'm sure it was something. Maybe something really old. Maybe even something a bit Roman,' she suggested, with just a hint of timidity, as if she expected Mr Dark-eyes here to correct her at any moment with his infinitely superior wisdom.

Across the shoulder-high remains of thistles, my eyes met Arwen's. OK, so it was an unlikely beginning to a friendship, but just now we were being bonded in a shared view of just how much Cadi was letting the female side down with this cringe-worthy performance.

'It may be nothing,' I said. 'But you can come up and look, if you like.'

Our visitors exchanged a quick glance. A conspiratorial glance, I decided, abruptly back into unease once more.

'I don't think' began Arwen.

'Yes!' said Drystan, at the same time. 'Yes,' he repeated, louder, as if to drown out any protest. 'Yes, please. We'd love to.' For a moment, I thought his companion was about to turn on her heel and stalk off, but then her expression softened into a kind of resignation.

'If it's not too much trouble,' she murmured.

'Oh, not at all,' said Cadi, before I could stop her.

So there we were, the four of us, making our way into Bryn Glas castle.

'You were Miss Tudur's gardener, Arwen,' I remarked, into an awkward silence, leaving Drystan behind to the tender mercies of my little sister.

'For a while. It was mainly just cutting the lawns and pruning, especially after she couldn't get out here very often. It would take a serious amount of work to get even the shrubbery back into shape.' I saw her bite her lip, a touch of colour flooding the sunburn of her cheeks. 'Not that I'm suggesting – '

'I know.'

'Good.' We were back to eyeing each other warily, for some reason. I pushed open the damp-swollen door into the conservatory, and stood back to let her step inside. Just for a moment she hesitated.

Of course! How stupid can you get? I've had enough gardens in my time to know just how much they become a part of you. You plan them, nurture them, watch them changing year by year. You murmur encouragement to the weediest stalks of delphinium that look as if they might not make it, and engage in trench warfare with the slugs and their dusk to dawn incursions into the marigolds and the lupins. You pray for the sweet peas to climb high and flower well, and pull up encroaching montbretia by the handful.

Whoever might own it technically, a patch of ground you nurture soon flows in your bloodstream. Arwen had probably worked here for years, popping in for cups of tea and a chat with Miss Tudur every now and again: the place must be full of memories for her, just as it had been for me that day young Aled Jones marched through in his immaculate suit.

'Doesn't seem right without Elinor and her plants,' I observed, casually. She eyed me sideways.

'No.'

'The only thing left was that fern over there.' I pointed to a large terracotta pot, dark earth escaping through the widening fissures of a crack shooting in a jagged fashion right down one side, with a sad looking shrivel of a brown frond peering over the side, and moulding compost spilling onto the floor. 'But looks like the frost got it. I'll re-pot it, but I'm not holding my breath.'

'Oh.' I felt her hesitate. 'I've got cuttings I made a couple of years ago. If you'd like some of them–'

'If you're sure, I'd love to.' I smiled at her. 'Thanks, Arwen. When the glass is repaired and I've got the heating working again, I'm hoping to get it back to the way it was as much as possible. Having some of Elinor's plants there would make it really special.'

'OK.'

'Great.' It seemed friendship might be back on the cards again.

'You certainly don't believe in wasting time,' said Drystan, as we reached the corridor connecting to the servants' stairs.

'This is a working castle, I'll have you know,' I retorted, swiftly. He was looking at me as if I was a lottery winner with ideas above my station. He probably thought I was a lowly and ever-so-'umble cleaner – which I have been when needs must and it was the only way to keep my children in winter boots (And no, not the labelled kind. Just the sort that don't let in snow and water.)

In fact, he was looking around as if he expected to see signs of gilding over every wall and leather sofas piled one above the other in every room, along with a motley of obese cherubs smirking from the dado rail. 'I don't have the means to be sentimental about it, much as I'd like to be,' I muttered. 'Not if I want to get the punters in.'

'With a four-poster bed in every room,' he returned, with a faintly scornful smile.

And just where did he get off, telling me what was what?

'Of course. It's what people expect.'

'You could always try giving them what they don't expect.'

I gave a loud snort. 'Not if I expect to pay the gas bill, I won't.'

I couldn't be certain, but I could have sworn I glimpsed Arwen poke him, hard, straight into the ribs, as she turned to follow me up the winding steps of the servants' stairs.

Anyways, Mr I've-got-an-opinion-for-everything subsided, and followed silently. I could hear Cadi twittering breathlessly in his ear.

My flat in the servants' quarters at least provided a welcome distraction.

'Oh, it's cute!' exclaimed Arwen, showing some enthusiasm at last. 'How clever! I'd never have believed you could have fitted in a kitchen as well as a bathroom. It used to be so grim up here, didn't it, Drys?'

Oh, so she had got around in the castle. And so, it seemed, had he. And I know exactly what sort of thing a dusty old attic full of dark corners would be useful for. I eyed them both, sharply. What useful things might they have stumbled across, the pair of them, between energetic bouts of grunting and gyrating? There must have been plenty up here, and if they were 'liberated' before the Tudurs got in to make their inventory, who would know?

'This is it.' Cadi had creaked her way across the bare floorboards of the living room and out onto the little balcony. 'Look! You can still see it. Hurry up, the sun will be gone in a minute.'

Sure enough, the markings on the grass could still be seen. Fainter now, as the light was broken into narrower and narrower shafts the further the sun sank beneath the trees.

'Extraordinary.' Even Drystan appeared impressed. 'You can't see a thing from ground level.'

'It's like those surveys you get from the air, when you can see old field patterns and roads, even towns,' added Arwen, sounding suddenly fired up and excited and forgetful of all that wariness bit.

'So it's not something you'd expected?' I asked.

'Oh no, not at all. I've never seen it from up here before. It must only be visible when the sun is in the right place. Well, and I never thought to look.' She was peering down, frowning. 'It can't be a building, surely? It looks far too big.'

'Even for a Roman fort?' I suggested.

'Wouldn't have thought so,' said Drystan. 'If it was a fort, or even a villa, then there would be some sign of internal structures. Besides, it doesn't look to me as if it is that deep below the surface.'

'Maybe it's a monastery?' suggested Cadi. 'Or a church.'

'Maybe.'

'But you don't think so?' I frowned at him.

'There aren't any records of anything that big being here.'

'Buildings are lost.'

'But they usually leave a mark. A church or a monastery would have had quite an impact on the local area. It would surely have left some traces on a map. In the names of places round about. Local legends, even.'

OK, he had a point. There were plenty of witches' caves and holy wells around Llanestyn. I'd always known not to go up to Llanestyn Falls around dusk unless I wanted to risk being swept into the dance of the faery people, and only emerge in a hundred years' time when everyone I knew had long gone to their graves. There was a vanished bride holed up as a skeleton in her hiding place in the trunk of a tree in Llanestyn woods, and on moonlit nights you could watch Rhiannon, the lady of the moon from the old Welsh stories of the Mabinogion, riding on her white horse, slowly, but impossible to catch, on her way back down to Annwyn, the underworld.

But a monastery, or a Roman fort? Not a dicky bird.

'So what else could stretch all the way down the garden?'

'No idea.' At that moment the sun sank to a far less branchy portion of the trees, and the light on the lawn brightened. Arwen gripped the side of the balcony.

'Look, Drys: there's another one. Running parallel.'

And so there was. Two lines running alongside each other right down and under the shrubbery.

'Like a path,' I said.

'Of course!' Drystan had caught her excitement. 'A path. It's not a building at all: it's a garden feature.'

Like decking, fountains running out of urns, and weird things made out of concrete and steel?

'A garden feature.' Cadi was frowning, as if she was sharing my doubts on this. 'That big?'

'Yes, look. That's where it would be, leading straight from the front of the house.'

'Castle,' I corrected.

'Not the castle, the house,' he retorted, impatiently. 'There was a mansion here before the castle was built. If the doorways were roughly in the same place, then that would lead straight from the main entrance.' The sun had sunk even lower by now. The slanting beams vanished abruptly, plunging the garden into shadow. 'Damn. Just a few minutes – '

'What do you think it is, Drystan?' breathed Cadi, sounding suitably awestruck.

'D'you know, from what I saw, it could be a parterre.'

'A what?' asked Cadi, who had studied history at university and had once gone on for months about the Elizabethans and Jacobeans, and their peculiarities when it came to gardening habits, and I could bet my bottom dollar (not that I have any, never having been to the States) knew every last thing about parterres.

'It's a way of dividing lawns and separate areas of gardens into patterns. Or, if we're really in luck, it could be the remains of an original knot garden.' I saw him catch Arwen's eye and clam up, sharpish.

Oh, Arwen knew what a parterre was, all right. I could see it in the sudden closing down of her face, and her turning back towards the stairs, as if on an urgent mission to get down to firmer ground.

Hell and high water! What on earth had persuaded me to take them up there in the first place? OK, I could let it go, pretend it had never happened, and I'd never been feverishly reading up on parterres and knot gardens, either. I could send them away, and there was nothing they could do about it. No self-respecting expert would come chasing after a mere shadow, and I could make sure neither of them ever got past the front door again. That was my intention. All my life I have been possessed of good intentions.

'You mean, it could be Elizabethan?' I demanded.

'Oh!' Aha! That clearly caught Arwen on the hop: signs of guilt, methinks.

'Possibly,' said Drystan, smooth as could be. I was rapidly coming to the conclusion that he was a rat of some kind, and I suspected 'love' had nothing to do with it. 'After all, Elinor did talk about the possibility of finding an Elizabethan garden here.'

What? My hackles were all over the place, in an instant.

'How did you get her to tell you that?'

'I beg your pardon?' I wasn't buying that look of outraged innocence for a moment. 'That's none of your business.'

'Well, I hate to point this out,' I returned, icily, 'but – given that I own this place, garden and all – it is.'

I know that is the moment he should have fallen madly, passionately, deeply, in love with me without my realising; pining for months for one tender glance from my deep blue eyes, before sweeping me mercilessly into an arbour of honeysuckle and bourbon roses to arouse my passion to glorious heights in one endless kiss.

Believe me, he didn't.

And my eyes are mud-pie brown, come to that, last time I checked.

'*Drys!*' I heard Arwen warn, quickly, before he could let rip with the comments I could see were just bursting to get between those rather nicely full lips of his. Pity, really: by then I was in the mood for a no-holds-barred humdinger that could justifiably have ended me in directing them both to sling their respective hooks.

'Look, *Ms* Deryn, I didn't "get" Elinor to tell me anything, right? She told me because she liked me – '

Oh, yeah? And pull the other one while you're at it.

' – and because she believed I might possibly take over the running of Bryn Glas from her one day.'

What?

There are not many times in my life when I am well and truly gob-smacked, but this was definitely one of them. Behind me, I heard Cadi begin to giggle.

'Elinor was Drystan's great-aunt,' said Arwen, who must have taken pity on my gulping-fish state.

Diawl! No wonder his introduction of himself had been so brief! You mean, I had actually allowed in, *invited* in, one of the race of Tudur within the walls of my lovely, precious castle? No wonder he'd been looking down that straight nose of his at the sight of the local peasantry daring to pollute the ancestral pad. He was probably plotting to have me out of there by the end of the week, and without paying me for the privilege, to boot. I spotted a malicious glint to his eye.

'I'm the black sheep of the family,' he announced. Rather unnecessarily, in my opinion. So was this a subtle hint that he was:

1. An axe-murderer.
2. A herbal poisoner.
3. Not fussed either way.

I spread my best deeply-bored expression all over my face:
'I don't doubt it.'

'So we understand each other, then, Ms Deryn?'

'Oh, perfectly, Mr Tudur.'

'Good.'

And just where is the rat poison when you need it handy?

'Tea?' I enquired, with my very sweetest of smiles.

CHAPTER 10

I WAS STILL FUMING WHEN KATIE ARRIVED, as promised, the following Friday.

I'd had plenty of time to let off steam on numerous occasions during the week, of course, what with tripping over workmen, and the finishing of my flat going predictably to the wire, with the last coat of paint still drying as the van arrived with the smaller bits of furniture I'd destined to keep around me in my private quarters.

Relations were becoming a little strained by Thursday, and I think we were all glad when Friday afternoon came around and Robin and the workmen left for the weekend.

'Although if you need any help – ' said Robin, as he shooed the last plasterer out of a downstairs loo, and returned to assist my final set of removals from my little camping ground in Elinor's room.

'Thanks, but that's fine,' I replied, hastily stuffing used knickers out of sight into my rucksack, along with all the other washing destined for the newly-installed luxury of a washing-machine. 'Katie volunteered to help me get settled in, so she should know what she's letting herself in for.'

Robin picked up the deflated mattress – destined for Katie's use in my sitting room for the next few days until I could sort out a sofa bed for future visits – and eyed me, his eyes soft, dark, and concerned.

'If you are sure, Lissa. It's just that you've seemed a little, well, stressed, these past few days.'

Stressed? Of course I was bloody stressed! I'd left my home and my friends of the past twenty years or so to take a jump into the unknown, in a rambling old castle that was in the middle of having its insides scraped out and turned into the biggest gamble of my life. Not to mention a former owner worming his way in under false pretences, and hints that my canny little nose for Potential had merely spotted something already known, probably thoroughly checked out for any real use, and generally *passé*. Followed by lurkings in the garden, a vanished chimney, and my favourite Kingston-upon-Thames belongings stacked upstairs any old how, and a daughter arriving any minute.

Stressed? What the hell else should I have been? But I was a grown-up: it came with the territory. And there was nothing at all he could do about it. Robin, being an old-fashioned kind of a gentleman, was likely to offer flowers, chocolates, and a night out at the local Italian restaurant as a means of stress relief. Which was all very nice, and normally I'd have appreciated the gesture, but at this moment it would mean negotiating a shower I'd never tried before under serious time pressure, finding my iron – guaranteed to be very low down in a box – and an outfit that didn't make me look like a bag-lady and attract the scorn of the swanky types that frequented Giovanni's *en route* to the opera in Llandudno. I am just too old to be Cinderella, and a girl does have some pride.

'I'll be fine,' I murmured. 'I'm just a bit tired, that's all. I'm sure Katie will be shattered after her drive, so I expect we'll watch a video and have an early night.'

'Oh, right,' he said, still hesitating. He knew from experience my daughter's appalling taste in sloppy films, and not even his concern could get him to volunteer to pick one up from the local Spar. I smiled.

'Perhaps we could meet up later in the week. Sunday, maybe. I'm sure Katie would love to see you.'

'Very well then.' I could see him clocking up plans by the second.

'I'll give you a ring on Sunday morning and we can decide then,' I put in hastily, before he managed to have the entire day arranged, complete with alfresco champagne and Shakespeare in the grounds of Penrhyn Castle, or Plas Newydd over on Anglesey.

'As you wish.' The worried frown had left his brow. *Bechod.* It took so very little to make him feel he was looking after me, and he did always so transparently mean well.

Unlike certain others I could mention.

I listened to him going clunk, clunk up the still-uncarpeted stairs, and looked around Elinor's room. The wall was still there. I'd been so exhausted all week I hadn't had any sleepless nights to start poking around and knocking it down, and I hadn't felt like bribing a builder to do the dirty for me. Not yet.

I had a feeling that whatever lay hidden there was probably going to send my blood pressure soaring, and I thought I could do without that kind of thing at the moment. But this floor was almost finished with its plumbing and tiling and due for a coat of paint: if I was going to investigate, then it would have to be soon.

But not just now. I put the idea firmly out of my mind, and followed Robin up the stairs to my new flat.

At least this part of the castle was beginning to feel like a home, rather than a building site. After Robin had left, I spent a relaxing time putting soap and towels in my little bathroom, and finding homes for tea and coffee in my kitchen. It all felt far too neat and clean, but a weekend of me and Katie together would soon sort that.

Robin had brought up the microwave to sit over my gleaming new oven, protesting that it was an old one and he didn't really use it, despite its straight-out-of-the-box gleam. The washing machine hummed and whirred happily. I made myself a cup of tea and some toast, and then settled down to a happy few hours unpacking boxes.

My only real doubts about the move had been during those days I'd been sorting out which parts of my life to take, and which to leave in the Kingston-upon-Thames charity shops. I'd lived surrounded by memories: all the things that had once been and would never come again. Being a wife; being a mother. Being young.

Strangely, crouched on the floor in my new living room, it had become like opening treasure troves. There was excitement in the air as I stacked my familiar books onto the shelves, along with the CDs and my old record collection. I fished out the two pairs of baby bootees I'd kept (one for each baby), placed in a box along with a sliver of net from my wedding dress, and a pressed rosebud the glorious Raphael had once sworn came all the way from the ancestral home in Tuscany.

Look, I believed him, OK? Probably still do, come to that. You see, the sex was –

Ah, well. I expect it rains all the time in Tuscany, too, if you live there. Bound to. And the ancestral home probably has the mafia installed next door, come to that.

Anyhow, I placed my precious mementos back in the bottom drawer of my bedside cabinet, where they had always been. I christened my new loo (always an important ceremony in a new place), made another cup of tea and headed for the next box, scissors in hand.

Ah, yes. Forget Tuscany: this was home.

CHAPTER 11

KATIE ARRIVED WITH A SKID OF GRAVEL ON THE DRIVE, and a ringing of my discreet, one tone, new bell.

'Wow, Mam, this place is amazing,' she exclaimed between kisses, as I opened the door. 'Much bigger than in the photos!'

She looked a little paler and a little thinner than when I had seen her last, and there was a noticeable absence of Tim. My daughter has always taken after Cadi rather than me: tall and willowy, with thick chestnut hair that always shines, and a sculptured jaw-line and cheekbones that will lend her beauty right into old age. Me, I've never been of the willowy ornamental variety.

Cadi, I'm afraid to say, can be *very* ornamental when she chooses: most particularly when boredom with her current career move has set in. My sister has always been possessed of a low boredom threshold: website design had lasted longer than most, but I was planning to get her to finish the one for Bryn Glas before Christmas, if you see what I mean.

For the past thirty years, Cadi has developed a nice line in gentlemen well-endowed in the monetary area, who all appear to believe that a could-be-a-model female on their arm dripping a few diamonds and hiding all evidence of brain will give them as much cred in the taste and sophistication stakes as their gold-plated loo-seats, Christmas-tree chandeliers, and imitation Versailles chimney pieces.

Mmm.

Cadi has done well in diamonds and cruises and functions amongst the minorly rich and famous. She even made it onto an inside page of *Hello!* once. However, this is not a career I have any wish my daughter should aspire to. Unlike my sister, Katie is still sweet, innocent, and possessed of a conscience I have a feeling would not allow her to stash cash, jewels, and the odd compromising photograph in case of a rainy day, in numerous deposit boxes around the globe.

Normally, I don't worry: my daughter is a twenty-first century woman with a career, a house of her own, and options. The only thing is that my sister's first little stray into the realms of Ornamental Female just happened to begin with a broken heart...

If Tim didn't buck up his act, pronto, I decided there and then, Alternative Arrangements would just have to be made.

'Tea?' I smiled, mentally flicking through my file of Eligible Young Men. I'd come up with pretty much zero even before Katie had grabbed her camera from the dashboard.

'In a bit. I'm going to see everything first. And take *loads* of pictures.' She slammed the car door shut. 'I can get my stuff later. Is your computer here, yet, Mam?'

'Er, yes, *cariad*.' Katie was clearly in manic mode. Impossible to deflect, in my experience: just hold on to your hat, girls, and prepare for a bumpy ride.

'Great. I'm going to e-mail loads to Merion tonight. He'll be *so* jealous I got to see your castle first.'

I didn't like to point out that, given the choice, her brother would still be scaling the Dolomites at dawn, pursuing just the right light for those stunningly atmospheric photographs of his, in the cause of furthering his burgeoning freelance career

105

to the point where he could give up the part-time job teaching photography at the college within easy reach of the Lake District.

'I'm not sure Merion will be able to open attachments at a cyber café,' I murmured.

'Well, he'll see them as soon as he gets back home, then.'

Right. OK. Time to just go with the flow, then.

So we were round Bryn Glas like a whirlwind, with Katie exclaiming excitedly at everything, from the views across to the mountains to the shining state of the loos. She even hauled me inside the old stables set along the wall of the garden beside the drive: vast, forlorn, and empty, and a problem for the future I was busily trying to banish from my mind. A castle was quite enough to think about for the moment, thank you very much.

Luckily, Katie was not in planning-Mam's-future-life mood, or we'd have had visions of swimming pools, Jacuzzis, indoor tennis courts, or – heaven help us – pony trekking. I like my manure well-rotted and ready for the garden, thank you very much. Instead, she was off up to my kitchen to work out the oven and cook the rapidly defrosting pizza I'd bought that afternoon. My fridge was up to speed by now, but the freezer was still settling down after the trauma of the move.

We had our pizza and chocolate cake (healthy eating would resume next week, this was a serious stress-busting measure) sitting on my little balcony in the dusk, burning citronella sticks for the midges, and sipping red wine.

'Well?' I enquired, sleepy and contented. 'Does it meet with your approval?'

'Oh, Mam, it's *gorgeous*. I'd live here, any day.'

'I'm glad you like it.'

'It's so, well, *romantic*.'

Oh-oh. I had a bad feeling coming on.

'It's a fake, darling. Not a real castle at all.'

'But that doesn't matter, Mam. It's how you *make* it that counts.'

Hmm. Things were definitely bad with Tim. Some girls eat for comfort. Some girls drink, have ill-advised affairs, or blow a month's budget on shopping. Katie, on the other hand, just loves to organise. I should have recognised the signs from the start: the alert, twitchy, ever-so-energetic air that had her still looking around even after the soporific effects of wine, pizza, and an overdose of Death-By-Chocolate.

'It'll just take time, darling,' I murmured. It was like putting a finger in a dike to keep the sea out: in the long term, no chance. Katie was off again, this time ready to decorate my life.

I should have known where it would start.

'Oh, Mam!' Her eagle eye had spotted something within minutes. 'You're not going to put those curtains there, are you?'

'Well, I know peeping Toms don't usually have a fire-engine's crane in their back pocket, and I'm not much to see, anyhow, but I do want something to keep out the outside world at night.'

'But *those*.' Mmm. When Katie ceases to be distracted by my attempts at humour, I know there is serious trouble afoot.

'They'll do. For now, at least.'

'Rubbish! I know your "will do". You got those from a jumble sale at my primary school, Mam. I bet they wouldn't even make it to a boot sale nowadays. They're pants, Mam.'

'They're not that bad,' I protested, hurt on the offending curtains' account. I felt deep attachment towards those curtains. I'd even grown used to the garish sixties pattern of apples and oranges, with a few lemons thrown in: we'd shared many a sleepless night, those curtains and I. My every last dream and worry had breathed their way into the weave. And so what if they were faded and a little moth-eaten? This was my space.

'Come on, Mam. You own a castle now. You've worked your socks off for as long as I can remember, and you hardly ever get anything for yourself. When was the last time you bought a new dress?'

'I like charity shops. Makes you inventive. Helps you find the unpredictable.' And when the kids were small, kept us in clothes and shoes and bed linen. Not to mention the carefully spotted new-looking items horded for the wider family at Christmas, to save my pride and a confession of just how near the edge we really were.

All right, so I had had more money in my purse these past few years, but I still felt a fraud in a boutique, or even a modestly-priced chain store. The credit card zinging up the noughts still had the power to make me nervous. I'd kept that credit card through thick and thin, used strictly for emergencies only (as in petrol to get to work, the heating going wrong; that kind of thing).

'But you're spending mega-bucks on the rooms downstairs!'

'That's different. That's business.'

'So you intend to have everywhere like a palace, and put the crap in your rooms!'

'Well, darling, if you go to any castle in the land, I rather suspect you'll find that is the normal state of affairs. All the best bits go on show.'

'Oh really!' she snorted, with the disgust of the have-everything-perfect-and-in-its-place (including the kids) before you move into the marital home. Nothing secondhand, mended, reconditioned or handed down for my daughter, nowadays. Not even the car. Just a weight of credit – even with the fully paid-up house – that made my eyelids twitch at the thought of it.

'Anyhow, I thought "vintage" was in, nowadays. That's second hand, isn't it?'

'Not any old second hand.'

'And mine is?'

'No, Mam. You have very good taste.' She eyed the offending material with a quick shudder. 'Normally. But you've always put Merion and me first, and now you deserve something for yourself.'

'You mean, a castle isn't enough?'

'I thought you said that was business?' And just where did my daughter learn to nit-pick her way out of losing arguments, I'd like to know?

'It's still a castle,' I growled. 'Many people in the world don't have a decent place to call a home.'

'Oh no, Mam. I'm not falling for that one. You've got a point, true, but I know you: you'll argue until the cows come home, and I'm not going to be distracted. Not this time. You need a day off, so I'm taking you to Chester tomorrow morning, and we're going to get you some real curtains. Really nice, soft, floaty curtains. Make this place romantic, like it should be.'

'Katie, I am not a floaty kind of person!' I was growing alarmed. I could see me being railroaded into miles of muslin, along with pale lilac chiffon, beaded scatter cushions, and hanging lamps suspending scented tea-lights all over the place. Ugh! And just where would my cred as a bolshy old trout be, then?

'OK, OK. Not *very* floaty, then. Just nice.' She smiled brightly. 'More wine, Mam?'

Mmm. Chester it was going to be: I could feel it in my waters. Katie has inherited a stubborn streak from somewhere (bound to be Terry, in my opinion, although there have been people who've disagreed), and she was clearly aiming to wear me down with argument or alcohol, or a mixture of both. Which wasn't fair, youth having a slight physical advantage in the practice of the first and the recovery stakes of the second.

'Thank you,' I said, with all the graciousness I could muster. 'Just half a glass. Then we'd better sort out this bed of yours, if we're going to be off early in the morning.'

Chester was, well, Chester. Lovely, even when you are not in the mood. I mean, who could stay cross with a gorgeous old walled town with half-timbered buildings and a collections of interesting little shops in between the usual stores?

I actually began to enjoy it after an hour or so. In fact, so much so I began to recall the location of every charity shop, and gave Katie the full experience, much to her mortification.

Although, as I pointed out, she wasn't going to meet anyone she knew there, and she was quite free to pretend she was only humouring an old bat of an aunt, if she was really that fussed.

Katie, still being within shouting distance of her teenage years, could fit into those mountains of clothes everyone else has expanded out of. So by the time she'd spotted the bargain of a Gucci dress that looked as if it had been worn once to a party and then discarded, and a velvet coat that must once have cost the proverbial arm and a leg and still looked stunning, I had her half converted to my point of view.

Only half, you understand. It's against Katie's principles to be converted to anything, and she did argue that this back-of-the-woods part of the country had just not caught onto 'Vintage' yet, and really both items should have cost twice as much.

Interesting argument.

I let it go: I needed to save my energies for the battle of the curtains. I spotted several serviceable, hardly worn-looking pairs, in only last year's colours, in Oxfam, but Katie remained adamant that on the subject of curtains it was new, or nothing.

In the end, we compromised. It was the port-hued velvet curtains in Help the Aged that saved my bacon. The worn-in variety, that would look as if they had been at my window for ever, and were probably refugees from some minor mansion being turned into an old people's home. Even Katie had to admit that she couldn't better them for love nor money.

In return, I let her loose on muslin and scatter cushions to her heart's delight, and the subject of that very tight, much too low evening dress I'd briefly dallied with in Save the Children, before concluding I would never wear it. But, as Katie pointed out, how could I not help starving children, and besides, every woman needs a slinky, clinging, emerald velvet gown, for emergency purposes only.

The upshot of all this was that we arrived back in Llanestyn far later than planned, ravenous, despite lunch and a break for afternoon tea, cake and all, and in no mood to cook. So what else could we do but the decent thing and order an Indian take-away, and then mooch around Llanestyn Spar for accompaniments while we waited?

In the end, we'd taken so long over the videos and DVDs, with Katie mourning the great lack of choice this far from the metropolitan centre, that it was time for her to dash to fetch our meal, leaving me to queue to pay for the rest of our provisions.

Now, there is one thing about living in a small community: with one Indian, one Chinese, one fish and chip shop and a single convenience store, you are just bound to meet someone you know getting last minute supplies for the weekend, or a bottle of wine.

'Oh! Hello,' I muttered, as a greeting had me turning round to the basket behind me, blocking my escape. 'How are you?' I added, feebly.

'Oh, fine,' said Arwen. Slight chill in the air there, and no wonder, given the abruptness of our parting and no mention of her, or that companion of hers, darkening my door again. 'Are you settling in all right?'

'Oh, yes. Fine, thank you.' The shopper before me was paid up and moving away. Which was when I discovered exactly what my daughter had been stashing in our basket.

Namely: one excruciating-looking video I had every intention of dozing my way through; two bottles of red wine; one bottle of whisky (OK, hands up to that one: shopping always did send me to drink); a large and gungy cheesecake, and a copy of *Heat* and *Everything You Want To Know about Soaps*. Oh, and a box of chocolates to complete the picture.

No doubt Arwen – who I couldn't help noticing was clutching a large pot of organic yoghurt along with a bunch of flowers and a bottle of wine, while wearing a long batik skirt and clearly off to the healthy-eating variety of party – would be laughing her socks off with that Tudur love-god of hers at my sad existence, surviving only on doses of Cadburys and endless re-runs of *Pretty Woman*.

'Mam!' Ah, the cavalry, in the form of Katie, stinking the place out with the unmistakable whiff of balti and naan bread, arrived just in the nick of time as I was stuffing everything as fast as I could inside carrier bags before anyone else could spot my purchases and assume the worst. I smiled at her.

Oh-oh.

I should have known from the brightness of her tone. The faint flush of her cheeks and the sparkle to her eye gave the game away, if nothing else. Now, much as I love Llanestyn, the talent – in the male department, you understand – is not exactly overwhelming. Which meant Katie's 'Tim? What Tim?' flutter of excitement could be due only to passing mountaineers returning from a day on Snowdon, or –

It had to be. I just knew it. I could even spot him through the window pane: all jacketed and spruced up, with flowers and bottle, and clearly heading for the same party as Arwen, and looking particularly heart-stoppingly gorgeous.

'Come along, darling,' I said, quickly, hoping if I ignored all this it would just go away. 'We'd better go home before our dinner gets cold.' But Katie was in unstoppable mode. A very bad sign, as far as my daughter is concerned.

'Mam,' she exclaimed, 'Mam, you'll never guess who I've just met!'

CHAPTER 12

ELIZABETH BENNETT NEVER HAD THIS PROBLEM, I can tell you. I mean, what self-respecting heroine ever finds a potential love-interest – even if she doesn't intend to touch him with a barge pole, nice assets, or no nice assets – only to discover herself in imminent danger of becoming his mother-in-law? I mean, his mother-in-law! The old bag comedians still can't resist making jokes about. The stock laughing-stock figure of the has-been older woman. I ask you! The indignity of the thing!

So I clearly wasn't going to spend my life fighting off Mr Drystan Tudor's advances when he finally saw the light and found he couldn't live without me. Not that I was that fussed, you understand, but a girl does like to think she still has choices.

And, somehow, we – or rather Katie – invited them both to dinner the next day. I could have dropped large hints about young Mr Tudur being Already Taken, and what about Sisterly Loyalty, apart from the fact that Arwen didn't appeared overly concerned with my daughter's undisguisedly star struck gaze when it came to her companion.

Mmm. Either she was very sure of him, or he was more of a rat than I thought and she couldn't wait to pass him on. This was not exactly what I had in mind when I was considering Alternative Arrangements to Tim.

But at least it cheered Katie up no end. She was off to Tesco first thing next morning, before whipping my new cooker into obedience before you could say homemade mushroom pâté and asparagus soufflé. She even made a fruit Pavlova from scratch, meringue and all: something I've always considered a severe waste of time when the frozen ones are quite delicious without the fuss. OK, they're not as good as Katie's, but they're a damned sight better than mine would ever be.

At seven-thirty, sharp, there was a knock on the door, and there they were the two of them, looking clean and young and beautiful, and elegant without trying, to boot, even with our agreement not to dress up for the occasion, given the delicate footwork still necessary to get up the stairs to my little retreat. Plus it put a stop to Katie's idea that I should wear the velvet evening dress. Mother-in-law fodder I could accept: I had a mother's love to guide me. But mutton dressed as the proverbial – no way. So trousers and the nice top it was: I'd ironed them, and that was a major concession in itself.

'Hello,' I said, accepting the wine bottles and bunches of flowers and trying to be at ease with all this.

'What a difference the furniture makes: it's lovely,' said Arwen. I smiled at her. To be honest, I felt bad that I'd ushered them both out quite so abruptly last time. There was still something about her I liked, despite her taste in friends/lovers. And, to be perfectly truthful, she felt like a last link with old Miss Tudur.

I might not have liked the idea of Arwen getting cosy with a Tudur, black sheep or no, but I still liked the idea of the continuity of the work on the garden, passing on from Elinor to me, as if the link between us had never been broken and the magic secret garden of my childhood still existed, somewhere out there.

'It's getting there,' I replied. 'It still feels strange living in a castle at all instead of a suburban semi.'

'Well, I'd say you'd worked wonders in a few days,' put in Drystan, all politeness. He was even smiling at me.

'Furniture always makes a difference,' I returned, stiffly. This was the second time he had made his way onto my patch under false pretences, and I wasn't about to let him forget it, daughter or no daughter. Katie, busily pouring wine, stopped in mid-pour, all attention.

'You didn't tell me you'd been to Mam's flat before, Drys.'

'Oh, didn't I mention they'd been up, darling? It was just briefly, just to look at the layout of the garden.' I hadn't meant to go on, but somehow I did. 'I was rather hoping Arwen would become my gardener.'

'Really? Oh, that's a really great idea, Mam.'

'If you're not totally booked up, Arwen, I was going to ask you to think it over.'

'Yes, of course.' Arwen sounded a little uncertain. Well, I could see her point: Katie was human enough, but as for her mother...

'Mam used to come here when she was a kid, you know. She used to tell Merion and me loads of stories when we were little about sneaking in and visiting an old lady in a falling-down old castle. We thought they were just stories. It sounded just too, well, Miss Haversham, to be really real. Strange, isn't it, that she's ended up living here?'

'It was only once or twice.'

'No it wasn't, Mam. It couldn't have been, you used to talk about her all the time. You used to visit her whenever we came up to see Nain, and she left you and Cadi the ammonites.'

'Oh, so that's where they went,' put in Drystan, slowly. My, those grey eyes of his could be sharp when he wanted them to be. 'Elinor's solicitor wasn't half cagey about them.'

'Thank you. And I suppose you want the two of them back, now you know where they are?'

'Good heavens, no! That was not what I meant – ' He frowned at me. 'Are you always this defensive?'

'Defensive?'

'Mam,' said Katie, gently. She can always spot me building up a head of steam. I put a lid on the blood pressure.

'Look, Ms Deryn, I know my family can be, well, difficult, at times...'

'Difficult?' I may not be able to bawl him out, but I could still scowl at him. 'More like a bunch of low-down, jumped up, unscrupulous little – '

'*Mam!*' My daughter was mortified; Arwen was choking in a corner. Look, Katie should know by now that you can't take me anywhere.

'And I take it you always speak your mind?' enquired Drystan, deftly removing Arwen's glass and slapping her on the back to assist the dispersal of the wine that had gone down the wrong way.

'Only recently. After a lifetime of trying to be nice.' I cleared my throat. 'Would you like a glass of water?' I asked of Arwen, who nodded, wordlessly, still in the process of trying to catch her breath. I escaped into the kitchen.

'Oh, don't take any notice of her,' Katie was saying as I returned. 'Mam's bark is much worse than her bite. We used to have the bailiffs round loads, trying to get our stuff, and all kinds of people trying to rip her off, after my dad left. It's just a survival thing, really.'

'Thank you, darling, but actually it's an age thing.'

'No it's not. You were always saying you needed to toughen up. And you always *sounded* brave, but you were always chucking up in the bathroom afterwards.'

Thank you, Katie. Both my guests were eyeing me closely by now. Probably waiting for my head to start spinning around, or something.

'Well, if you want to talk about surviving,' I said hastily, 'Elinor was the real survivor, living to over a hundred, like that, and dying in her own bed at the end.'

'Yes, yes she was,' said Arwen, still sounding hoarse and raw about the throat. 'I can't imagine living that long and seeing so many changes.'

'D'you know, she once told me she knew someone who'd been in the Boer War,' I said. 'You don't imagine memory stretching back that far. That's real history.'

'You mean, like the garden?' said Katie, blissfully unaware of the undercurrents she was sailing over.

'The garden?' frowned Arwen.

'Didn't she tell you? That's why Mam really bought this place. She just loved the garden, and she said there was a mystery about the place, something the old lady was always talking about.'

'Not always, darling. And, anyhow, I'm sure our guests don't want to talk about the garden all evening. There will be plenty of time for that, later.'

'Oh,' said Katie, taking the hint. She turned to smile at Drystan. 'It must be strange coming back, Drys, with someone else living here, after Bryn Glas has been in your family for so long.'

'Not really. As I told your mother, I'm afraid I'm seen as the black sheep of the family. I used to visit my great-aunt when no one was looking, but other than that I wasn't allowed near the place. Might pollute the atmosphere,' he added, with a grin.

'Really?' I could see he was growing more attractive by the minute in my daughter's eyes: she never could resist a touch of danger in a man. And I thought my youthful weakness for male beauty was bad... 'What makes a Tudur a black sheep?'

Living?

Hey, I didn't say a thing. I didn't even express a thing with my eyes, well, not intentionally.

'Oh, easy,' Drystan was replying. 'A failure to restore the family fortune, I'm ashamed to say.'

Oh God, a gold-digger, then. Right, I was publicly writing my daughter's husband out of my will altogether, first thing tomorrow morning: not a penny to pass through his grubby little paws, whatever the circumstances.

'Really?' Katie's eyes were sparkling. Predictably. She hasn't lived as long as I have, yet: she hasn't yet learnt that a touch of danger in males normally denotes utter domination of all remote controls in the house, a distinct unwillingness to pay bills, and a lack of turning up for dinner when expected. And that such habits are bloody annoying, in the long run.

'Mm,' Drystan was replying, all smiles. 'dot-coms.'

Mam bach; so not even original, then.

'You started a dot-com?' I heard Katie breathe, in undisguised awe.

'With a couple of friends. Guys we'd been at college with were making fortunes selling widgets and web-space, so we jumped on the bandwagon, selling adventure holidays to over-paid, over-stressed business managers.' He caught my eye. 'I know; not exactly ethical. Anyhow, like thousands of others, we were a bit late: the bubble burst before we could float the company and clean up. I was once told I was worth thirty million pounds, believe it or not: for all of one week, and entirely in fantasy, of course.'

'But that's awful!' Nothing like heroic failure to keep female attention, I'm afraid. 'Like winning the lottery big time and then not being able to find the ticket. It must have made you sick!'

'At the time, it did. But then, well life goes on and you get to thinking "what the hell would I have done with thirty million quid?" ' Katie's round eyes showed a certain eagerness to assist him see the light on this point. 'I mean, even if you change every hour, there are only so many clothes you can wear, and unless you want to die an early death, there is only so much food you can eat. While champagne all day just means a rich alcoholic rather than a meths-swilling one. And do I seriously need six houses in exotic locations and a tribe of servants in each one?'

'But you wouldn't have to spend it *all*. You could give loads away to charity.' Katie was organising him already, and they hadn't even exchanged meaningful smiles yet.

'And have everyone clamouring at my door, and a bodyguard even when I have a shower just in case someone kidnaps me to help themselves to a ransom? No thanks.' He grinned. 'OK, most of my family will never speak to me again, but I'm sure that's no great loss. Eh, Lissa?'

'Hrmph.' I wasn't in the mood for conceding points, not even this one.

'And I suppose, in the end, it gave me the freedom to do what I wanted to do, and to hell with trying to impress anyone else. Funny, but I rather suspect that might well have been the one luxury I could never have bought with a hundred million.'

D'you know, he almost sounded as if he meant it, too. And he did look particularly fetching in the warm light of the candles.

OK, perhaps I'd leave my will alone for the moment.

CHAPTER 13

'SO WHAT *DID* YOU WANT TO DO, DRYS?' asked Katie, smiling at our guest in undisguised anticipation.

'Eco-dwellings.'

Oh, bloody hell. Don't tell me Drystan was really some crusty alternative type, heavily into raw manure and alfalfa sprouts? I couldn't see Katie squatting in a teepee while the council did their best to eject her out of sight of the castle-viewing tourists.

'Eco-dwellings?' The concept was an entirely new one on my daughter, I'm ashamed to say, despite my best efforts in the recycling department.

'Houses that use natural energy and don't damage the environment.'

Which put me and my castle in our place, all right.

'Re-ally?' Yep, Katie was wavering. I could see the mind ticking, and that even her limited experience could conclude that microwave dinners, knee-length leather boots, eye-shadow, waxing-creams, and cashmere sweaters were probably off the agenda, then.

'Drys used to work at CAT,' explained Arwen, who'd been watching all this with a faint smile on her face as she recovered her voice.

'Cat?'

'C.A.T. The Centre for Alternative Technology, down near Machynlleth.'

'Oh.'

'You've been there, darling. I took you and Merion once, not that long after it had opened: the place with the windmill and the solar panels to make all their energy, and the reed-bed sewerage system and the polytunnels.'

'Oh, that one. With all the mud.'

'It was early days: I don't suppose it's muddy now.'

'Certainly not,' said Drys.

'Yeah, but your place is,' said Arwen, tartly. 'Just remember to take your wellies if he ever invites you there. My shoes have never been the same again.'

Well, well. Now that was unexpected. A Tudur with compost toilets and a solar panel roof was an unnatural occurrence. Rather an intriguing one, really.

'Was that for gardening?' demanded Katie, suddenly seeming to become aware that Arwen was a very attractive woman.

I'm afraid to say that, with the utter thoughtlessness of youth, Katie had showed every sign of deeming Arwen, though nice, of course, to be far too ancient to be of any interest to her male companion at all. Suspicion appeared to have aroused its head, at last.

'Not exactly.' Arwen blushed. Yes, actually blushed, right down to the neck of her jumper. Aha! So not so disinterested, after all! Maybe my first assumption of their extramural activities in the attics had been right, all along. In which case – 'But I am helping Drys with his veg plot. I've worked organically for years, and gardening isn't exactly his thing.'

'Is that what you did here, at the castle?' demanded Katie, still eyeing her closely. 'Organic gardening?'

And so we were back to the garden again. It seemed quite determined to stay in the air that night.

'Where I could. Much of it was simply pruning and keeping the lawns down, I'm afraid. Boring stuff. Not that I found it boring,' she added, hastily. 'Elinor did think of doing other things.' She cleared her throat, as if the wine hadn't yet entirely dispersed yet. 'But she was very old.'

'What things?'

'Oh, re-doing parts as they used to be. Growing vegetables in the walled garden and getting the greenhouses back into working order: that sort of thing.'

'And the Elizabethan part?' I asked.

'Oh.' She and Drys exchanged glances. 'Elinor did begin looking for it. We just never got very far, and then – well then she seemed to lose heart, and just wanted to keep it the way it was.'

'But there must have been some records.' I frowned at Drys. 'The Tudurs must have something. I thought all old families kept things like that. Family Bibles and what not. You were quite sure there was a house here before the castle, Drystan, so it could have gone back to Elizabethan times. Wasn't anyone curious?'

'Of course.' He was smiling. 'There were always supposed to be plans of the house, and the garden, too. The place was turned upside down after Elinor died, but nothing came to light. My Uncle Griffin fumed for days.'

I bet he did. I'd never actually met the head of the Tudur clan, even though I'd been in a room with him several times over the years, and had conducted swingeing negotiations – always through intermediaries, of course – on the subject of buying his castle.

As far as I could remember, Griffin Tudur had always made no bones that his Aunt Elinor had no business being in Bryn Glas, even after his father – Elinor's younger brother – had partaken of one-too-many brandies in the Snowdon Arms one night and sent his car hurtling over the side of a cliff on the way home, leaving Elinor as the last representative of the older generation of Tudurs.

In fact, it was a fairly safe bet that Griffin Tudur would *never* know of my existence, despite being installed in the family pad: I had the wrong blood, the wrong address (before the castle, naturally) spoke the wrong kind of English, the wrong kind of Welsh. I was road-sweeping fodder, while Griffin Tudur was heading for the Community Council, the Council proper, right into the robes of the Gorsedd of Bards, and straight for Arch-Druid. Even a Lloyd Jones was not good enough for Griffin Tudur, and – in Llanestyn at least – that was saying something.

'So why was Elinor convinced there was an Elizabethan garden here, stashed under the shrubbery?'

'Oh, there were always stories in the family,' said Drys, casually. 'You know the kind of thing.'

'Stories?'

'That Elizabeth the First had spent a night here once: visiting her cousin, Sir Tudor Tudur, and he'd had an entire garden laid out for the occasion.'

'An entire garden?' breathed Katie. 'You mean, made especially for her? Like the Chelsea Flower Show?'

'That sort of thing,' said Arwen. 'It's possible. The Earl of Essex made one when she visited him on one of her progresses, complete with an orchard, and a ripe cherry tree out of season.'

'Ah, that's so sweet!'

'Sign of ambition to get inside her imperial knickers, more like, and have her crown off her head like a shot,' I muttered, darkly.

'Oh, don't be so cynical, Mam.' Katie tucked her arm into mine. 'I think it's a lovely idea. It's such a pity no one ever found a way of getting the garden back to the way it was then.' The arm tightened, meaningfully. 'But you could, Mam.'

'Oh, yes? And without any plans and any evidence, and the possibility it was never there in the first place?'

Not to mention the mutterings in the village about the present race of Tudurs being nothing of the sort, just offshoots of a Parry who'd once made it big in the cotton mills of Lancashire in the 1800s, until – growing tired of exploiting his English workforce of women and small children – he'd returned to exploit his fellow-countrymen instead, taking the name of 'Tudur' to dignify proceedings, along with his building of the castle. The whole Elizabeth the First connection could just be a piece of local colour, too.

'Except for the parterre,' said Arwen, slowly.

Except for the parterre. Or knot garden.

'Parterre?' demanded Katie. I looked down into the dusk of the lawn as Arwen explained. There was nothing to be seen: just the green of the grass darkening to grey as the light faded.

I could hear the delicate rush of water down a rocky incline into the pond and the bats were out on business. It was the half-light again, the time that was neither one thing nor another, when my Celtic ancestors steered clear of swamps, and the shadows of clearings where worlds might just collide...

'Oh, you've just got to investigate, Mam,' Katie was saying excitedly, 'just think how exciting it would be if you really did find an Elizabethan garden!'

'I'm sure the Tudurs tried, *cariad*.'

'Well, my Uncle Griffin did. He badgered Cadw and the National Trust, and all kinds of museums, and the archaeology departments of several universities. No one was interested, with no evidence at all.'

Aha! So there was hope for the Gorsedd of Bards, yet. I knew from my sources (to be unnamed; of the Deep Throat, variety, suffice it to say) that they had been resisting Griffin Tudur for the past twenty years. They must surely take heart from the fact that not everyone just rolls over and dies when the self-styled patriarch of the race of Tudur rolls into town, demanding this, that, and everything, with only world domination reserved for next year's agenda.

'But now you have the parterre,' said Katie.

'Which could be anything, darling.'

'OK: well, you'll just have to find some evidence. There has to be something, Mam. And with all the building work – '

'Oh.' I said. I must have said it in a peculiar way, because there they all were, staring at me, expectantly.

'Mam?'

'Oh, bugger.'

I was in the kitchen before you could say 'pissed as a newt', and pouring out a large slug of whisky into a glass.

'Are you all right, Lissa?' asked Arwen. They had all followed me in and were watching me, anxiously. I wouldn't have been surprised if they'd locked the balcony window, just in case I'd seriously lost the plot and they had a Jumper on their hands.

'Probably not.' And that was the understatement of the century. I downed the whisky in one, and was off down the stairs like a rabbit. By the time they all caught up with me, I was standing in Elinor's bedroom, gazing at that wall, lump hammer at the ready.

'Er, look, Ms Deryn – Lissa – perhaps we should discuss this...' Well, it had to be Drystan they nominated as chief straightjacket catcher. He was a Tudur, after all, and so used to dealing with the delusional, the batty, and the downright nutcase.

'It's now or never,' I heard myself mutter. The whisky, along with a glass of wine, and an absence of dinner as yet, had gone straight to my head, and I was off in foreign shores, watching the whole thing from a vast distance.

'Yes, I'm sure it is, Lissa.' His hand reached over mine. Well, he didn't smell of chemical toilets: just a hint of wood fires and a touch of soap. Could quite go to a girl's head, that, even without the whisky. 'Only perhaps we should eat, first?'

Certainly not! I might come to my senses.

I gritted my teeth.

'I don't care if there are a hundred skeletons in there,' I said, shaking him off. 'It's where it's got to be.'

'Where what's got to be, Mam?'

'Evidence,' I said, grimly. 'Now stand back.' I took a swing with the lump hammer – rather expert swing, I'm afraid to say, given my early history of DIY, before I could afford to pay others to do the dirty work. Nothing lady-like about it. The hammer went straight through the plasterboard, shattering pieces about me.

'It's hollow!' exclaimed Drys.

'Well, of course it's hollow. It's a false wall. There used to be a fireplace there, when I was a kid. It's where Elinor always kept the ammonites.'

I gave a few more bashes, and we pulled away the pieces with our hands. The wall practically crumbled around us, until there was a gap just large enough to step through.

Well, it didn't smell of dead bodies, but then the whiffable parts would have rotted away years ago.

Arwen had already fetched the large rechargeable lamp on the staircase, ready for the emergency of a power cut. She handed it to me. Well, there was no going back from this now.

I took a deep breath, and stepped gingerly inside.

CHAPTER 14

OH, THERE WAS PLENTY TO SEE, ALL RIGHT.
The torch streaked over the mantelpiece, just as I remembered it, with the pillars at the side, and the heavy slate above. No mirror, no tapestries, medieval or otherwise – and thankfully no bodies, as far as I could see.

'That looks Victorian, to me,' said Drys, peering in behind me. 'No one thought about the fireplace. We assumed it was just blocked off and the surround removed when the radiators were put in.'

'So why go to all the trouble of building a false wall? That's the bit that has been puzzling me. There has to be some reason. If it's just ordinary Victorian, there would be no need.'

'Could be damp.'

'Don't be so boring!' I exclaimed, frowning at him. The whisky was wearing off, and I was beginning to see how I might just look like a prize twit, especially if this turned out to be the major damp-proofing efforts on this side of the castle. Robin would never let me live this down. He'd never let me loose on one of his projects (even if they were technically mine) ever again.

'Only pointing out it could be an attempt at dry lining,' Drys returned. Rather mildly, I suppose, given the circumstances.

'Mmm,' I muttered, swinging the torch around in reckless manner: OK, at this point I'd have taken skeletons, mummified remains, the works, and risk footsteps creaking along the corridors at dead of night for ever after. Anything to prove this was not a functional partition.

'There!' Drys grabbed my arm, steadying the beam of the torch back towards the mantelpiece. His breath fell on my cheek, with just the faintest Mediterranean hint of red wine and olives. Blimey! He was crushed right up against me: we were practically entwined. I didn't move.

Oh, all right: he didn't notice, OK? Satisfied? Hey, it was a nice thought, and probably my last chance in life to be in an almost-clinch with a tasty looking man a good ten years younger than yours truly, and with a rather neat little bum on him to boot, so who could blame me?

'What?'

'Up there!' I leant back (against him, of course: I mean, there was very little room in there) and followed the beam of the torch. Something flickered on the wall. This time it was an involuntary squeal I gave. Most undignified, but it did have its compensations. 'Hey, it's OK. They're only plaster figures,' said Drys, steadying me with his free arm, so we were almost completely intertwined this time.

Damn! And he still didn't notice! Oh well, mother-in-law material I would just have to resign myself to be. Heigh, ho. I suppose I've been through worse things in life before. Besides, curiosity was getting the better of me.

'Oh,' I said. My eyes adjusted. Even a manly arm around my shoulders couldn't distract me now. I straightened up. 'So *that's* what was under the mirror.'

'What is it?' I'd almost forgotten Arwen and Katie – oops! Forgotten I was getting cosy (well, failing to) with a possible Alternative Arrangement to Tim – what kind of mother did that make me?

'Two figures.' I called back. 'A man and – a woman, possibly? Some kind of pattern around them. It's difficult to see with this light. But there is definitely something there.' Unencumbered by my not-insubstantial figure, Drys was raking the chimney breast slowly with the torch. This time he did notice, but unfortunately only to jump in response to my sudden squeal. 'Look, look, look!'

'What?'

'That was a ruff. I'm sure that was a ruff!'

'Could be a collar.'

'I'm sure it was a ruff. That really would make it Elizabethan.'

'Not if it's a collar.'

'Do you always have to be right, Mr Tudur?'

'Lissa, I was only pointing out the possibility – '

'Oh for heaven's sake!' Katie wriggled her way halfway through the hole. 'It's like listening to a kindergarten in here. Where are these figures?' Drys obliged. And he certainly noticed Katie was next to him, up close and personal, as far as I could see. Suddenly it wasn't quite so much fun any more. I slipped out and made my way back to Arwen.

'They look like plaster,' I said, trying not to listen to my daughter's excited squeaks within the partition. And he didn't seem to be making any objections to them.

Honestly! Men! Good job I gave them up years ago.

'Oh.' Arwen was chewing her lip. Her eyes were excited, but that chewing was definitely nervous. Mind you, she had been standing out here listening to first me then Katie alone in a dark place with the possible – probable? – object of her desire, and while I couldn't possibly be taken seriously, my daughter could.

Fortunately, Katie re-emerged at this moment, and hustled Arwen inside. No squeaks or squeals this time. Just silence. Then a brief murmur, too low for me to hear. It almost sounded as if Drys was reassuring her. Something rather nasty and cold went down my spine.

Don't ask me why, when I was standing on the brink of the greatest Potential of my life: but it did.

'I suppose we really ought to leave it for the builders before we do any damage,' said Drys as he and Arwen emerged, dowsed in white plaster dust and smeared in soot.

'That would be the most sensible thing to do.'

'Oh, Mam!'

'Although just a little more shouldn't do any harm, I suppose,' he added, with a faint grin.

'I'm sure it wouldn't,' I replied.

So we pulled down a little more of the wall, shedding a little more light inside. But the figures above the mantelpiece, with an intricate pattern of stylised flowers forming a diamond pattern around them, remained in shadow, emerging only briefly in the rippling light of the torch.

My bathroom was well and truly christened that night. We all ended up trying to wash as much dust and soot as possibly from out of our eyes and behind our ears, before settling down to Katie's meal, which was by then just a little overcooked, but nobody seemed to notice. In fact, it was very hard not to be cheerful.

Nothing like a bit of soot and a mystery to break the ice.

Once we'd run out of every possible permutation of knot gardens and Elizabethan remains of every variety possible, even Arwen ended up laughing at Drys's tales of his machinations in order to buy a piece of land and get planning permission for a windmill and solar panels this close to the rarefied air of Snowdonia National Park.

I'm afraid Katie – who was in fine form that night – topped it all with a rip-roaringly and only mildly accurate account of my various career moves in order that we could stop dodging the bailiffs on a regular basis during the first years of my single mum existence, followed by a rundown of the décor of my first purchases in the property department.

'You're exaggerating,' I protested at last, wagging a finger at her. 'None of them were half as bad as you're saying.'

'Some of them were. Life of grime, or what, that one in Teddington! We used to smell you coming a mile off while you were doing it up.'

'Well, maybe that one.'

'And the others! And then there were the scrap yards. You couldn't *move* in our front room at one point for loo seats and hand basins, and all the old doors and bits of wood.'

'Beggars can't be choosers,' I replied, primly. 'And anyhow, it wasn't for long.'

'Phew, no. Once Robin took over, it was just your smelly feet we had to put up with after work. Honestly, you used to look like a labourer at times, Mam.'

'I was a labourer. Basic stuff I could do, up to a point. And the gardening.' I smiled at Arwen. 'I used to like doing the gardens. It was only just simple stuff, of course, that didn't take much maintenance. Most of the tenants didn't have the interest to keep them up. A few did, which was always a bonus.'

'So you were a wicked landlady, then, Lissa,' remarked Drys, who had been watching me with quite unnerving closeness for the past few minutes. Looking for the hard hat and the boiler suit, no doubt.

'Of course. Until I could afford to pay someone else to do my dirty work. Just like the Tudurs here, and I bet I was a lot fairer than they were. My rents were always at the lower end of the market price, I'll have you know, and I was a dab hand at the maintenance. Never a dripping tap or a damp wall in all my properties. Good business practice.'

'Fine. I believe you. I wasn't suggesting anything!' I eyed him suspiciously, but he had already turned away to ask Katie something, and I safely avoided his eye for the rest of the evening.

'I'll get the builders on to it on Monday morning,' I said to Arwen as the two of them left, once the pubs had finished chucking out the last of the Saturday revellers and settled down for the traditional lock-in.

We hadn't drunk enormous amounts, but still rather more than either of them had expected in all the excitement, and Arwen was voting to leave her van safely in my drive. I had offered to phone for a taxi, but they both said they preferred to walk. So I waved them off down the drive, hoping Katie did not notice the salient fact that they had only one torch between them on a dark and gloomy night.

Mmm. Yes; the jury was still out on that one. And nice bum or no, young Drystan would still get the same treatment I'd be handing out to Tim (if I ever caught up with him), if he dared to do the dirty on my daughter.

'They're nice,' said Katie, sleepily, tucking her arm into mine as we trudged our way wearily up the stairs once more.

'Mmm.'

'And I think you should take Arwen on as your gardener, Mam. She seems to know lots, and she does know the gardens.'

'I suppose so.'

'And isn't it exciting, Mam! We really found a bit of the old Elizabethan mansion!'

'We don't know it's that, *cariad*. It could still be Victorian.'

'Oh, I bet it is. I know you're trying not to let me be disappointed if it isn't. But I just bet it is. I can feel it.'

Whatever Katie might feel, Robin was furious.

He tried not to show it, but I could always tell. Rather an irrational fury, if you ask me. I mean, what harm had we done? And the builders could well have spotted the false wall when they came to decorate – the ease it came down, as I pointed out in no uncertain terms, it could have fallen to pieces with the first layer of wallpaper paste, in any case. And, anyhow, just whose castle was this?

'It was a damned stupid thing to do, Elissa. The whole thing could have come down on top of you all, and heaven knows what might have happened. That Tudur fellow always was a reckless one. Old Griffin would never let him near the place, and no wonder, if those are the kind of stunts he's likely to pull.'

'It was my idea,' I retorted, through gritted teeth. I mean, not even being allowed to make your own cock-ups! Not that it was anything of the kind, of course.

Robin clicked his tongue disapprovingly, to let me know his opinion that I had allowed myself to be led astray on this matter, and had the entire work team in Elinor's room within the hour, leaving the rest of the castle to fend for itself.

The wall came down easily enough. It was gone by the end of the day, with the last pieces being barrowed off into a hastily commandeered skip, and the dust being allowed to settle.

'Well, well, well,' said Robin, slowly, as we all downed tools and gathered to gaze at the unexpected find appearing through the white clouds of plaster dust. Nobody else said a word.

'That's Elizabethan,' I said, at last.

'Looks like it to me,' said John Parri Jones. He perched himself on a stack of boxes and rolled a cigarette thoughtfully. 'Who would have thought it, eh?' He gave me a slow, expressive wink as he moistened the paper. I eyed him without comment.

John Parri Jones, of Parri Jones & Son, Builders, was about my age. He'd have been the Son part of the business when the partition was put up, and Elinor, being a sharp old bird, could hardly have been ignorant of the fact that the only builders you could seriously trust in Llanestyn were Parri Jones & Son, and always Parri Jones senior, until Son had been whipped into shape.

'I bet the Tudurs will be pissed,' remarked Steve Parri Jones, the current Son, a leaner, less bejowled version of his healthily stocky father. 'Annoyed, I mean,' he corrected hastily, with an apologetic glance in my direction.

'I expect they'll be bloody pissed,' I replied. 'Missing a thing like that.' If it was as old as it looked, then it could well have meant listed building status, grants, National Trust, Cadw, the Lottery, the works. Instead of a common or garden Victorian Folly, they could have had the real McCoy on their hands, and a priceless one at that.

I loved it. I could just imagine them all peering over the paintings to find a lost Turner, or Rembrant, and rifling every cupboard for the family jewels that had been sold off years ago to keep the roof in working order. And there it was, all the time, under their noses. I was sure Elinor was laughing her socks off somewhere.

Although it was a rather strange thing to do, all the same. Surely leaving the whole caboodle to the National Trust – or even to the local cat sanctuary – would have made her point just as well, and with not nearly so much effort? Very odd.

'Mmm.' Robin peered at the figures of a man and a woman on the chimney breast, with the weaving pattern of Tudor roses in between them. 'It is clearly very old. An expert needs to look at that, if you ask me. I can phone around if you like.'

'Fine,' I replied. 'Thanks. You're right: we do need to find out exactly what this is before any more is done to this room.' Robin, being a Lloyd Jones, knew anyone who was anyone within a fifty-mile radius, so a few university professors wouldn't be difficult for him to grab hold of. One thing at a time. I wasn't about to mention gardens at this point: I had a sense life was about to become complicated enough, as it was.

After they had all left, Katie and I crept back for just one more glimpse, just to make sure it really was there and not a dream. At least, that's why I was there – not that I was about to admit such irrational feelings, of course.

'So there must be an Elizabethan garden out there,' said Katie. 'Aunt Cadi will love it! She just adores being in at the beginning of things, especially exciting things like this.'

'Mmm,' I replied. Katie is far too young and sweet to suspect which particular bit of all this her Aunt Cadi might be looking to adore. Beautiful and dangerous: not something my little sister was likely to let slip easily through those elegantly manicured fingers of hers.

I looked down into the garden, sleeping peacefully under the drizzle of fine rain. A peacock feather lay on the lawn right beneath me, shimmering iridescent green and purple as a ray of sun broke through the cloud, leaving a hint of rainbows beneath the oaks.

What was it Arwen had said? That Elinor had started restoring a part of the Elizabethan garden that had occupied her mind so much over the years, and then stopped, and let the gardens be. Elinor was a survivor and a doer, not a dreamer. I was quite sure if she really set her mind to something she would see it through, especially something I knew was so close to her heart as this.

So why had she stopped? And why had she blocked up the chimney, hiding away the evidence of anything older than a cotton millionaire's gothic playground? Supposing Bryn Glas had been turned into a hotel or an old people's home and the delicate plasterwork had remained in their seclusion forever, or swept away by some plasterer keeping to a tight schedule? Something must have stopped her.

I had a nasty feeling I wasn't going to enjoy finding out what, exactly.

CHAPTER 15

B Y THE TIME KATIE LEFT – most unwillingly, and with promises to come back as soon as she could – the press had already been.

When I say press, I mean the Llanestyn Herald, who sent out one of their freelance reporters, with a large camera and an eye for a pretty girl. (Katie, not me, naturally.) We (or rather, Katie) ended up on an inside page as *Piece of Local History Uncovered*, with a quick run-down of (Katie, presumably) finding evidence of an earlier dwelling on the site of Bryn Glas castle, and a breathless musing (hey, it was past Summer Fair time, there were no exam results to fill up the pages, and the National Eisteddfod had finished weeks ago – they were desperate) on the exciting finds that might yet lie undiscovered.

It was Robin who contacted them. He was quite right, of course. I mean, with half a dozen builders in on the act, we could hardly swear the whole lot to secrecy. And better stay in control of the publicity, rather than wake up to some half-baked tale circulating round the village with an unfortunate hint of diamonds that might bring every housebreaker flocking around to try their luck.

'And you know, Elissa,' he reasoned, reasonably, 'there are grants and such-like out there to help you, and publicity like this always counts.'

'I suppose so,' I muttered, trying not to sound ungracious. My personal opinion was that it was far better to stick my head under a pillow and hope the whole thing went away. Which was not the grown-up thing to do at all.

It was exciting, of course it was: but sometimes the worst curse that can be laid upon you is for your wishes to come true. It was hard to explain, but somehow my beautiful, wonderful, absolutely perfect castle didn't feel like mine any more.

Was that what Elinor had seen, I couldn't help wondering?

After the press came the media. We were the 'feel good' factor of the day for the local bulletin, and even made it briefly onto the national news a few days later.

Tilly from next door in Kingston-upon-Thames phoned up in a high state of excitement to tell me so.

'I couldn't believe it when I first saw it, darling,' she crowed, delightedly. 'I was only half watching – you know how it is when you're running around getting tea – but it just had to be you. I recorded the later one; I'll send you a copy. I still think you should have got them to interview you. Ageist, that's what it is. Age-*ist*.' Tilly is sixty-five if she's a day, so this is a subject close to her heart.

'Katie enjoyed being interviewed,' I muttered, apologetically.

Tilly would never had stood aside and let youth be pushed to the fore. She might appear elegant and tiny in her well-cut suits and flaming red hair, and never a touch of lipstick out of place, but she still works as a Personal Trainer, pounding and pummelling the would-be skinny and fragile-looking of Richmond and Hampton Wick into the obligatory shape. And she had sent a few stray bailiffs packing, in no uncertain terms, when the kids and I first arrived next door, with the mysterious vanishing of Terry's car (or rather the monthly payments of his finance deal) still dogging our footsteps.

'I could see she did,' said Tilly. 'And she handled it really well: the camera just loves that girl, Lissa.'

'For heaven's sake, don't start putting ideas in her head!'

Tilly chuckled. 'Darling, as if I would. I was proud of her, that was all. She's turned out all right, you know, has that one.' I could hear the pride in her voice.

Tilly was such a part of our lives, all those years: at that moment I just wished I could have brought her up with me, lock stock and barrel, and sent the new mums of Llanestyn circling Llanestyn Falls with their pushchairs with all the panache of their English sisters trotting past Teddington Lock, or loping round the Serpentine in Hyde Park in lycra jogging shorts and cropped tee shirts, one hand on the designer three-wheeler buggy, the other clutching a copy of *Low-Carb Revisited*.

'You and Coral are still coming for Christmas?' I was suddenly anxious.

'Of course we are, darling. If you're sure you'll be ready on time.'

'Oh, I will be. Robin made damn sure the penalty clauses will half bankrupt the builders if they miss their deadlines. And, to be honest with you, there really is just the kitchen to put in now, plus the finishing touches Katie's volunteered herself for. Robin's already got the building inspectors and the fire people all lined up. *Then* all we'll need is the Tourist Board and their stars for the brochures and the website, and I'll be ready to roll.'

'They should give you full marks just for that garden, by the look of that TV report.'

'I rather think it's bathrooms and ambience that count.'

'Oh, we can help you with the ambience bit, all right. Mind you, I'm not having you practising breakfasts on us all day until New Year, Elissa Deryn: I know you. It's the full turkey experience or I, for one, am off to the Ritz.'

I giggled. Tilly has a no-nonsense, buck-yourself-up-girl approach to life that always had me snapping out of any lurking self-doubts, pronto.

'Oh, you've got to have some breakfasts, Tilly, that's the deal, you know: you're my trial run before I open for real. You've got to have a least one piece of frazzled black pudding and soggy croissant before I hand over the key to your room.'

'Black pudding? I thought you were going healthy and organic?'

'Organic black pudding, then.'

'Never heard of such a thing,' snorted Tilly. 'I hope you're planning to offer a healthy option as well.'

'Nothing wrong with a good fry-up before you tackle Snowdon.'

'Darling, I have news for you: I am not tackling Snowdon. Not in the middle of winter, and definitely not at Christmas. No way, my girl. This is my one time away from physical exercise, I'll have you know. Besides, it interferes with the gin.'

'OK. I might let you off with wholemeal toast and muesli one day. But the rest of the time I'm practising my bacon and eggs. I need to get this slick before my first paying guests, you know.'

Tilly laughed. 'Forget guests, darling: at this rate you'll have Hollywood calling: atmospheric old houses are all the rage, nowadays.'

Well, I did my best: I set up the answering machine with my best husky voice. But Johnny Depp never called.

Ah well: his loss, not mine.

After the media came the experts. Not the bigwigs from Cardiff, but a semi-retired history professor, with a particular interest in the Elizabethan period, who had been at school with Robin and had moved in the Lloyd Jones circle ever since.

Professor Gwynne turned up, complete with white beard, crumpled linen suit and bow tie, and muttered in an excited fashion into his whiskers, before consuming enormous amounts of tea in the conservatory while waving his arms in a flurry of such long words – both the English and the Welsh – that I soon gave up and took to admiring the vivid blue of his eyes instead.

He was followed by a colleague from Bangor University, who turned out to be a younger, less bearded version, who became equally excited and incomprehensible, and uttered the ominous words 'rare', and 'national treasure', and told Robin that he really should consider getting the place listed.

I beg your pardon?

And no, I did not pour hot tea over either academic head, neither the young, nor the old: which I, personally, considered to be the very model of restraint.

'There you are, you see,' said Robin, as silence descended in my domain once more. 'I told you you'd uncovered something remarkable.'

'Hrmph.'

'Don't you see, Elissa? This changes everything. And if the garden itself turns out to be half as unique as they believe it could prove to be –' He gave my hand a reassuring pat. 'Well, then, Elissa Deryn, we could have a national treasure on our hands! How lucky that you took such a fancy to the place, and it wasn't some developer who'd got their hands on it. We'll have to seriously look at the plans for the renovations again, now.'

No, I didn't throw tea over his head, either. Instead, I smiled sweetly and packed him off home so I could sit down with my old friend the Australian Shiraz and think about this. It was all getting, well, just a little bit out of hand. Not that I had much time for thinking, or even considering just how out of hand this might all end up becoming.

For after the experts, came the Tudurs.

No, not the delectable (if slightly shady) Drystan, suddenly seeing the light and wanting me, body and all, this minute, now, and all the long moonlit night long. Drys had buggered off and lain low ever since all the hoo-ha began. OK, I hadn't invited him back, so this could have been a sign of politeness. I'd spoken to Arwen on the phone with a run-down of the experts, and told her to come over any time to see our discovery, but she seemed to be lying low as well.

Mmm.

No, the Tudurs came, one and all – and from time immemorial, I suspect – in the shape of Griffin Tudur marching up to me as I sat on the steps outside Elinor's conservatory, enjoying the evening light with my first glass of Shiraz and too lazy to get up and see if it was Robin returning for round two of the National Treasure argument (and a rapid introduction to the boiling oil solution to friendly disagreements) who had just pulled up in front of the house in a hail of gravel.

'Miss Deryn.' I put down the glass before I spilt it all over my shabby old working trousers and completed the picture of a raddled alcoholic taking her poison. Thank heaven the bottle was in the library – to make sure I didn't drink it all at once – and safely out of sight.

'Good evening,' I spluttered, staring up into a mass of grey-streaked tawny hair, bristling eyebrows – a touch of fox in there did I detect? – and pale eyes of a most unnerving orange glow, too gobsmacked to tell him to get off my land, and contact my solicitor in the morning.

He clearly took my discomfort as a sign of awe. He took position in front of me: a shadow blocking out the slanting brilliance of the evening sun, legs apart, one hand resting on the ornate hilt of a walking cane. There was very little point in my standing up: I remembered he even towered over Robin, which not many men can do. So I remained seated.

'Miss Deryn. I've been reading quite a bit concerning you, recently.'

Shotgun licenses? Death warrants? Mafia contracts?

'Really.'

'Oh, yes.' There was a moment's silence while he stared down at me. 'It seems your purchase of Bryn Glas was rather a fortunate one.'

'It was?'

'Oh yes. Given recent developments.'

'Looks like a lot of hard work and responsibility, from where I'm standing,' I remarked, mildly. Sitting, I should have said. But I had a feeling we were not engaging in niceties at this moment.

'Who would have guessed it.' And no, it was not a question.

'Who, indeed.' There was another silence. I could feel him staring down at me impassively from his self-created shadow.

'I believe you were friendly with my aunt, for a while.'

'I was twelve. She was nice to me.'

'But you visited her on several occasions since,' he shot back in, with the clean thrust of an unscrupulous barrister nailing his quivering witness.

I sighed. Look, didn't he know I was a single woman? Well, actually, he most obviously did: I'd bet my last pair of shoes he'd be nowhere near the place if he thought for one minute I had a male of any kind stashed around the shrubbery.

Yes, I should have known some Tudur or other would be stomping, sooner or later, over my flowerbeds, with all the strut of the acknowledged master of the universe come to sort out the pond-life of existence with heavy disapproval and an undercurrent of physical violence – not to mention a bit of the old thrill in the nether regions, I wouldn't doubt: oh, joy! Something they really could beat up if they wanted to – at last!

I gritted my teeth. 'I did visit Elinor, yes.'

'Aha!' Judge, jury and executioner, no less. OK. If I let that motor-mouth of mine get the better of me, I could be in trouble here.

And where is the knight in shining armour when you need him? In his elegant dining room laying out my future over grilled chicken and salad and a chilled glass of Chardonnay in one case, and no doubt cosying up nicely with a younger woman amongst the solar panels, in the other. I wouldn't have minded if King Arthur himself had appeared: I've have faced Guinevere later.

But, of course, he didn't.

I'm not sure I like all this 'grown up' business. Much too scary, if you ask me.

'Look, Mr Tudur, is there a point to all this?'

'You visited her.'

'Yeees.'

'So you could have discussed things.'

'Things?'

'Things.'

'I expect we talked about something, Mr Tudur. I don't remember any long silences. It's usually the weather, on these occasions, isn't it?' He leant forward, so his face was just above mine.

'She had no right to give you things.'

'I beg your pardon?'

'You heard, Miss Deryn.' You mean, he was getting his Y-fronts in a twist over a pair of old fossils? Not even the entire set, given that there were three. And the entire set being priceless? I'd eat my socks if that were the case. 'You thought we didn't know about those papers, did you?'

'Papers?' Newspapers? A secret will? A letter saying the castle belonged to the current inhabitants of Buckingham Palace and could on no account be sold to riff-raff?

'Papers.'

This could go on for some time, I could see. I blinked at him. I suspected he was all bluff, but in this life you never can be entirely sure.

'Well, if I come across any, I'll let you know,' I replied, with my best bland smile.

Just for a moment, I thought Griffin was about to wallop me over the head with that ornamental cane of his. But even a Tudor must be aware that, in these degenerate days of social equality, horsewhipping the peasantry is known as GBH, and frowned upon even by the local constabulary, who in these exceedingly degenerate times are no longer in the pocket of the nearest landowner – the small technicality of having got shot of the land (along with the castle) for loads of lovely sponduliks, making no odds with Griffin Tudor, I had no doubt.

'I'm sure we'll be discussing this again, Miss Deryn.'

I was effing sure we wouldn't be. Not on a one-to-one basis, and in absence of any knight available for hire, shining or not, anyhow. I mean, a girl can get seriously weary of this kind of treatment on the steps of her own castle.

'Of course, Mr Tudor. Now if you'll excuse me...'

I left my wine where it was and strode back into the conservatory, pulling the door shut behind me. I didn't look back, or stop to lock up properly. The glass was so fragile it would have been a simple enough matter to break in, in any case. I went straight inside the walls of the castle and turned the lock of the substantial door to the library.

Then I went round every door and window I could find and checked the locks. I heard the Range Rover cruising magisterially down my drive, but still I kept on checking.

God bless the Victorians, is all I can say: when they did something, they did it right, and that included solid doors, solid windows, and some pretty impenetrable-looking shutters.

Only when I was quite certain no one could get in without the aid of dynamite, or a small army, did I go and throw up in one of my nice new loos.

After which, I headed upstairs for hot tea with plenty of sugar to consider my plan of action.

'Garden archaeologists?' Arwen sounded wary.

'Yes. You've worked with some, haven't you?'

'Yes. A little. Mostly the Llanestyn Garden Society. It's a hobby, really, for most of them.'

'That's OK. D'you think they might be interested in looking at Bryn Glas?'

'Interested? It's all they've been talking about since that article in the Herald, Lissa. You just try and stop them!'

'Great. Can you bring some along in the next few days?'

'The next few days?'

'Yes. Like, tomorrow?' I just about kept my squeak at bay. 'I mean Saturday,' I added, hastily.

'There are one or two I could ask, and maybe some students.' I could almost hear her frown. 'Look, are you sure about this, Lissa? You could get *loads* of professional help. Robin was talking this afternoon about getting some expert in from London.'

First I'd heard about this, of course. And just how do you go about boiling oil? In Medieval, castle defending quantities, that is.

'Oh, quite sure. I want to do this my way. No interference.'

'Are you OK?' Her question was so unexpected, it threw me for a moment.

'Yeah, of course.' I bounced back: a Deryn unfazed. 'Never been better. And I would like to employ you to oversee the restoration of Bryn Glas gardens. But if you'd rather not – '

'Oh, I'm interested all right.' Aha! Now that reply came back fast. My bet was wild horses couldn't stop her.

'So tomorrow, then? Look, I know it's short notice, Arwen, and I'm not expecting anything: just a quick look to see if it might be possible to find whatever that shadow might have been on the lawn.'

'I know it's a knot garden, Lissa. I just know it is.' Heavens! She was taking this to heart already.

'I hope it is. And if it isn't, we can always make it up.' Oops! I could almost hear the reverberations of shock in the ensuing silence: I considered now was probably not the time to suggest she might lighten up. Maybe this whole thing was a bad idea, after all. I mean, I didn't really know her. And hadn't

I only thought of her because she was some last link with Elinor, and I was feeling in need of as many bodies as possible wandering around my castle, just now?

Warm, live, friendly bodies, you understand. Just to give my ghost of the morning light, not to mention the delightful Griffin, something to think about. Besides, Plan B might involve being seriously nice to Robin for a while, which – apart from being the most dastardly dishonourable tactics a girl could consider – might lead to all kinds of difficulties in the future.

'Lissa...!'

'Only joking. Wouldn't dream of such a thing. And anyhow, I'm sure you're right: it's bound to be there. Why shouldn't it be?'

There was a further silence. *Diawl*! She was probably weighing up the likelihood of me demanding she grow opium poppies in the walled garden: between running the illicit still and the gambling den in the old stables, naturally.

'Lissa – ' she began, at last.

'Yes?' I tried to sound encouraging.

'Oh, nothing. See you tomorrow, then?'

'Great,' said I, merrily.

CHAPTER 16

MISS ROSENSTERN NEVER UNPACKED HER BAGS. Not even, said Mam, when she retired from nursing at the local hospital, and eventually grew too frail to live alone and moved into Plas Hyfryd, the old people's home just within sound of Llanestyn Falls. Mam used to visit her there every Sunday, never fail.

'Poor dear, she looks so tiny nowadays,' she said once, as we helped her with the annual cake-making bonanza for Plas Hyfryd's Christmas Fair. Cadi was creaming the sugar and margarine in a large bowl and sneaking a finger-taste of pure sweetness when Mam wasn't looking, as she always did. Cadi was never a one to resist sweetness, even then.

I was spooning flour into the oval container on the kitchen scales, watching for the magic moment when the round metal weights at the other end lifted slowly and hung in the balance, just like the figure of Justice on the town hall. So did grown-ups shrink, I wondered? Children grow up, so why shouldn't grown-ups shrink down? Like Alice in the rabbit hole: up and down, up and down. I wasn't sure I liked the idea at all.

I used to dream about Miss Rosenstern. Always the same dream: there I'd be, walking through Llanestyn park, ducks calling in the frosty air, the muddied smell of fallen leaves rising all around me. And there she would be, sitting on her bench, packed bags all around her, while the heavy drone of an Enola Gay made its way with its mushroom cloud, inevitably towards us.

I hadn't had that dream for years: but I had it that night, in my fitful dozing between every creak that stirred my poor old castle between the dark settling around me and the slow dawn rising.

Oh, sod Griffin for putting the wind up me with his blustering!

Of course, that was it. Finito. No more.

Wasn't it?

Bound to be. He'd made his point, hadn't he? Let off steam. Viagraed the ego no end. I was just playing into his hands lying here in the dark, quivering.

But then you hear such stories. Stalkers. Madmen. Shotguns in the dark. Blood oozing slowly down the stairs... Oh why did I ever watch those horror movies of Merion's? I knew at the time I should have swallowed my pride, confessed to being a wimp, and shut my eyes tight to all those visceral visions I still could call up at a moment's notice.

Slit throats just ain't entertainment when you're alone in a castle with a Tudur on the warpath outside. Besides, the Tudurs had always been known to be a bit ropey on the sanity front – at least, as far as Llanestyn was concerned. Rumour went, Elinor's father had been trying to get an invitation to Windsor Castle on the grounds of being a close relative, for years.

Now, I ask you.

Was that what the papers were? The thought went slithering down my spine. Were they some batty version of cast iron proof the Tudors should never have vacated the throne and Griffin should take his rightful place amidst the ermine?

In that case, he could have them, no worries, and good luck to him. Scotland Yard, MI5, MI6, CIA: They'd keep him occupied and off my back for years. I'd have searched, turned the place upside down, handed everything over right then. Except the builders had done that for me, and nothing, as far as I knew, had been found. Not even in the cavity behind Elinor's false wall.

Which was no reason for Griffin to stop thinking there had been. And this being life, I couldn't turn to the back page of the story and see if I survived, and then decide whether I was going to carry on reading, or not.

Bugger.

I'd never been so glad when Saturday came around and brought the distraction of Arwen and her merry men.

They were a motley crew. Not all men, either. And not all young. I spotted at least three women past retirement age, clothed in cotton trousers, stout walking boots and fleeces, giving off an unnerving air of healthiness and energy that put me well to shame. The rest were mostly of student appearance, all ethnic sweaters – Fair Trade, handmade in Peru, most probably – along with well-worn climbing boots that had clearly stomped the tops of Snowdon and the Carneddi in an earlier manifestation of their existence, and combat trousers that had seen better days. Not an ironed shirt between them. Wonderful.

I watched them unloading all kinds of fearsome implements from the back of an ex-BT van, which had been hand-painted a grassy shade of green with 'Llanestyn Historical Garden Society' in swirling purple letters on the side, and fairly rubbed my hands in anticipation.

Oh, stuff Griffin. I hadn't got time to fend off poisoned arrows and battering rams set against my castle wall, especially now it was daylight and there were people all around me: now this was my kind of thing!

'Hi,' I said to Arwen, approaching without the presence of her usual sidekick, but trailing a whole host of far less eye-catching, but much more useful, bodies instead.

'I hope it's not too much of an invasion, Lissa.'

'Oh no. Absolutely not. The more the merrier.' I caught the slightly strange look she gave me at this rather overdone show of enthusiasm, and smiled instead at the large Viking of a man loping up behind her. All blue eyes and white-blond hair, just slightly receding, along with a prominent nose and a mouth that appeared far too wide for his face. He gave me a broad smile over slightly crooked teeth, and I was charmed.

Well, I needed a few more men around the place. On a part-time basis, you understand. Definitely the more the merrier. Did Arwen have any more of these stashed away?

'This is Hugh,' she said. 'He's a real enthusiast for garden history.'

'Pleased to meet you,' I beamed. 'I can't wait for this.'

His large paw enveloped mine. 'This is so exciting, Ms Deryn – '

'Oh, do call me Lissa, please.'

'Lissa. We've not had anything on this scale before. We'll try a few trial trenches in likely places, if that's OK with you, and find this shadow of yours.'

'Fine by me,' I grinned.

Hey, this was as good as being on *Time Team*, and I'd always had a bit of a thing for the one in the stripey woolly jumpers. Things are definitely looking up!

Robin made no bones of his disapproval that I had taken matters into my hands in such a high-handed way, especially after all his efforts to lead me unto the paths of righteousness, as far as the official academic circles were concerned.

'Oh, well, they offered, and they seemed so eager,' I smiled, innocently. 'I really didn't like to say no.' Robin knows me and the innocent look. He eyed me with a stern gaze. As usual, I took no notice.

He gave a deep sigh, shook his head despairingly, and stomped off to inspect the installation of the final loo with the air of the wronged Sheriff in one of those old cowboy films – you know the kind: where the women do a lot of soulful gazing and sacrificing of themselves, and would clearly not have lasted a day on the pioneer trail amongst the tough old birds who survived that little lot.

And Clint Eastwood could have taken care of a Griffin in a black hat without so much as disturbing the ash from his cigar.

Ah, now, those were the days...

'Well, looks like we might have found your shadow,' Hugh announced.

'Can you tell what it is?' I murmured, gazing down into a muddy patch of earth and trying to look as if I knew what I was looking at.

'Sorry, no.'

I gazed around at the long rectangular trenches that had appeared in my lawn throughout the day, with bodies still digging and scrapping and brushing away into the descending gloom of the evening and its accompanying drizzle of rain.

'But there could be a knot garden?'

'Possibly,' said Hugh.

'Yes,' said Arwen at the same time.

'So worth continuing with the excavations, then?'

'Of course,' said Hugh. 'If the lawn has been reasonably undisturbed, we could well find some evidence for the way it looked.'

'Like Hampton Court, you mean?' They'd found whole beds there, just as they'd been dug. Whole huge swirls of them. I'd seen the photos each time I'd been to visit the restored Privy Gardens of a Sunday afternoon, which had always been my day away from Potential, to dream about the extensive garden (which in Kingston would have cost more than my castle, and without the earning potential) I would potter about in my old age.

The Privy Gardens were from a little later than Elizabethan times, admittedly, but the principle was still the same.

'Well, perhaps not in so much detail, and we don't have the same resources.' Hugh was looking faintly alarmed.

'Oh, just the smallest corner of a real Elizabethan knot garden will do for me,' I replied. I could feel the grin stretching from ear to ear.

OK, so I had an entire castle to clean of builder's dust, furniture arriving in a few days, and children arriving to inspect progress at the weekend, and in need of large amounts of food (Merion, despite being scrawny in build, is still a bottomless pit as far as nutrition is concerned) and beds to sleep in.

I should have been grown up, responsible, and shot off instantly in search of the hoover and the supermarket, leaving my willing volunteers to continue their rectangular explorations in my lawn.

Which was why Cadi found me, scrabbling in the ground with a small trowel and up to my ears in mud.

'Aha! Caught you, Deryn,' she said, looking down at me in the bottom of the trench, swanlike and elegant, without a hair out of place (Cadi, not me, naturally). 'I just knew you couldn't resist, *cyw*.'

'Well, they're all volunteers, I couldn't just leave them, could I?'

'Of course.'

'And I found stuff. Look.'

'Stuff.' Cadi peered down with some distaste at the small piece of pottery I handed over. 'Yeah. Great. Fascinating, I'm sure.'

'It's Elizabethan,' I replied, crossly.

'Really.' She eyed the muddy sliver with undisguised scepticism.

'Yes, really. Gwen at the end there is an expert: according to her, it's real Elizabethan, and just at the level where it looks like there has been a row of hedging.'

'Oh, fields.'

161

'No, not fields. Not that kind of hedging. The ornamental kind: box, privet. That kind of thing. The kind the Elizabethans used in knot gardens.'

'I thought Elizabethans didn't approve of box. Didn't like the smell,' said Cadi, sweetly.

'OK, well not box exactly. Whatever they used.'

'You mean thyme, marjoram, rue, santolina – '

'Cadi!'

'I was being supportive, sweetie pie: I looked it up on a website,' said Cadi, with that faint smile of hers that always appears when she knows she's winding me up.

'Ha!' I stood up with a creak of the knees. Look, you can get lost in the sniffing out of broken pot and elusive, doubt-defying coins, OK? I'd been there rather longer than I'd planned. My shoulders ached and it took me a while for my back to straighten to its usual upright.

'What happened to the yoga class?' said Cadi, who I am quite certain can still touch her toes and be quite unnecessarily athletic when it comes to –

'I'm still looking.'

'Well if you're going to get up to these kind of antics *and* run a B&B, you'd better find one quick.'

'OK, OK. No need to rub it in. I've quite enough with Robin muttering beneath his breath each time I pass.'

'Don't knock it, Lissa: Robin's an old sweetie, and you're very lucky to have him.'

'I don't "have" him, in any sense of word,' I snapped, irritably, attempting to rub the particularly tender muscles between my shoulder blades.

'Well don't blame me if you find him slipping through your fingers.'

'And what does that mean?'

'Oh, nothing.' She smiled. 'Come on. You make me a cup of tea and I'll give you a shoulder massage. Deal?'

Oh, it was a deal, all right. My sister's massages are legendary. Best not ask how she learnt them, and why: just breathe in deep and savour the moment.

As I made the tea (a lengthy process with builders and excavators to keep happy as well) Cadi rooted around my castle, tutting at my oversight concerning the necessary essential oils, along with a distinct lack of a dust-free surface and the necessary privacy for her to really go to town.

So we settled for the steps outside the conservatory. The sun was out and warm for the time of year. The peacocks (who had not taken well to proceedings after years of the quiet life in control of the place and tended to let rip with indignant shrieks each time one of our human moles moved too quickly) emerged from the shrubbery to join us, pecking at the grass, one eye for the main chance in the cake and sandwiches department (invaders having their little compensations, at times).

'Mmmm,' I said, as the knots down my back were firmly untangled and I began to feel human again. Bliss. 'I don't know how Mair and Alison do it, day after day. They must be in their seventies, at least.'

'Habit,' said Cadi, beginning to work on the steel ropes in my neck. 'Training the right muscles and knowing when to stop.' She paused for a moment, concentrating. 'I expect,' she said, as she cupped my chin and gently manipulated my head, 'they'll still be out there in their nineties, finding lost gardens. D'you know, I really envy them.'

'Envy? Cadi, you never get your hands dirty. You hate mud. And you complain about the slightest bit of rain. You wouldn't last a day.'

'Not of the excavations bit, idiot.' She released me, and I turned to look at her. She was watching the diggers on the lawn, a faraway look on her face. 'The sense of purpose. Something you really, passionately believe in, so there's not enough hours in the day, and you just can't wait to get out of bed each morning. Like you with your castle, Lissa.'

'You have your websites, and meeting loads of interesting people.'

'That's just a job. It's not me, not really.'

Oh-oh. My sister's low boredom threshold surfacing yet again. I frowned at her.

'And you've led a much more exciting life than me.'

'For heaven's sake, Lissa! I'm not going to just live on memories for the rest of my life.'

Oh. More than just the boredom threshold: the 'help I'm nearly fifty, what have I done with my life, what do I do to make the most of the rest of it with the body growing unreliable, and the mind heading that way?' scenario.

Tell me about it.

'You have so many talents, Cadi. I'm sure you'll find something.'

Cadi wasn't listening. 'Maybe I should have had children.'

Ah. So the first signs of the no-turning-back, your-fertile-days-are-over had hit at last. I looked again. Cadi has the obligatory teenage figure, wears the obligatory tight-fitting, up-to-the-minute clothes: I'd never thought of her as anything but gorgeous. Which she is.

But our eyes are attuned to our age, as if we carry our mirror with us, stretched across the inner vision of our eyes: even thirty-year-olds are starting to look like children to me. I looked again. Fine lines were beginning round her mouth and the corners of her eyes, despite the cartload of creams and potions I knew very well she kept on her dressing table.

'Children leave, Cadi.'

'But they come back. They'll always come back.'

'But you're never the centre of their lives. Not once they leave. They are too busy trying to get their own futures together. Kids aren't always an answer, you know: you can't rely on them to give you a purpose for the whole rest of your life. That's the hard bit, letting them move on, and finding somewhere to move on to yourself. And, anyhow, you did loads of things because you didn't have a family to tie you down.'

'I suppose.' She began squeezing my shoulders again. 'I'm just not sure about living on my own, for the rest of my life.'

'Who says you have to? There are plenty of men out there!'

'Not nearly as many as there used to be, *cyw*. When you get to our age the best ones are taken. And the ones who aren't, or have been thrown back into the pond – '

'I know. Beware, beware.' I smiled, encouragingly. 'Lots of women live on their own nowadays and have a whale of a time.'

'Mmm.' She was clearly not convinced.

'It seems scary when you think about it. I just wanted to give up and die at first. But now I can do what I want, when I please. The bills and the workmen trying to rip you off are a pest, but most of the time I have utter and total control of my life. Don't surveys always say the more control of your life you have, the happier and least stressed you can be? Well, I've got it. The ultimate. Nowadays, I can't image things any other way.'

Except when Griffin Tudur came baying for my blood, of course.

'Really, Lissa? You mean that?'

'Oh, yes,' said I, nodding sagely.

'Right.' And there was silence for while as she concentrated once more on the particularly knotted bit between my shoulder blades.

Absorbing my words of wisdom, and rearranging her life accordingly, I smiled to myself, drifting off into a pleasant haze of warm sun and the contentment of limbs relaxed by physical exertion in the fresh air.

I mean, what else are big sisters for?

CHAPTER 17

ALL IN ALL, I WAS SAD WHEN THE WEEKEND was over and the old green van was being packed away for its final departure. I hadn't had so much fun in ages, and my castle had felt, well, lived in and intruder-free at last.

At least Cadi was staying overnight, on her way to Manchester at some ungodly hour in the morning to catch a flight to New York. To meet a client, so she said. Hit Bloomingdales at top speed, if you ask me. I mean, a girl who doesn't eat has to have *some* kind of high in her life, and Cadi had been trying to give up the cigarettes for years, so even that was a guilty pleasure, nowadays.

But that left an entire working week before Merion and Katie arrived. OK, I'm a coward, right? I just didn't fancy five clear days and nights for Griffin to stage any resumption of the intimidation tactics. I hadn't said anything, of course, but Robin – bless him, he did have my interests at heart (even if this probably meant he viewed them as somehow his own) – had by now ensured the security system was up and howling, and linked to a direct line to the local police. Female on her own in large castle, and all that.

This was sort of reassuring, but I still wasn't entirely convinced in my own mind that any lone constable summoned at dead of night – or even in broad daylight – would stick around very long if he found Mr G. Tudur, Esquire, caught in his beam, whatever the said Mr G. Tudur might be doing at that precise moment (i.e. slicing up little me for breakfast).

Given the choice, I felt I'd stick with my ghost of the early morning light. At least there was an outside chance they might prove reasonable and let me try and settle whatever it was that was still keeping them hanging on in there. I had a feeling that with Griffin there was no chance. Not a snowball's hope in hell. It was a well-known fact that once a Tudur got up a head of steam there was no stopping them, and reason had nothing whatsoever to do with it.

Which meant I needed the distraction of my long-lost garden like nobody's business.

'So?' I demanded, as I made my way down to the excavations to say my thanks and good-byes. 'What d'you think?'

'Great,' said Arwen.

'Stunning,' said Hugh. Enthusiastic agreement rose in a murmur around us.

'We've had a great time,' put in Mair, the smallest and frailest looking of the energetic septuagenarians, who, as far as I could see, hadn't stopped from the moment she got here. 'Thank you so much for the opportunity, Lissa.'

'Brilliant,' echoed Phil, a particularly stringy variety of student, who had been far too shy to even meet my eye until now.

'And good luck,' put in Gwen's digging-mate, Sylvia, who had once been a headmistress and was not the kind you'd argue with, even now.

'And it's definitely a knot garden?'

'As sure as can be, without further work,' said Hugh.

'Great stuff.' I went all wobbly in the tummy, and this time it had nothing at all to do with Griffin. 'So it should be possible to uncover and restore it?'

There was a moment's silence. Arwen took to scraping the last of the mud from a spade in a deeply engrossed manner.

'You could uncover it,' said Hugh, at last. 'It would be a big job.' Aha! So that was it.

'Expensive, you mean.'

'Ah – yes.'

'I see.' Look, I appreciated them all doing this in their free time, and I didn't expect them to all carry on for nothing, not when I was living here in a castle. But until my paying guests started coming in and paying, I needed to keep a tight rein on the remains of my budget. My funds were not limitless, and heaven knew how long I might have to survive on them until Bryn Glas began to make a profit, let alone allowing for emergencies.

I cleared my throat. It doesn't look good, pleading poverty with a battlement as your roof and expensive showers and bathroom fittings making their way down your drive on a regular basis, not to mention the deliveries of towels and bedding that had taken place under their very noses. But I was going to have to say something.

Money, eh? Always the realist, is hard dosh; stopping you dead in your tracks, however hard you worked for it, and however worthy the cause. I've never quite got over a sneaking, childish envy of those gilded few for whom the supply appears limitless without all that amount of effort. But then I suppose I appeared gilded to the casual observer who hadn't been party to all that hard graft across the decades and didn't have the considerations of me surviving solo for another fifty years without ending in the gutter.

Diawl.

Of course, I did have my contingency fund, in the form of a bolthole back to Kingston that not even Robin knew about – although I rather suspect he suspected it. Robin knows me and my abject terror of the cardboard box – even though the arches beneath Hungerford Bridge have been cleaned out and tarted up into expensive shops, nowadays – so he must have suspected me of something. But contingency funds are not *exactly* there in aid of a spot of gardening.

'The thing is...' It was Arwen who came to my aid in this. 'There just could be a solution.'

Oh-oh. I had a bad feeling about this.

'Which might,' added Hugh, 'help to cover at least some of the costs.'

'Oh?'

'The thing is...' He retreated into a cough, leaving Arwen to finish the job.

'The thing is, Lissa, those news items about you stirred quite a bit of interest. Did you know you made it to the nationals?'

'Mmm,' I conceded, warily.

'Well, a friend of Hugh's – ' A friend of a friend, eh? Always bad news. 'Works for a TV production company, and they might interested in following the progress. If you decide to restore the garden, that is.'

'The progress.'

'Yes. Finding it, the detective work. Restoring it. They'd come at intervals and follow what you are doing. They're looking at a six part series initially – '

'Initially?' Lights, camera, action, and full-of-themselves media types running loose over my castle from now until the dark and distant future!

'There's lots of interest, Lissa. Even the BBC. Gardening is very popular, you know.'

'Hrmph.'

'They'll pay.'

A-ha!

'Rather well, as it happens.'

I saw what they meant.

'And there are grants,' put in Hugh, earnestly. 'I can talk to a few people, if you like. Sound them out.'

'I'll have to think it over.'

The hell I would! I wanted this garden, even more than the four-poster beds and the gleaming new kitchen, which were for my guests and not really for me, in any case. But a girl does have her pride, and, besides, I needed to make a show of consulting Robin's superior wisdom on all matters upon this earth, if just to keep the peace.

The BBC, eh? This is big time, Lissa! I suppose it's far too late for a facelift and a tummy tuck?

I decided it was. I'm not into pain. Much less the spilling of my own blood unless it cannot possibly be avoided. As for voluntarily going anywhere near a hospital and a surgeon's knife and all the possible complications – nah, it would have to be for something as good as eternal life, and even then I'd need to think about it.

'Of course, it's unlikely we'll be able to establish the entire layout of the garden from the archaeology,' Hugh was saying.

'Oh.' Ah well, back down to earth with a bump.

'Of course, it doesn't have to be exactly how it was. Gardening was hot in Elizabethan times, too. There were books, and plenty of detailed records. Patterns for knots. Plants they used. We can go on those to recreate an impression of just how it might have been.'

'You mean, *The Gardeners Labyrinth,* and *The Compleat Gardeners Practice:* that sort of thing,' I put in, wisely. I hadn't been boning up on knot gardens and parterres for nothing, you know.

'That's the one. And there are quite a few restored knot gardens we could look at. Hatfield house, those kind of places.'

Great! Visiting posh houses and gardens to die for. Just my kind of thing.

Except I had a Bed and Breakfast to set up and run, of course.

Damn.

Maybe I could just marry Robin and be a kept woman for the rest of my life? Then I could just garden to my heart's content.

Yes, I know: the thought was unworthy of me. But wouldn't you be tempted? And he wasn't a bad old stick, really, as far as middle-aged men go, and he'd never yet been able to keep me in order.

Ah, but it wouldn't be *my* garden.

A thought struck me.

'There wouldn't have been plans for this garden, would there?' As in paper plans. Papers. Papers! Something Cadw and the National Trust might go all weak at the knees for and possibly stump up all the necessary readies to keep a Tudur in clover for years to come. I had papers on my mind.

'Could have been. If the gardens really were created for a visit of Queen Elizabeth there could well have been records kept. For the Tudurs to show off their achievement to anyone who couldn't get here. If we're really lucky, there could still be planting lists amongst them.'

I looked straight at Arwen. Time for the direct approach.

'So is that what Elinor was working from?' I demanded.

'No.' She didn't quite meet my eye. 'Well, not exactly.'

'What not exactly?'

'There *were* plans. At least, I think there were. Elinor said she might have seen them when she was little. They were amongst the papers her father was using for his book.'

'And you didn't think to mention this before?'

'Elinor wasn't sure. Besides, she said her father burnt everything, right after he'd finished his book. I know she looked for them, but she never found them. That was when she decided to give up the whole idea of restoring the garden.'

'Oh,' I said. 'I see,' I said. I smiled. 'Ah well, *The Proffitable Arte of Gardening* it will have to be, in that case. *Do* let me help you load those wheelbarrows, they look so terribly unwieldy.'

Right, that was it. I was not being the fall guy for some inter-Tudur family feud and general double-dealing, smash, grab, and thievery. If Griffin Tudur thought that I had buttered up Elinor just to swipe some ancient plans of the garden, on the off-chance that I might own the place one day, then he had another think coming.

This was no time to hang about: the moment the green van vanished between the branches of the driveway, I was in my car and hot on the trail of the prime suspect.

'Plans?' Drystan Tudur stood in his front porch and showed no signs of inviting me in. Much as I would have liked to suspect he had a naked bimbo stashed away in there, and didn't want me to snitch to Arwen, I had to conclude that this had more to do with me looking as if I might be on a mission to murder him. Which, if I didn't get answers, and quick, I was quite likely to do.

'For the garden.'

'Garden?' I knew those tactics: I used them myself.

'Quit stalling, Drystan. Plans for the garden at Bryn Glas. The original garden. And I want to know who has got them.'

'You could try asking politely.'

'Stuff politely. That bloody uncle of yours is convinced I've filched them from Elinor's purse and is threatening to tear me limb from limb if I don't produce them.'

'Ah. I see. You'd better come in, then.'

Oops! And there I stepped, right into the dragon's lair.

I'd been in such a temper up until that point I hadn't thought to look around the place. I'd found him easily enough: everyone knew where the weirdo trying to live at one with Nature hung out. A Tudur weirdo, to boot. I'd vaguely been aware of an open gate and a long drive through green fields up to the house tucked away under the mountainside.

174

Of course I'd expected an eco-house: turf roof, below ground, hobbit-like bolthole smelling of damp leaves and earthworms. The door I stepped through was into a traditional cottage: small, and low, but unmistakeably stone walls and slate roof, with deep set windows to reveal just how thick those walls had been built. Inside it looked quite normal, too. Large scrubbed kitchen table: an old-fashioned range alongside a cooker and a washing machine. No bimbo draped across the appliances waiting for a resumption of services, thank heaven.

'You've got electricity!' I remarked, accusingly. He turned and grinned at this.

'Yep. Right up the valley from Llanestyn. Spoils the view, but everyone who has lived here since the Sixties has gone for the home comforts over the aesthetics. I take it you're not heading back to lighting fires in grates in Bryn Glas except for aesthetic purposes?'

'I should think not! I'd freeze. But then I'm not masquerading myself as an eco-house.'

'A work in progress, Lissa. A work in progress. Surely you should be one to appreciate a work in progress?'

'Hrmmph.'

'And anyhow, these old cottages are well on their way to being eco-houses to start with: you don't get insulation like these walls, nowadays. Don't you worry: by the time I've got the solar panels heating my water, and my windmill generating the rest, I'll be selling power back to the mains, just you see.'

He switched on the kettle. 'Come on, we can sit in the sunroom.'

The sunroom was an addition at the side, jutting out into a neatly laid-out vegetable garden. The old sofa was large and soft and settled itself around me in a rather comforting manner.

'Thanks,' I muttered as a mug of tea – normal, not herbal, thank goodness – was placed in my hands. I was shaking ever so slightly, I noticed with unease. Now where did that come from?

'OK. My dear Uncle Griffin.'

I shuddered. 'He accused me of having papers. Well I'd no idea what he was on about, I thought he meant a will, or something. But when Hugh was talking about garden plans today, well, that's when it struck me. That must be what he meant. It would all be too late for a will, now, surely? And the only thing that would make Bryn Glas worth more than I paid for it – '

I came to a dead halt. Talk about fraternising with the enemy! Mr Failed-dot-com here would have wanted his fair whack and more from the castle. I swallowed.

Oh, bugger the lot of them: I was out of here.

'Would be the garden,' Drystan finished, before I could extricate myself from the treacherous curves of the sofa holding me in place. 'You think they hadn't worked that one out already?' I frowned at him. 'Lissa, they were scouring the place for those papers old Tudur was supposed to have used for that book of his, right up to the moment you got the key. No one else might have taken the rumours seriously, but every paid up Tudur amongst them was praying.'

'Including you?'

'Oh, come off it, Lissa, wouldn't you at least be curious if you were in my shoes?'

'Hrmph. All right, so what happened to all the copies of the book? None just hanging around, I take it?'

'Not now. Not as far as I know.'

'Damn.' I wasn't sure I believed him, but it was as sure a brick wall as I had come across. 'Then how the hell am I supposed to convince Griffin that I don't know anything about them?'

'I'll have a word if you like. Not that he'll take much notice of me, I'm afraid. He probably has me down as having filched them in the first place.'

'And did you?'

'My dear Ms Deryn, do you really think I'd be sticking around this dump with that kind of dosh in my pocket? I'd be off down the Nile, and then on to New Zealand for the quiet life.'

'All right, all right. No need to be sarcastic.' I sighed. Suddenly I felt tired, and ready to fall into bed.

Mine, not his. Do get your priorities right!

'More tea?'

'No thanks. I must go. Early start,' I muttered, waking up to the fact that I was lounging, yes lounging, in a very comfortable space with a rather delicious younger man – and delicious he was, however lacking in taste any of his morals might be – with no one else remotely in the vicinity, and wouldn't Llanestyn just love to get hold of this one? 'I'd have liked to have seen what the garden really did look like. Now I suppose I'll just never know.'

'Not exactly.'

'What?'

'Not exactly.' He cleared his throat.

'You have got them!' So what had made him change his mind? My heart speeded up like there was no tomorrow.

'No. And I don't know where they are. I swear, Lissa, on whatever you care to name.'

Diawl uffern dân!

'So what, then?'

'But I do have a copy.'

'What?'

'Look, don't get excited. It's only part of the garden, and it's a crude, hand-made copy Elinor said she made when she was a kid. More like a doodle, really. But it is a copy of the original layout, I'm sure of it. There's no detail of planting, or anything like that. But it might be a start.'

'And you had this all along.'

'Er – yes.'

'And I take it Arwen has had a glimpse of this?'

'No!' He scowled at me. 'Of course not. You don't think Arwen would have kept quiet about a thing like this, do you? She's been dying to restore that garden for ages. If she'd any idea I'd have got such a thing wild horses wouldn't have stopped her using it.'

I scowled back. I wasn't entirely convinced, but it was not the time to argue. One Tudur after my tail with an axe was quite enough, thank you.

'And so what, exactly, were you planning to do with it?'

'To be honest, Lissa, I didn't know. Elinor gave it to me, almost the last time I saw her. Asked me to keep it safe.'

'But she wouldn't have meant never to have used it!'

'It's not as simple as that, Lissa.'

'Not convenient to show it to me, you mean.'

'No, that is not what I mean. You can have it, and welcome, if you think it might be of use to you. But use that head of yours, first, Lissa. Just supposing – and I am only supposing – that my dear Uncle Griffin has glimpsed the original, or even the copy. If you follow the sketch now, well, you can guess what he's bound to think.'

Ach a fi! If Drys was a liar, he was a very convincing one. He had me twitching to the bottom of my toes, no messing.

OK: his bed. Just so long as I never had to leave it, and never had to be on my own, ever again.

'Oh,' I said.

'You can see it, if you like, Lissa. I'll scan it for you. Take the original, if you prefer. But please think about it, before you use it.'

I took a deep breath.

If I thought about it, I'd never even want to look at it. If I thought about it, I'd never touch that garden of mine with a barge pole, ever again.

'Oh, bugger Griffin,' was what I said.

CHAPTER 18

WELL, AT LEAST I SURVIVED THE WEEK without being chopped into pieces and scattered to the winds. Just. I couldn't entirely escape an uneasy sensation of being watched from the time the builders left in the evening until the time they arrived next morning. And there was only the kitchen to finish now. A couple of weeks and they would be gone. Leaving me entirely on my own from dawn till dusk, and open to menaces, for I wasn't officially opening for guests until after Christmas, when I'd have the safety net of my trial run under my belt.

Needless to say, after days of this uncertainty, I was a trifle jumpy. Hugh, on the other hand, was over the moon.

'And you just came across this?' he demanded, excitedly, as I spread out my scanned copy of the map on the coffee table in Elinor's room.

'It was found.' I smiled, blandly. 'The original is quite safe.' I couldn't help a glance at Arwen, but she was bent over the spidery little drawings as if she had never seen them before.

'They're like a child's drawings,' was all she said.

'That's what they are. They were made by Elinor when she was a little girl. Apparently from the original plans.'

'Amazing.' This seemed to excite Hugh even more. 'That really adds to the story. "Garden saved from being lost to the nation by extraordinary detective work", and all that: TV just loves that kind of thing.'

'It wasn't exactly detective work – ' I looked down at the drawing. To the casual eye it looked just like a child's rather wobbly pattering of four squares with squiggles filling the inside of the squares and blank spaces on the outside. I'd have never given it a second glance myself, except for the line of a wall at the far end, stones clearly marked, and a door in the centre and steps leading down. Clear enough when it was pointed out to you, and you knew the layout.

'Four knots.' Hugh peered closer. 'Yes, I believe that could fit with what we found on the ground.'

'So those must be paths all around,' put in Arwen.

'And that round thing at the centre.' Hugh screwed up his eyes as if attempting to imagine the whole thing in situ. 'A pond, perhaps, like at the Manor House at Hatfield?'

'Or a sundial,' said Arwen.

'Oh, a sundial,' I put in, quickly. 'Definitely a sundial. I like the idea of a sundial at the centre of my knot gardens. Besides, if I can find a reproduction Elizabethan one it'll look really olde worlde for my guests.' Arwen gave me an old-fashioned look. She hadn't forgotten my ill-timed crack about making everything up. 'Well, it isn't clear, and I suppose we can have some leeway.'

'If this is anything to scale, Lissa, it really is big. If we recreate all four knot gardens they'll take most of your lawn space, you know,' said Hugh, still peering.

'That's OK. We can still put grass around the edges and plenty of benches. And, anyhow, weren't loads of herbs used to fill in the patterns of the knots? I like the idea of my guests wandering in between beds of lavender and lemon balm. I think it could be rather soothing after a hard day sightseeing. I am going for the upper end of the market, after all.'

I know Robin said it was the wrong way round, but while I was waiting in Kingston for contracts to be exchanged and the real planning to begin, I did spend quite some time reading every help book I could lay my hands on, and researching the unique selling point of my castle (as far as potential guests were concerned, that is). It didn't take much brain to spot that hikers, dogs and muddy boots were probably not my most likely clientele. Katie did spend some time trying to persuade me I could make a fortune catering for pop idols, playboys and movie stars (as in Johnny Depp and Justin Timberlake), but I just knew I would never make it past the first limousine and attendant reporters, and if I wanted to run a Hollywood hotel I'd have gone and got experience in Hollywood, thank you very much. I'd soothed her ruffled feathers with a quick round of research in every likely B&B we could find, from Dorset to Chester.

Cosy and comfortable, quiet and stylish, with old-fashioned friendliness and charm: that was my brief for my old-fashioned and style-of-its-own castle. No conferences, no management meetings, and not that much to interest children. Not that I've anything against children, you understand, just that I was more of the peace and quiet variety of holiday aiming for working couples taking a weekend break, and retired couples exploring the countryside. And just wait till I put my knot garden on my in-progress website!

'Pity there isn't a planting scheme,' said Hugh.

'Can't we just go for the kinds of plants in *The Compleat Gardeners Practice*, and the rest?'

'Can do. Although many people chose to do an "interpretation", rather than follow old planting slavishly.'

'A lot of modern gardens use box,' put in Arwen, frowning. 'Which the Elizabethans tended not to use.'

'Well, couldn't we compromise? Have two genuine and two with box? Or use all kinds of different hedging for the patterns?'

'That might work.' Arwen traced the squiggles within the squares as if willing them to speak. 'It didn't look as if there was enough there to see what the original knot patterns might have been. I can bring you some copies from books for you to see, if you like.'

'Great.' This was going to be fun!

Hugh phoned me later that afternoon. The production company were in ecstasies. The American market was being mentioned. Fine by me. What better way to market your B&B? There were all the negotiations to be done, but I determined then and there it was a sure thing, and in the bag already.

'Not the walled garden?' I dared to enquire, mildly.

'Not yet, Lissa. You've got to keep something for the follow up.'

'Follow up?'

'In case the series is successful.'

'Oh, right.'

'Besides, you don't know what we might uncover in this part, and then there will be the researching of knot designs, the choosing of planting schemes, and then putting it all together, and watching it grow. I'd say you've got at least one series, if not more, just in that alone.'

Semi-permanent TV coverage. The nation, if not the world, gazing in on my garden. So much for the quiet life, Lissa.

I wonder if Ioan Gruffudd or Brad Pitt are into gardening?

As soon as the workmen had left that evening I had a shower and fluffed myself up into reasonable shape, with a pretty, but comfortable, autumn type dress lurking in my wardrobe.

With the dinner cooking nicely away in the oven, I sat for a while on my balcony, shoes kicked off, feet up, sipping tea (in mother mode, so having to be a good girl for this evening) and admiring the view over my soon-to-vanish lawn. Some of the best shrubs had gone already, taken out of the excavator's way by Arwen and replanted in a discreet corner of the walled garden, ready for future use. The rectangular molehills of the trenches lay open to the sky and full of promise. This was going to be even better than I had imagined.

After Hugh and Arwen had gone, Robin had muttered about the mess, and putting off guests by an earth-moving work in progress, which had led to slightly heated words on the wisdom of undertaking the restoration at all in my first year.

All right, it was crazy, and not the textbook way of approaching things, but at my time of life I don't have a year or two to waste. And besides, couldn't I make my restoration a feature of my guests' visit? Spend your resting hours watching a genuine Elizabethan garden take place? Maybe a bit part in a TV series, as icing on the cake. Everyone wants a chance to be on the telly, nowadays, don't they?

I sighed, and glanced down at my well-thumbed history of the knot garden, idly flicking through for inspiration, as you do. Low hedges of box, and topiary. In my mind's eye I could suddenly see it all: patterned and formal, blue with drifts of lavender contained within the patterns of box. Grey-green santolina intertwined with rosemary. The kind of garden Shakespeare would have seen. My tummy gave an odd twist. This was definitely excitement.

Hey, who needs rampant sex, bruised egos and smelly socks when there is a garden out there to be working on?

Stuff Robin for being such a stick in the mud and insisting I do things by the book, when he knows damn well that – legal necessities apart – I'm not that kind of girl.

Stuff Griffin for not having the guts to intimidate me in public and risk the law on his doorstep, and sending me wide awake at the faintest creak of the rafters.

I had the scent of box and lavender in my nostrils, and no one was going to stop me now.

'Men', I snorted to myself. 'Who needs 'em?'

The doorbell rang. I hadn't heard a car, but then I'd been lost in thought, so I must have missed it. I craned my head over the balcony, but Merion (or possibly Katie getting away from work early) was out of sight underneath the porch.

'I'll be down in a moment, darling!' I yelled down into the abyss. I was down like a shot, without even bothering to put on my shoes. 'I'm sorry,' I said, breathless, as I pulled open the door. 'I thought I would have heard the engine – '

Well, nothing like the total lack of vehicle to bring a girl to a dead halt. There aren't many times I'm rendered speechless, but this was one of them.

No, not my son, and definitely not my daughter.

Oh no. Definitely not.

Not Ioan Gruffudd. Or Heath Ledger. Not even Aragorn, taking time out from elves and hobbits and magical rings.

My visitor stood there, smiling at me, eyes soft, and oh-so winsome.

And there I was, barefoot, most definitely not pregnant, but far, far too late to shut the stable door, if you see what I mean.

'Hello, Elissa,' said he, serenely. 'Long time, no see.'

CHAPTER 19

'COME NOW, ELISSA, BE REASONABLE...'

'Reasonable? *Reasonable?* You walk out, not a word from you for years, and then you just roll up unannounced, and expect me to welcome you with open arms?'

'I really think it would help you if we discussed this over a cup of tea,' he smiled. 'Tea always seemed to soothe those nerves of yours.'

'Tea?' My squawk outdid that of the peacocks in raucousness. I could hear them, all around the grounds, shrill with conviction they had a new rival amongst them. Which they had, I simmered to myself. Just not quite the kind they imagined.

'Yes. I'll make it for you, if you like.'

Oh, no you don't!

'Tea won't change the fact that you left me. Now just go away, will you.'

'As you wish, Elissa. But there's no need to be quite so touchy, you know. I would have thought you'd have been able to move on by now, and I do think Katie will be most upset – '

'Bastard!' He blinked at me with those big blue eyes of his.

'Katie is my daughter, too, Elissa. I like to know what is happening in her life. She just happened to mention – '

'And that Merion is arriving today as well, I suppose?'

'A family reunion, Elissa. A time to hold out the olive branch, don't you think?'

187

He meant me, not him. He was as peaceable and olived as can be. Fairly oozing with the stuff. Time had not withered Terry. Not touched him at all, and that's a fact. A few grey hairs at the temples to add a distinguished air to the easy-on-the-eye features. A touch of creasing in the sunburn around the edges of his eyes, just so they could crinkle even more seductively than ever.

Apart from that, he was as lean and clean-cut as ever. He could have walked straight onto the set of any TV programme, the usual twenty-year-old blonde at his side, a decorative sidekick. He could have walked onto the set of the latest James Bond movie and knocked Pierce Brosnan, or whoever, off his perch, no worries, and waved to the scarcely-clad babes to come flocking in.

'I er – ' Not only rendered speechless, but my stomach was into a quick lurch, and my knees had gone all peculiar.

'Good girl.' He smiled, and stepped inside.

Did me a favour, really. Might have taken me at least half an hour, otherwise, for the dazzle of his beauty to wear off. My knees regained their poise, instantly, and my stomach came to its senses.

'Terry, why are you here?'

'To see my children,' he explained, very patiently, as if I had turned deaf and more than a little senile: almost as if I had aged to the point where I could have been his grandmother. The only possible response to that was a loud snort.

'After thirty years, you just happen to stumble across us?'

'You have been in my mind these past months, Elissa. I knew there must be a reason, something calling me towards you. I'm extremely sensitive to such things, you know.'

Blimey! And this was the man who once told me female intuition was a weakness in my hormones and to start reading *New Scientist* and get real. I eyed him suspiciously. In my first shock I'd missed the air of utter calm that hung about him like the haze of a baking afternoon. The still and timeless day-at-a-beach kind. I could almost smell the sea, and hear the drone of light aircraft overhead as children splashed in a sea of innocent blue. He smiled, and whole schools of dolphins danced in the waves.

Oh, and don't tell me: down on the shoreline a lion was just lying down with a lamb for an ice cream and a spot of sunbathing.

'You're not on something, are you?'

'I don't need artificial stimulants,' he explained, in that newly kind tone of his. 'Why should I, Elissa, when I have life?'

Good job I hadn't had my dinner yet: it would have made an instant reappearance on the spot. Terry had never been religious: he hadn't needed to be – he'd always had himself to worship. Now, it seemed, he had turned this into an entire cult.

'So you found yourself, then,' I said, nastily.

'Oh, I don't think any of us can say that, Elissa,' he replied, in the manner of a teacher gently correcting a pupil. 'I think *that* is a life-long study, don't you?'

Maybe I should have installed boiling oil on the battlements, after all.

Don't get me wrong, here: I'm not a violent person. Not normally. I can't bear the wildlife programmes where you know the baby creature is bound to get it. Or even if it might. I may have remained cool during Katie and Merion's horror movie phase, but I'm behind the sofa now (as in, the remote is always at hand) when the crime is committed – in the most flashily and bloodily technically realistic way possible in a bid for the next TV awards – for the detective to have a murder to solve.

I looked at Terry. He looked at me. And it may have been weakness, but I could hardly throw him out on his ear with the dogs snapping at his heels (so to speak), in the best lady of the castle fashion, with our children about to arrive at any moment.

'So do you still take sugar in your tea?' I muttered, as I led the way down to the half-finished kitchen in the basement. (I wasn't letting him up into my domain, no way. Terry, on past form, was quite likely to get ideas into his head without that kind of thing, thank you very much.)

'Herbal. I gave up caffeine years ago.'

'Well, the builders haven't. So tough.'

'Just hot water will do, in that case. When you've lived in the desert you come to appreciate just what a miracle water is.'

I knew I should have stocked up with the weedkiller. Nice quick trip to the garden centre, anybody?

The tap might hold miracles, but the kitchen was a shambles. They were still at the tearing-out phase, with the vile old units stacked in all their grimy wonder in a corner. I filled the kettle, with its decoration of black fingerprints all over, at the sink, and placed it on a fridge clearly on its way out in more than one sense.

'We can take these up into the conservatory.' I busied myself spooning out instant coffee for me, and rendering a tea-stained mug reasonably clean for the miracle of water.

'You're having a lot of work done.' Terry had dumped his well-worn rucksack on the ground and was perched on the edge of a stool, gazing around with interest.

'A bit,' I replied, warily. Terry had rarely shown any curiosity as far as my activities were concerned when we were married, and I didn't see any reason why he should start now. Well, actually, I could see a reason. Rather a large reason. A reason with battlements and a better earning potential than my ex-husband had ever displayed in the years I'd known him.

That was the bit that worried me.

You mean, I didn't believe for one moment he had gone through enough bimbos to see the light at last, and realise what he had been missing all this time? Per-lease. My cynicism has been carefully garnered over decades: it's the major comfort of my advancing years, and I'm not about to let it slip away into the ether now, thank you very much.

'It's a very big project for you, Lissa.' He sounded concerned. I yawned.

'It's a challenge. But I have had help.'

'Help?' Now he was fishing. Temptation nearly got the better of me, but I was fairly sure Drystan Tudur would turn up sometime during the next few days, if not hours, and I didn't think he'd play ball being passed off as my billionaire toy-boy lover with a yacht in the Adriatic, a pad in New York and a timeshare in a Bedouin tent – and those just for starters. Especially not with Katie around.

'Robert Lloyd Jones, if you must know.'

191

'Robert? He's still around, then. Good old Robin.'

'He's not that old,' I retorted, bristling. 'And he's been a good friend when I needed one.' Terry shot me a sideways glance, but then obviously decided to ignore the dig.

Mmm. Either he had metamorphosed into a saint, or he was really after something.

He was after something.

'And so you have a conservatory, do you?' he murmured, as I handed him his water, spooned sugar into my coffee, and led the way over broken bits of wood and coils of extension cables into civilization once more.

'I wouldn't exactly call it that, yet. It's very run down.'

'But plenty of possibilities, eh?'

'I expect so.'

'Conservatories are very useful as eating areas, you know.'

'Really.'

'And with that kitchen being so dark – '

'It's for catering, not for entertaining.'

'Catering? Oh, so you mean to run this as a commercial enterprise, then?'

Damn. Why couldn't I keep my mouth shut? But then I'd assumed Katie would have spilled the beans.

'Bed and Breakfast,' I said, shortly.

'Oh, but it would make such a wonderful hotel. You could furnish it in the grand style and advertise it as luxury accommodation. Mini-breaks are big business nowadays, with most people working so hard and having fewer long holidays. Then there's the conference market. That's always big. With proper planning and marketing, you could make a fortune, Elissa.'

'I don't want a fortune. I don't want to live in a hotel, thank you, and I definitely don't want conferences.'

I have had more intimate experience of conferences than most. One of my first cleaning jobs (crap pay, but a nine-thirty to two-thirty shift especially to capture single women with kids at school and not a lot of choices) had been in a big chain of hotels. They had conferences coming out of their ears. I had the vomit and the used condoms under the bed coming out of mine. The boys and girls away on a paid jamboree without the family – no thanks. Not in my castle.

'In business you have to go where the money is, Elissa.'

'Mmm. So where did you say you were on your way to, Terry?' I enquired, casually, as I drew up dilapidated bamboo chairs for us to sit on. The sun was slanting through the trees and across the expanse of lawn. I could see the midges dancing in the rays: the damp of evening was arriving. It would be dark soon.

'You could really do this up smart,' he said, by way of reply, looking around the bare, genteelly falling-apart of Elinor's domain. 'Could be a real feature, could this, done right. It would need new glass, of course. Cost a bit, but it would be worth it.'

'They're starting at the end of the week. Scotland, is it? Or didn't you have an aunt in Belfast?' I knew damn well he didn't, but it was a good opening line to a subject that needed to be sorted now, this minute, without Katie to jump to his defence and demand provision of a bed for his fatherly head.

'I'd thought of visiting Findhorn. There are good people there. Strong, deep, spiritual people. Good to be amongst, you know?' I nodded encouragingly. 'It's a long way.' He smiled.

'Plans can tie you down, you know. If we spend our lives planning for the future, it's as bad as living only through our past. We need to learn to live in the present. Be open to everything that is around us, now.'

Mmm. So that would be in the potential leg-over and a free breakfast department, would it?

'You could have brought your car up to the front. There's plenty of room to turn round, and it would have saved you a walk down the drive in the dark.'

'Car?' He smiled benignly at my *faux pas*. I should have known. 'I have done without a car for years, now, Elissa. They're utterly wasteful. They are ruining our environment, you know. One of the major causes of global warming. And so many people in the world have no access to their own transport, except their animals. A far more earth-friendly way of living. I learnt so much from the experience of being able to live amongst such people. I'd never own a motor vehicle again. And you meet people, when you are hitching, you really meet people, you know? Not like being shut away inside your own car. And people are so kind, so obliging. Like the guy who brought me up from Abergavenny. Just a guy up on business. I said Bangor would be fine, but no, he insisted on leaving the A55 and bringing me right to the gate. I did invite him in. You'd have really liked him, Elissa, but he had a meeting to get to in Llandudno. Great Volvo. Really fast. Must have cost him a bomb. And I bet he didn't earn peanuts, I can tell you.'

'There are several hotels and guest houses in the phone book,' I persisted, grimly.

'Hotel?' He laughed. 'Have you any idea what a rip-off those places are, Elissa? You don't think I have that kind of money, do you?'

OK. Tent? Teepee? Yurt? Igloo in deepest Antarctica? Or would Sir prefer a nice warm coffin in the garden, perhaps?

I could feel a hot flush coming on. I went over and opened the door to the conservatory. The air drifted in, cool, and with an elusive edge of frost that sent my senses tingling and sent the hot flush wafting safely out of sight over the garden wall.

Of course, he was my ex-husband, and nothing, technically, to do with me at all. I've come a long way over the past thirty years: I stood there and debated whether I had come far enough to sling him out and risk his meeting our mutual offspring coming up the other way and my heartless behaviour doing the rounds of Llanestyn for the next twenty years or so. I don't mean Terry would have to run around complaining to all and sundry. News works in the osmosis fashion in Llanestyn: it oozes out before you know it yourself.

Suddenly, I didn't care. Hadn't I given up on men years ago? Hadn't Terry done me the biggest favour in the first place running out on me like that? OK, if he'd stayed I might never have found myself cleaning regurgitated lager, curry and chips from beneath the rim of conference loos. On the other hand, I would never have had those stolen nights under the stars with Raphael, who knew how to tweak a lady's buttons, all right, and I most certainly would never have become the lady, and sole owner, of Bryn Glas.

The sex – as Raph had taught me, if a little belatedly – had never been up to much. The cash, from what I had seen so far, was still pretty well non-existent. And hadn't I earned enough for my own needs in the first place? Let's face it: what on earth else could I possibly want him for?

'Miss Deryn!' I nearly died. Of course, I should have realised: from the outside of the conservatory Terry was tucked away safely out of sight within a deep beam of shade, leaving me standing alone by an open door, gazing wistfully out into the gathering gloom, a temptation to any passing Tudur, hell bent on a mission of his own. Knight in shining armour, Excalibur in hand, ready to preserve my long-lost virtue, he was not. Unable to resist the temptation of a lone female, ripe for the terrorising – you bet.

'Yes, Mr Tudur?' I murmured, trying not to squeak. In the excitement of the last half hour I had, for the first time in over a week, entirely forgotten Griffin's existence. Now he was standing right next to me, face close to mine, orange-tinted eyebrows bristling in outrage.

'Miss Deryn, I've just been speaking to that television production team of yours. They tell me there is a plan of the garden. Of the original garden. Perhaps you'd like to explain that to me?'

'Not particularly.' Beetroot just couldn't match the colour of his face. I hoped he didn't existed on a diet of beef burgers and chips: he was heading straight for *Ysbyty* Gwynedd with a coronary, if he had.

'You told me you had no such plan.'

'That's right.'

'And now there is one. Pff! Just like that. That calls for an explanation, Miss Deryn, don't you think?'

'It's not a plan, Mr Tudur. Just a rough copy someone found and lent to me. There's a lot of interest in the restoration of Bryn Glas garden, especially now the TV are involved.'

'Hm. That "somebody" wouldn't be my nephew, by any chance, would it?'

'Really, Mr Tudur, the plan was given to me in confidence. I'm really not at liberty to say.'

'So it *was* him. The conniving young – Shouldn't be allowed to carry the name of Tudur, and that's a fact. And I suppose that Jenkins woman was in on it too?' I frowned, and folded my arms across my chest, trying to look inscrutable and not in the least bit intimidated. 'Well, let me give you a friendly word of advice, Miss Deryn. There are things here no outsider should meddle in: not unless they want to get their fingers seriously burnt. And I mean seriously. As for Drystan – never could stop money running through his fingers, that one. Knew I was wise to him, that I'd stop him getting his hands on Bryn Glas, for all his little schemes. So don't you go fooling yourself on his account. And don't think I haven't seen the way he looks at you: woman of your age ought to know better. Most undignified.'

'Have you quite finished?' I demanded, as icily as I could manage with my voice threatening to waver all over the place. 'And will you please go.'

'Not until I've seen – ' He came to an abrupt halt.

Well, well, well: so Terry did have a purpose in life, after all. Don't get me wrong, he wasn't waving a sword and shooting past me to slay the dragon spitting fire and brimstone all over my conservatory. He had merely uncrossed his legs and re-crossed them again the other way. But that simple gesture had created a creak in the supporting bamboo that drew Griffin's attention like nobody's business.

Now, I'm not in favour of using people, you understand. Not in principle, anyhow. But I figured Terry owed me one, and, hey, what the hell?

'I don't think you've met my husband, have you, Mr Tudur?' I murmured, sweetly. 'Terrence, this is Mr Griffin Tudur. His family used to own Bryn Glas. He's been taking quite an interest in my work on the place.'

'Really?' said Terry. I didn't expect him to be macho about this. Terry has never really got on with his fellow man: not enough potential to impress, if you take my meaning. He always preferred the company of women. It had been one of his main attractions – after the sheer beauty of him, of course. I'd thought at the time it was an indication of his refined and sensitive nature. Until I noticed it was the very young and wide-eyed that he really went for, and once I'd moved past that stage myself (innocence being very difficult to preserve for ever), he rapidly lost interest.

But he was male. And nominally in possession of me, and that would do me fine, for now. Just for now.

'Good evening, Mr – ah – ' Griffin knew very well I was a Deryn, born and bred. He was always most accurate in the amount of nose he could look down at each of the local degrees of riff raff, and the Deryns came fairly well at the bottom of the pile.

'Hamilton,' I provided, helpfully. 'I'm afraid I always use my professional name. Confusing, I know.' I fluttered an eyelash, recklessly. Not, need I add, in my erstwhile husband's direction. That would never do.

'Mr Hamilton.' Griffin was gruff.

'Mr Tudur.' Terry was serene. A rather ominous silence fell. Look, couldn't they just talk about the footie last night and the price of beer, or some such masculine thing? I could see I was not out of the woods, yet.

'Perhaps you'd like to join us for some of the filming of the restoration of the garden, Mr Tudur?' I murmured, demurely. 'I'm sure the film crew would be really interested to hear your views on the history of the Castle. It's still your family's history, after all.'

'Hm.'

Well, I thought he'd be flattered, but those eyebrows were back bristling again. You can just never win with some people! I racked my brains for a safe topic of conversation. My companions were not in the least helpful. They just kept eyeing each other. Sizing each other up, no doubt, ready for a spot of mutual head bashing outside, in the best sheep territorial battles tradition.

But the gods were on my side that day. A smart little car pulled up, and unfolded Merion, to loom at a great height, towering well above Griffin, let alone his father.

'*Cariad*! Darling!' I cried. 'Over here!' Out of the corner of my eye I could see Griffin stare. Probably under the impression I had a whole harem of men of all shapes and sizes. And ages, too, after that highly uncalled-for comment concerning Drystan. Fine, well if that was how he wanted it. I ran over and gave my son a good old-fashioned hug. 'Merion, am I glad to see you!'

'Hi, Mam,' he said, grinning his wide, lopsided grin. He's got to the age where I can kiss him in public without him trying to sink through the floor, so I did. He even planted a kiss back on my cheek.

'How was the trip?'

'Brilliant. The best. I've brought my laptop and loads of photos – ' He came to a dead halt.

'Merion – '

'Mam, what on earth is he doing here?' And he did not mean Griffin, currently hot-footing it into cover of the trees as a second car came speeding up my driveway. Mmm. Terry had not thought to announce this little visit to his son, it seemed. Interesting tactics.

'D'you know, I'd really like to work that one out myself,' I replied, thoughtfully, as Katie's car drew up in a swirl of gravel.

'Hi Mam, hi Dad!' she called. No Tim still, but plenty of starry-eyed enthusiasm.

Uffern dân! Not the spectre of happy families! Not now. Not with my castle at stake!

Please.

CHAPTER 20

'BUT MAM,' PROTESTED KATIE. 'You can't just throw him out. You *can't!*'

Oh no? Just watch me.

'So what do you propose we do with him, then?'

'Look, I'll pay for a B&B, if he hasn't got the money,' said Merion, frowning. 'There has to be a room still free somewhere.'

'Nice idea, *cariad*, but no.'

'Mam, I can afford it, and won't it be worth it just to have him out of here?'

'He's our dad!' cried Katie, indignantly. 'You can't just get rid of him, like a sack of potatoes.'

'I'm not getting rid of him,' I replied. OK, I'd conceded a point and stretched the family dinner to include Terry, and even allowed him up into my sanctuary. I handed her a glass of wine. 'Now go and take this to your father and keep him company while Merion and I finish the dinner.' And if Terry had given up alcohol, that was his look out. Somehow, I doubted it.

'I mean it,' said Merion, stirring the sauce, viciously. Poor Merion. He'd always felt the lack of a father. I could cover for the girly things with Katie, but not the Sunday afternoon five-a-side in the park. I did my best, but I knew I wasn't the same.

'Where's yer dad, then?' had always been the taunt at school. He never said so, but I knew it. Broken families weren't quite so normal back then. Terry wasn't dead, so we were a failure, somehow. Mostly me, of course. Not good enough in

201

the kitchen and the bedroom and the listening department to keep my man from straying. 'Stand By Your Man' warbled Tammy Wynnette on the radio. I most obviously hadn't, and who else would ever give me a second glance? And as for those poor kids of hers, growing up without a father. It was a real shame, it was: a real shame.

'It was a nice thought, Merion.' I cleared my throat. OK, this might make me sound the bitch of the century, but Merion was a grown-up now, and I'd always tried to be as straight as I could with my kids, and it just had to be said: 'But once you start paying for one thing, where do you think it will end?'

He winced. I winced. He kept stirring. So the thought may not have exactly crossed his mind before, but it had registered there now, and he wasn't hurling pots and pans at me. Well, they say it's a wise child that knows its own father – and I don't mean in the genetic identity stakes, here.

'Thanks for the offer, darling, but it's not your responsibility. You've got your own life. I'll sort your father out: after all, I was the one who married him.' He frowned at me. Ah, *bechod. He* wanted to protect me, too. I didn't take offence: just as a sign I'd done something right in his upbringing, in spite of everything, and even though I say it myself. 'Now, would I *ever* regret having you and Katie?' I demanded, fiercely.

'No, Mam.' He smiled, and looked a little happier.

'Come on, then: let's get this dinner under way.'

So, there we were: the Hamiltons *en famille*. Well, three Hamiltons and a Deryn, to be exact. And two of the rest might have 'Hamilton' on their birth certificates and passports, but if I had my way, I'd be down to the General Register Office with the Tippex in no time flat, leaving just one Hamilton sipping his wine (I told you he would), and supping on the finer things of life. Although, to be perfectly exact, there might just as well have been just that remaining Hamilton there, since he paid for his supper by regaling us the entire evening with the defining (and I suspected heavily-censored) highlights of life (as in, his) for the past thirty years.

Katie was all wide-eyed wonder. Just like I used to be at her age.

'And you really met the Dalai Lama, Dad?' Her father poured himself another glass of wine, and nodded.

'A remarkable man. A truly remarkable man.' He beamed around at us all, benignly.

'Oh, I so wish I'd travelled. I really wished I'd travelled more, Dad,' she breathed. 'I wanted Tim, my boyfriend, you know,' (I gave her a sharp glance at this, but she didn't notice) 'to take me to see the Grand Canyon. But he's always so busy with work and his flat and stuff, so the furthest we've ever got is Malaga.' She sighed. 'You could feel the desert wind blowing across the sea from Morocco. But Tim was worried about drugs and stuff.'

Oh, for Heaven's sake! Don't they make them young any more?

'I thought you and Tim were history?'

'Oh no, Mam. We had a really long talk and sorted things out. We're fine now. He's changed, Mam, really changed.'

'Oh.' I cleared my throat. 'I thought you said that last time,' I murmured, gently.

'Oh, but this time it's different.'

'Oh,' I said, resisting the urge to wrap her up in cotton wool and rush her off to a safe place full of ice cream and rose-petals, and no worms in the bud, munching away, slowly, to the anguish I could just see was waiting for her.

It's only living that teaches you that people can change – but that it's rare, and takes a lot of hard work, and is never overnight. But I knew there was nothing I could say. I've learnt from hard experience that wishful thinking is always blind: all I could do was to keep quiet, and be there to pick up the pieces.

'So what was the very best bit of all, Dad?' she was asking.

'Difficult to say, my dear. Very difficult to say.' He stuck his spoon into the lemon torte (Katie's contribution) and licked it slowly and luxuriously, as if he'd been fed on beans and yak's milk for the past decade or so. Which he could well have been. I yawned, loudly. 'Of course, sunrise over the Himalayas. Base camp at Mount Everest. That was unforget-table. Niagara Falls were simply superb. And the Great Wall of China, of course. Amazing construction. But, do you know, my dear, I think it was the people that I will always value the most. All the people I saw and met and talked to. A remarkable experience. A real lesson in life. There is nothing that can beat it. Seeing the world is the thing, you know. Seeing how people live in other places. Gives a sense of perspective. Makes you realise just how pointless all this rushing around after fame and material possessions is in the great scheme of things. Makes you realise what is important in life.'

Good grief! Hadn't anyone ever told him that the Sixties were done and dusted years ago? It would be a kindness (as well as a pleasure) to do the job myself.

But Katie was still wide-eyed and awed, sitting happily at the master's feet. (I must have gone wrong somewhere). Merion, on the other hand, had turned pale. Right, that was *it*. I could feel the pressure rising as my brain came up to the boil.

'Really?' I murmured, sweetly. 'I've always held with the Miss Marple theory, myself.'

'Miss Marple?' Katie was looking at me as if I'd gone slightly mad. Merion had his head bent over his dessert, but I caught the faint hint of a smile.

'You know: that you can live all your life in an English village, and by learning to understand the people in it you can know the world.'

'You're not still reading Miss Marple, are you, Elissa?' said my absolutely never-to-be-more-than-ex husband. 'I thought you'd have given up escapist fantasy by now. It's not all cosy English villages with roses round the door, you know. There's a real world out there.' He lifted another spoonful of torte to his lips. 'A big bad world, where unpleasant things happen, all the time, even though some people don't like to think about them.'

'Of course the theory implies, conversely,' I resumed, even more sweetly, 'that it is possible for one to travel the entire globe and see nothing at all.'

Our eyes met across the wasteland of empty dishes. Sweetened lemon oozed from his poised spoon and dripped, drip by drip, back onto the pristine cream at the bottom of his dish.

I made damn sure his eyes slid away first: this was my territory, and I wasn't having it. So he could like it, or lump it. And preferably bugger off, pronto. I watched as Terry's lips closed slowly, and the piece of torte vanished into the deep and meaningful depths of his wonderfulness.

'So which grand room have you been given, Katie?' he enquired, placing his spoon back into the cream, and reaching for the wine glass.

'It's beautiful, Dad. Overlooking the garden. Next to the room with those old plaster things on the wall.'

Fortunately, Terry showed little interest in this piece of information. I could see my daughter about to launch into the tale of our remarkable discovery – and just when I wanted as few attractions as possible to remain within my walls.

'And Merion is in the only other room with a bed in it on that floor,' I remarked, pointedly.

'Dad can have my room,' said Katie, quickly.

Oh no he couldn't. One floor down was far too close for comfort, and, besides, he might just get curious about Elinor's room and I wasn't having him touching my Elizabethan mouldings. Not on your life, matey; it might give him ideas. Or, rather, even more ideas than he appeared to be harbouring at the moment: nothing like the cool wind of middle-age whistling down towards you to make you dream of a comfortable bed at nights, wisdom, or no wisdom.

'There's the room next to the library, on the ground floor,' I admitted, grudgingly. 'There is a bed in there.' I smiled. 'It's just still in pieces. Real antique, it is, so no instructions. If you can put it up you can use it.'

'Mam!'

'Well, the mattress is new and so are the bedclothes. Besides, it's going to be the best state bedroom, I'll have you know, for seriously posh guests only. It's just a little bare at the moment.'

'Oh, but only for now,' Katie added, cheering up no end. 'I'm going to help Mam do the rest of the furnishings. She says I've got taste.'

'Did I say that? I'm sure I meant stamina, *cariad*.'

'Rubbish,' said Katie, who knows me by now. 'I heard you say taste, so taste it is.'

'Well, just so long as the Tourist Board agrees with you, darling, and gives us over the odds with their stars, I don't really mind.'

'I know.' Katie began collecting the dishes, giving me a quick squeeze round the shoulders as she passed. 'You've only got eyes for that garden of yours, now it's become so important to so many people. It shows your sweet, unselfish nature, Mam.'

'Hrmph,' I muttered, gruffly. I knew buttering up when I heard it: and no, I was not giving her father a permanent foothold into my castle and playing happy families with me into my grave; daughter, or no daughter.

And so to bed.

Ha! I might have known it would end this way. It was only as I was sipping the carefully-saved last of my wine on the peace and quiet of my own balcony that it struck me: there was Terry, tucked up royally in the king-size four-poster with the velvet hangings, in the best state room in the castle, while I was stashed up here in the servants' quarters.

Mmm. Now just how did that happen?

Robin fulfilled the invitation to lunch the next day in a high state of disapproval.

So my domestic arrangements – vastly and scandalously embellished, no doubt – had rushed around Llanestyn already. Terry was sipping camomile tea (the only herbal variety Katie could find in the local Spar) in the conservatory when Robin arrived. There was a mutual sizing up, after the manly fashion.

'Terrence.'

'Robert.'

They nodded at each other, each keeping their distance. OK boys, we get the message: you don't fancy each other, just couldn't possibly, and you'll be throwing down a glove later in the day for pistols at dawn over me and my castle. It's a man thing.

'Tea, Robin?'

'Thank you, Lissa. That would be nice.' He smiled at Merion. 'How was Spain?'

'Brilliant. Really good. The best ever.'

'I take it you managed to get some good photographs?'

'Not bad.'

'Not bad?' I looked at him indignantly. 'They're gorgeous, the ones we saw last night. Get Merion to show them to you, Robin. You'll be impressed.'

'So you're still planning to give up the day job, then, Merion?'

'Soon as I can. I'm starting to get a few commissions in, so hopefully it won't be long.'

'Good, good. I admire your dedication. I know how hard it must be to break into something like that.'

'Very,' I put in, firmly. My friends in Kingston had always sighed over my son's one-track dedication to his career and lack of any enthusiasm to make me a grandmother in the foreseeable future. Personally, I was quite happy for him to stick to mountains for a few more years, at least.

I mean, aren't grandmothers white-haired, decrepit; on their last legs, serenely crocheting pink and blue bootees for the rising generation, ready to fall behind and die in the snow to give youth the chance to reach the hunting grounds in time?

Um, well, actually, not nowadays, Lissa. Remember the Saga brochures? The moment they'd begun dropping through the door I'd known I'd have to get into training to keep up with that lot. Grandmothers, nowadays, are more likely to be trekking across the Alaskan wastes and stomping around Inca temples than knitting bunnies and boiling jam.

I mean, have you seen the packs of Ramblers storming up the flanks of Crib Goch of a Sunday morning? Terrifying. Absolutely terrifying. I always knew I'd be the one left behind croaking feebly for water and a stretcher while the sixty- and seventy-year-olds strode their way across the tightrope ridge and reached Snowdon's summit before the helicopter could winch me up to the short ride to the nearest hospital. Where I would, no doubt, just simply die of shame.

I needed at least a year or so until I was ready to face grandmotherdom.

There was a ring at the door.

'I'll get it, Mam,' said Katie, quickly. I nodded and headed for the kitchen to brew tea. With that enthusiasm in my daughter's voice, it looked as if I might have to sign up to the nearest gym, sharpish.

Of course, that hadn't been in my mind when I'd extended the lunch invitation to Drystan and Arwen. Drys might not exactly be my ideal of a son-in-law (too many questions over his head) but he could be just the distraction Katie needed at this moment. Put Tim and his miraculous transformation into angel, lover, and general good-guy into the shade.

There, you see? I can be self-sacrificing when I need to be. No love hath any mother... What's a nice bit of eyeing-up and daydreaming when a daughter's future happiness is at stake? Some people might call it facing reality: I'll stick with self-sacrifice. It sounds better.

I returned to the conservatory just as introductions were being made all round. Merion was looking relieved at the arrival of a member of the male species within his age bracket. Robin was scowling. Terry's eyes had narrowed, just a fraction.

'So you are a neighbour of my wife's, Drystan?' he was saying.

'Ex-wife,' I shot in, sharply. Rather too sharply, it seemed: Terry's eyes narrowed even further. Oh dear. He wouldn't – no, surely he couldn't possibly honour me later that evening with a lecture on how that young man with no visible means of support was after my castle?

Would he?

Knowing Terry, he would. No doubt straight after the lecture on that old man with very visible means of considerable support (not to mention the brother a judge) being after my assets. While he, Terry, was only after my best interests, and hadn't even noticed my assets at all. Naturally.

I caught Drystan's eye. Well, and I didn't see what he had to grin quite so fiendishly about. Good job I hadn't pressed him into service as the toyboy lover with a pad in the Bahamas and a chateau in the south of France. I could just see from the glint in his eye he might have had a whale of a time in such a role, and overdone things quite disgracefully. Apart from the treachery to Katie, I'd have never lived such a thing down.

Although the thought did send a rather pleasant quiver shooting all through me, in a rather unexpected fashion. Now get a grip, Lissa. Beauty (as I've found to my cost) isn't everything. Down girl, down!

'That'll be Cadi,' I said, quickly, as the doorbell rang once more. I shot out into the cool of the hallway before a hot flush could drag me down into the fiery furnace and keep me there, going all-peculiar all over.

Hormones, eh?

CHAPTER 21

THAT LUNCH HAD SEEMED A GOOD IDEA AT THE TIME. But, somehow, in the end, it felt like the moment everything went pear-shaped.

And it started so well.

'Yes, they're really keen,' Drystan was saying, as they all helped carry pizzas and salads down from my little kitchen into Elinor's old library, which had now been metamorphosed into a dining room.

Yes, I know it had been destined as my guests' lounge, but we'd had to make a few last minute adjustments after the discovery of my Elizabethan inheritance. With a bit of elegant juggling (and muttering from the builders) we'd transformed Elinor's bedroom into the lounge and the original dining room into a bedroom. This way, my dining tables could, if necessary, spill out into the conservatory, for candle-lit suppers under the stars. Dead romantic, if you ask me.

I wasn't intending to offer evening meals for my first season, but I wanted to keep the option open. Several tables that would normally be scattered around the dining room to provide privacy for breakfast, had now been slotted together to create a large table in the centre. With the kitchen not yet fully operational, this could hardly be dignified with the name of trial run, but it would still be a useful reality check in the logistics of serving meals here.

'You didn't say you were going to be filmed, Lissa,' said Cadi, accusingly, as I placed a large basket of French bread in the centre of the table and sat down.

'Didn't I? Well they haven't really started, yet.'

'Exciting, though.' Cadi was smiling. Now that the crisis of getting the meal down long flights of steps to the table in one piece was over, I had leisure to eye her suspiciously. I knew that smile. Besides, she was looking particularly young and pretty, which meant she had taken even greater care with her make-up than usual, and was newly emerged from the attentions of her hairdresser. 'Don't you think, Drystan?' she was adding, in tones of breathless wonder. I shook my head sadly to myself: no chance, in that direction, girl: no chance.

'Very,' Drys was returning her smile.

'Do you like gardens, then, Drys?' Katie wasn't taking her aunt's charm offensive lying down: she was in there like a shot. Atta girl!

'They're OK.'

'OK?' Arwen handed him the breadbasket with an air of indignation. 'OK? Don't like to get your hands dirty, more like. I'll have you know I dug every centimetre of his vegetable patch.'

'Rubbish. I did my bit. I only drew the line at the manure,' he retorted, grinning away. 'Anyhow, I don't even pretend to be an expert on organic gardening.'

'That's your excuse.'

How I wished I could make those two out.

I could see Cadi following their every move: the same thought was clearly in her head. Katie, on the other hand, appeared too busy trying to think of her next thing to say, to notice.

Of course, they could turn out to be brother and sister. Isn't that how these things are usually resolved? I eyed them both for signs they were twins, long lost, naturally, after being separated at birth by a cruel twist of fate. Nice try, but a similarity in being well-toned, healthily tanned and simply plain gorgeous, did not exactly imply a close family resemblance.

'I suppose I'm not very good at planning for the future,' Drys was saying, just a little wryly. 'An act of faith, that's what a garden is, isn't it? You plan a vision, create it, and then wait for years to see it grow. Whenever I used to go to Penrhyn Castle or Bodnant Gardens, I could never get over that the people who planted them never had the benefit of their maturity.'

'But isn't that what you're doing with your solar panels, planning for the future?' said Katie.

'In a way. But I do see more immediate results, you have to admit.'

'And it's so what everybody should be doing.' She sounded quite wistful. And I could bear witness he did live in a rather nice cottage, not a teepee. It looked as if the charms of leather boots were rapidly losing the battle for her allegiance.

Well, it was what I wanted, wasn't it?

'Ah,' Drystan was returning, dryly: 'once you hit forty, you know, you have to feel you're making your mark on posterity.'

I looked up at that. I couldn't help it. You mean, I wasn't old enough to be his mother? He caught my look and smiled. I could feel myself turning pink round the ears, so hastily resumed a profound interest in my salad. Look, it was only a thought, OK? A girl can think, can't she?

'So, has any more transpired concerning the garden?' said Robin, sounding irritated. Well, after all, he was used to being the centre of attention when he dined with me and Katie.

'Ah yes, the garden,' echoed Terry, who seemed to think he *was* the centre of attention, beaming at us all through his beard, as if he had just put our little discussion to rights with that knowing smile of his.

'Drys was looking,' said Arwen.

'Oh, I didn't find much, I'm afraid. Still no evidence that Queen Elizabeth the First ever came to this part of Wales. But I might have a possibility for the woman on that frieze of yours, Lissa.

'Really?' I caught sight of Terry's hand pause in reaching for the cheese board, but I was far too intrigued to care.

'Well, if the man is Sir Tudor Tudur, as the family believes, then she should be his wife, Bess Tudur. The dates seem right, and from the dates on the family tombs in Llanestyn museum, she survived her husband by almost thirty years. I also found a short paragraph about her in a local history. The only thing it really said was that she was noted as a gardener, which would fit with the decorations of flowers. She was even said to have written a book about it, which was unusual for a woman at the time. In which case, she could have been the creator of your knot gardens, Lissa.'

'Fascinating.' I should have been over the moon, inter-rogating him on his sources, planning a trip to the local museum myself, readying myself for the sniffing out of Bess Tudur's lost missive...

But all I could think, as I sat there, was of the slowly moving figure making its way through the mist on that first morning, and the cold shivers were back, travelling slowly up and down my spine.

'There you are, Mam.' Katie had forgotten her future happiness and was practically bouncing up and down with excitement. 'You've always loved Miss Marple! Now there's a real mystery to solve.'

'I thought Miss Marple was supposed to deal with murders?' smiled Terry, lowering himself to join the conversation at last.

'We shall just have to see about than, then, won't we?' I murmured, nicely.

Merion left a few days later. As I walked him to his car to say goodbye, it was clearly on his mind that he was leaving his father behind in possession of my best state bedroom.

'Mam, are you sure?'

'*Duw*, don't you worry about it, darling.'

'Mam, you won't let him, well, um... you know.' The weight of the entire world seemed to be upon his slender shoulders.

'No, I don't know, but I can probably guess.'

'Because I can tell him, if you like.'

Ah, *becod*! I could see him curling up inside at the thought of having to directly communicate with the individual who had been doing his best to ignore his existence from his first birthday until a few minutes ago.

'Now, darling, you don't think I've been practising becoming a vicious old trout for nothing do you?' He grinned at that.

'You're not vicious, Mam. You're not even old. In fact – '

'What?' He was eyeing me closely.

'Oh, nothing.'

'Then I'll be as much of an old trout as I want to, thank you very much.' I pulled the zip of his fleece up to his neck, and removed a few specks of building dust from the shoulders.

'Mam!' he protested, mildly. 'I'm not a five-year-old.'

Ah, *cariad*, but you always will be to me, however hard I try. A small, eager five-year-old in the yellow wellies I'd just pounced on in the local charity shop, jumping into every puddle and holding my hand tight when the thunder came. I gave him a firm smack of the lips on one cheek before he could escape, and propelled him into the driving seat.

He eyed me, as he often does, as if wondering if I am entirely all there: but then what child doesn't? I know I thought my parents were a decidedly weird species, when I was young. It was only the passing of time that taught me to walk the mile in their moccasins, or whatever it is you're supposed to do. I'm sure Terry would know the correct phrase.

'Have a good journey, *cariad*.'

'I could stay another day, if you like.'

'No, you couldn't.'

217

'But you will phone me, Mam, if you need anything?'

'Of course, darling.'

I stood and waved as he vanished down the drive.

I've got used to my children's absence, and I know it would drive me barking in a week to have either of them living with me again now I've grown used to my space. But I'm allowed a little tug of nostalgia for the smell of baby soap in impossibly fine hair, and the warmth of little bodies curled up against me, half asleep over *Snow White*, or wide eyed and thoughtful through every Narnia book, and *The Hobbit*, not to mention our long dwelling in Middle Earth and agonising step by step on the way to the fires of Mordor to get that dratted ring destroyed.

And of course I remember the other bits when I was too overwhelmed and frazzled, and the ritual of grunting insolence of the teenage years. And I know there's no use dwelling on the past; it will never get a castle done. All the same, I didn't quite feel up to the plunge straight back into Katie and Terry in domestic harmony around my dining table. Instead, I crept up the back way (i.e. the servants' stairway), and into Elinor's bedroom.

The frieze leapt out at me, as it always seemed to do, startling me with its pale, slightly battered, serenity. Was that really the creator of my garden, I wondered, trying to make out the stylised features of the woman amongst the intricate decorations of flowers. And if it was, surely she wouldn't object to my attempts to resurrect her creation? Would she? I sighed, and turned to the window. Below me the lawn stretched out: in my mind's eye I could almost make out the pattern of gardens secreted beneath the grass.

And if Bess Tudur had left a book describing her garden, just what exactly had the Tudurs thought fit to do with it? A book was papers, come to think of it. Surely Griffin couldn't think I had such a thing? I mean, I'd love to. Even if all it had was the original pattern for the original knot gardens. But I didn't, and I couldn't. Hadn't Drys said the Tudurs had scoured the place from top to bottom before I'd taken possession? How did they think I was likely to find something they'd so manifestly failed to dig out of the woodwork?

It was weird, looking at that fireplace, just as Bess Tudur, who had maybe created the garden, would have seen it, five hundred years ago. Spooky. A strange crackling went up and down my spine.

From everything I had read over the past six months about the lives of the Elizabethans, Bess would have been responsible for an almost entirely self-sufficient estate: enough to put Drys and his vegetable plot and plans for solar panels entirely in the shade.

It seemed a pretty scary idea to me, being in charge in a world without supermarkets. No fallback between her family – maybe an entire village, too – and starvation. Well scary. She would have had to ensure the crops were planted, then properly stored. Fruits preserved for the winter. Clothing spun and woven. Medicines made from the herb garden. A life tied to the land, and the surviving of the turning of the seasons, that had stretched back towards the beginning of time. Just for a moment I stood there looking through her eyes.

Oh, and I wanted to see the garden! Her garden. Just as it had been, all those years ago, royal visitor or no royal visitor. The room echoed, emptily, as I creaked across the uncovered floorboards towards the window.

As if from a far distance, there came the faint echo of laughter. *Duw*, I was halfway out of the window before I realised the sound really was coming from a distance: from my little kitchen up above, to be precise. I gritted my teeth. I wasn't going to be able to put off dealing with my domestic arrangements for very much longer, and for all my practising at being a bolshy cow, I still hate confrontations.

I could always send Robin or the police to deal with any tenants seriously out of line. There were contracts, laws, rules about that sort of thing. The inhabitant of my best stateroom was a rather more difficult prospect. This grown-up business is a definite bummer at times, despite the freedom to do what you want and have as much sex as you please (given the chance, of course). Right, I'd better go.

All felt peace and quiet here, but duty called: I'd a castle to furnish, and a daughter seriously addicted to happy families – not to mention retail therapy – to deal with. Plus an ex-husband already straining his keep-Griffin-at-bay advantages, and rapidly outstaying his non-welcome.

The film crew arrived for their first serious filming the next day. I made sure everything was shipshape and just what they needed. I was nobbled for an interview, which I suppose was predictable. I tried not to scowl or look too suspiciously into the lens, and at least it was lucky Katie and I were on our way to shopping heaven and I was looking respectable.

Filming, as I quickly discovered, is not as glamorous as it looks, and seems to consist of a lot of waiting around and repeating the same thing over and over. At least so far as I could ever see. Finding toilet-brush holders and soap dishes really did seem a more exciting way to pass time, I considered, as I was driven on the way to some serious shopping.

In the past, I've always enjoyed the last touches bits, but then I've never had a castle to accessorise before. Katie would have blown my entire food budget for the coming year on table lamps and pot-pourri holders, but I managed to keep her more or less within bounds, despite her protests.

'This is a work in progress,' I found myself muttering, at regular intervals as I was dragged in and out of every furniture shop and antiques place within driving distance.

'But Mam, that chest is so Tudorish, so perfect. And I know just where it will look great.'

'Not at eight hundred quid, it won't.'

'But Mam, you've got to do this properly.'

'The basics now, the frills bit by bit when I've an income coming in. After all, darling, I'm going to have to have something to put against all this tax I'm just bound to be earning in a few years' time.'

'But this one will be gone then.'

'And there will be others. In this life, there are always others.'

'But it won't be the same. And, anyhow, you don't really mean that, Mam.'

'I do. In this case, I definitely do. Right, now some nice, tasteful vases. Window shopping over for the present.'

'Oh, Mam!'

The cameras had gone when we arrived back late that evening – without the over-priced, decidedly dodgy-antique Elizabethan chest, I should hasten to add. The next day the remainder of the stuff I'd placed in storage arrived to keep us busy.

All right, I have to confess that I could be calm about the chest largely on account of a busy six months scouring every antique shop, junk shop, auction room and salvage yard within easy reach of Kingston-upon-Thames. The storage and removal fees had sent Robin clicking his tongue, but was I glad I'd done all that scouring before I had a castle well and truly on my hands, builders, gardens and all.

The bedding and the curtains had to be fireproof and regulation acceptable, of course. The rest – well that had been ripe for all the fun of no mercy for the over-priced and trying-it-on variety of dealer: the best stress-busting I knew while negotiations for the purchase of a castle are turning their slow wheels within wheels and leaving my life up in the air.

Katie shot me an accusing look for daring to make such decisions without her approval or expertise, but she was soon lost in the delights of opening boxes and planning where each of my carefully collected pieces should go.

'It's so lucky so much looks sort of Tudorish, Mam!'

'Mmm,' I grunted, innocently. Katie has somehow grown not to be the suspicious type, and Terry was nowhere to be seen at the sight of such frivolous domesticity as ottomans and chests of drawers, so there were no awkward questions concerning my fortunate premonition of the glories hidden beneath my Victorian folly. 'I never was much into stuffed foxes in cases,' I murmured, by way of an excuse.

'Yuck, Mam! Pants, or what. I should hope not.'

I'll tell you something for free: I never want to hang another curtain again, just so long as I live. By the time Katie's stay was drawing to a close we'd dusted and polished and hoovered and re-hoovered an entire castle, and sorted out enough towels and bed linen to keep an army. With the curtains up, and the bits and pieces placed around the bedrooms, the horribly bare, newly painted look was beginning to soften into a kind of pristine homeliness.

Downstairs, the last of the kitchen units were finally fitted, and the quarry tile floor completed. Of course, Bryn Glas wasn't perfect, there were still improvements to be made, but it was good enough for now, and the rest could be done, bit by bit. The conservatory was waterproof and with its radiators in place, all ready for a gradual return of the jungle.

That night the workmen finally left, never – barring major disasters, or so much success a new wing was needed – to return *en masse* again.

My castle was an up and running concern, at last. Now all I needed was a successful trial run at Christmas in the company of friends, and to take a deep breath and the plunge into my new life of taking paying guests in the new year.

Plus find a way of disposing of my encumbrance in my best bedroom, without alienating my daughter for life, of course. After that, I had a feeling the most troublesome of B&B guests would seem a piece of cake.

Right. This is it! Make way for a Deryn on the warpath – and beware, all ye who stand in her way...

CHAPTER 22

OH WHY, OH WHY, IS LIFE NEVER SIMPLE?
Warpaths can take so much more of a direct route when all you have to concentrate on is beating the hell out of someone who seriously got up your nose, or are being paid in hard cash (plus whatever jewels you can stash along the way) to do someone else's dirty work for them.

Look, call me weak, call me pathetic, but I had a daughter whose feelings I didn't want to hurt, OK? It was her last night here with me and her dad, and she was looking happier than I'd seen her for ages, so I couldn't start an aerial bombardment just then, could I?

Yes, I know I was slipping on the bolshy old trout front, but my youthful incarnation as a Nice Person, ready to be walked over by all and sundry, just would keep making these embarrassing come-backs every now and again.

So I cooked dinner without a mutter, and called Terry – who had spent the day deep in one of my books in one of my chairs, on my balcony, overlooking the progress of Arwen in my garden – to come and join us. Yep, I was heading straight for sweet as apple pie on the outside, steaming blue murder on the inside, mode, and straight for the whisky bottle, high blood pressure, or possibly both.

Heigh ho, such is life.

'I'm so sorry to be leaving, Mam,' said Katie over lasagne, which, being her favourite, I had made myself. 'Just when everything is getting so exciting.'

'If you had a videophone you could send a picture to her every day,' remarked Terry, prodding his pasta in an experimental fashion.

'Well, I don't have one,' I returned, mildly.

'You could always get one. They're not that expensive nowadays.'

Mmm. And who would get the most use out of that toy, I wonder?

'I'll think about it.' Typical woman. I could have hit myself the moment the words were out of my mouth: always trying to keep the peace, always leaving the opening for him to try again. Learn, Lissa, learn!

'Is this spinach in here?' Terry appeared to be in search of razor blades in his lasagne. Now that *is* an idea...

'It's organic,' I replied. 'Frozen, of course, but organic.'

'Strange thing to put in lasagne.'

I sighed. 'Not in my lasagnes, it isn't.'

'This part of some diet thing, then?'

'You don't have to eat it, if you don't want to,' I said, loudly.

'Only my little joke, Lissa. Surely you've learnt not to take things so personally, by now?' I ignored him, and turned back to my daughter.

'I'll e-mail you pictures, if I can work out the digital camera. And Cadi will have the website up in a few weeks' time. That should all keep you up to date. Then, before you know it, there will be the first of the TV programmes.'

'If they come back,' said Katie. My bristles were up in a moment.

'If they come back? Why shouldn't they?' I followed Katie's eyes. Sure enough, they rested on her father.

'Nonsense,' he said. 'They'll see sense in the end.' Under the circumstances, I kept remarkably calm. I didn't shout, scream, or hit anyone. At least, not yet.

'What sense?'

'Oh, come on, Lissa, it was a rip-off!'

'A rip-off.'

'The amount they were paying you. They quite clearly thought they could get away with it. Have you any idea just how much those guys just rake it in? They must have been laughing! Really, Lissa, didn't you at least take professional advice before you signed that agreement?'

OK, he'd got me there. I hadn't. Maybe I had been a fool? *Duw*! I'd forgotten just how Terry could have me doubting myself with just the faintest query to his neatly shaped eyebrow.

'It was such a good opportunity for publicity,' I murmured. You could hear the defensive tones from a mile off.

'Exactly,' said Terry. Those blue eyes of his nailed me, quivering, to the floor of his superior world-knowledge as the light of triumph beamed in their depths. 'And don't you think they play on that? And don't you think they are perfectly aware that everyone wants their fifteen minutes of fame, nowadays?'

I was twenty-two and entirely inadequate. I was twelve with Dad (for the very best of intentions, in his eyes, I'm quite sure) telling me if I didn't pull my socks up I'd never amount to anything and did I know what kind of girl wore that stuff round her eyes in public? I was two, with the world a very big and scary place out there.

My entire past life passed before my eyes.

All I'd ever wanted, when I was a little girl, was for the nice, strong, dependable, prince, with a face to die for, and assets the envy of the entire western world, to come climbing up the drainpipe to my under-the-eaves bedroom in Tyn-y-Coed, and whisk me away to my own little kingdom where I could sit pretty and for ever avoid the scary bits of rulership: like Bess Tudur's carefully working out of how everyone was going to eat, stay clothed and healthy, this year, next year, sometime and forever.

OK, so a Welshwoman's home is her castle. Which is all very well, except when the enemy has undermined the walls, scaled the battlements, and is sitting there, lording it over your dinner table, with a fresh young princess as hostage to your good behaviour. The time for boiling oil was passed: eye of newt in the cauldron in the basement was definitely next on the agenda.

Katie was frowning. She was trying very hard to play happy families, but I could see that even *her* optimism was curling at the edges under this onslaught. I caught her eye, and smiled at her. Best for her to escape first – even if it was to the rather dubious arms of Tim – before the frog's toes began to take effect.

'Pudding?' I smiled, through my teeth.

***

I ushered Katie out by the secret passageways before dawn – oh, OK, by means of the front door, then. I was quite sure there were some secret passageways, somewhere. I just hadn't found them yet, and that's no excuse to spoil a good story. Anyhow, she was off on her white steed (sad lack of rescuing prince, but you can't have everything in this life) and *en route* back to Croydon.

Then I sat on my balcony drinking coffee and downing headache cures to dull the after-effects of one (OK, maybe two) large whiskies in the small hours, and waiting for the rest of the world to reach their desks and I could start phoning.

I'd done half a day's work grovelling to a very nice representative of the production company on the subject of misunderstandings, mixed messages and how you just can't get the right kind of staff these days – unfortunately even the butler seems to think he has to put in his pennyworth – by the time Terry appeared, showered, shaved and immaculate, and ready for his breakfast.

'Toast?' said I, with dangerous quiet. Anyone who knew me would have acquired instant indigestion, there and then.

'That would be nice.' Terry sat down, poured himself a cup of coffee from the cafetière, and opened the paper. 'Katie get off all right?'

'Oh yes, she was away before six. She'll have missed the worst of the traffic. Should be halfway there by now. She'll phone as soon as she gets in.'

'Good, good.' He was deep in interest rate rises and a cabinet reshuffle, and, clearly feeling he had done his duty in the conversation stakes, was settling down to a comfortable morning at my table, before removing to the armchair in my sitting room.

'Eggs, bacon?' Raph would have been cowering beneath his chair by now, eyeing the nearest routes of exit. Even Robin – not that I had ever cooked him breakfast, I hasten to add – would have been diving out for the roses and the chocolates and the most expensive bottle of champagne Llanestyn could provide, and I'm sure would have added a small and cuddly teddy had he dared.

'Toast will do fine.'

'There's marmalade on the table. Or would you prefer lemon curd?'

My children would have been high-tailing it to school at this point, before the Death Star had a chance to hove into view, muttering: 'That's no moon, that's a space station!' as they shot outside the door. And do I look like Darth Vader? OK, OK. No need to answer that one. The question was purely rhetorical, I can assure you.

'Do you have that home-made marmalade?' His head appeared above descriptions of a hurricane in some safely remote part of the world. I pulled open the fridge, sending the bottles in the milk compartment rattling, and brought out the fancy jar with the homemade label (nothing to do with me, I paid good money for the privilege).

'Of course. Anything else?'

'No, no. That will do fine.'

'If you're sure.' The cool weight of the marmalade jar was very tempting.

I turned back to the toast, timely popping up from the toaster, dropped the pieces onto a plate, and laid them down in front of him. I stood there, with the advantage of being in the standing position, towering over him. I took a deep breath.

'Thanks, Elissa.' Pardon? Appreciation? A whole word of it! Did I hear correctly? The shock took the wind out of my sails for a moment. Right, OK, deep breath number two. 'You do look after me.' That breath went the way of the first, but even more so. He was patting my hand. He was actually patting my hand. 'And it has been so nice being a family again these past few days, don't you think?'

'I – er...' Yes, I admit it: I spluttered. I dissolved into inarticulate growling.

'I know.' He was stroking my hand now, slowly and gently.

Oh, shit.

'Look, Terry – '

'No, no,' he was patting my hand, and smiling at me. 'There's no need for you to answer now, Elissa. I know you'll need time to think it over.'

What?

'Terry – '

'Shh. It's all right. It's really all right. I understand. It's been a long time.' His smile deepened into serious concern. 'But this is such a big place for you to manage, Elissa. I know you're doing marvellously, but it's too much, it's much too much.'

'Really.'

'Of course. Do you think I have been taking notice of what's going on? I admire you for being so brave. That's what I've always admired about you, Elissa, you are so much more down to earth than I ever was.'

'Really.'

230

'Do you think I don't know you, Elissa Hamilton? Always the brave face. Always doing your best for everyone around you, never putting yourself first. But it's a jungle out there, and some people take advantage.'

'You don't say.'

'This castle, now. You could make a fortune, you know, with the right marketing, and the right management. This garden thing, once those people have finished, you could do some real, accurate, restoration work. There's nothing like that round here. You can get grants, you know. There would be plenty of help out there to turn it into a heritage centre. Those old stables would be just the thing for a little museum.'

'Museum?' My, he had been busy.

'And a café, now that's where the money really lies, you know, really good profit margin. You could even have weddings. People love that sort of thing. The National Trust charges the earth to get into their properties, I don't see why we shouldn't do the same here.'

We?

'Look, Terry...'

'You need someone to help you, Lissa. You must be paying a fortune to Robert Lloyd Jones, just think how much we'd save if I took over the management side of things. Then you would be free to concentrate on your garden. I know you always liked pottering in a garden, Elissa.' He gazed into my eyes, like a puppy making damn sure you take it home and feed it and don't notice too much about the potty training. It was really quite mesmerising. 'We can take things as slowly as you like.' Ah, so would this be a full six minutes instead of the usual three? 'Just say you'll think it over.'

'No, thank you.' I pulled the hand away, briskly. 'I appreciate the offer, Terry, but I'm quite all right as I am. Thanks all the same.'

'Look, Elissa, I know you were hurt when I left, but I thought you understood the reasons why. I was being stifled by my life: I was no good to anyone, least of all you and the children, like that. But we're grown-ups now, and surely, after all these years, you can let bygones be bygones.'

'No. Not really. No. Damn; bit of a bugger, that, I'm afraid. And your toast is getting cold.'

'Is there someone else?'

Here we go. Brad Pitt? Heath Ledger? Johnny Depp? Clint Eastwood? Perhaps we need the scary option: the entire male population of the Mafia? Or, even scarier, how about Griffin Tudur? Maybe not: the mere thought of him with his trousers down made me shudder. Right, Lissa, honesty is the best policy.

OK, it seemed a good idea at the time, right?

'No, Terry, there is no one else.'

He relaxed. I saw it. Damn. The bastard thinks he's still the only man who ever slept with me.

'I'm in no hurry, Elissa.'

'No. The answer is no, Terry. You left me. Thirty years ago, remember? We've both moved on. Now just drop it, will you.'

'I realise that you are hurt.'

'I am not hurt. I just know my own mind. Stick to the toast, and let's get on with the day, shall we? There are plenty of other things we need to settle.'

'That Robert Lloyd Jones – '

'None of your business.'

232

'Aha! So he *is* after you.'

'Maybe he is, maybe he isn't. Personally, I'm not bothered, either way. And the answer is still no. Once and for all no, Terry.'

'And that Tudur guy?'

'You mean Griffin?' I was weakening. Perhaps I could hold up Griffin as the love of my life. He was scary enough when he got going to give even Terry second thoughts.

'No, no, the young one.'

'*Drystan?* Oh, come off it: I'm nearly old enough to be his mother. Get real, Terrence.'

'I saw the way you two were eyeing each other. And some people will do almost anything to get back inside their ancestral home: it does happen, you know, Elissa.'

'Fuck off!'

Oops! Bad mistake to let the red glaze get to my eyes. Temper, Lissa, temper. Lose that, and he's got you banged to rights: just remember the old days and calm down.

'OK, OK. I'm just trying to make sure you don't get hurt, Elissa. No need to get upset. I didn't mean to touch a raw nerve, there.'

Right, that's it.

'Terry, I do not have a man in my life. I do not want a man in my life. I have a castle. I am quite happy just as I am. Now, can we leave it at that, and move on.'

'Oh.' He seemed convinced, for the moment, at least. He had leant back in his chair, and was not attempting to catch my hands. I gave a sigh of relief.

Much too soon.

'You're not, well, you know, are you?'

'I beg your pardon?'

'You know. Batting for the other side.'

'Batting for the – ' Oh, for heaven's sake! Can't you be original, just for once?

Since re-emerging as a single woman, I have, of course, found myself at parties where the wives think I must be after their husbands (per-lease, lady, give me *some* credit for taste and a will to live), and the husbands think I must be after their wives. (My only purpose in life. Naturally. I mean, what else is there?). And I wouldn't have gone back, even if I'd been invited.

OK, so all I need to do is say 'yes': pile *Fingersmith* and *Tipping the Velvet* to the conspicuous fore of my bookshelf, dig out the pink overalls and Doc Martin boots, and phone Tilly for the necessary details. Tilly (who'd been all for hiring a hit man on my behalf from the moment the dining room chairs made an enforced exit from my home) would have a hoot, and Coral would be tickled pink, if you'll excuse the phrase.

OK: here goes. Deep breath number three...

'Oh, Elissa, that's really not you.'

Oh-oh. Hadn't considered that angle. Every man likes a challenge, and what better challenge than being the one, the only one, to show the poor sad dyke the error of her ways and just what she has been missing all these years? Even more stimulating for the older man than a fresh young virgin, I suspected. I mean, fresh young virgins must grow a little tedious after a while, surely? A little on the predictable side, I would have thought. And usually not clued up enough to do the necessary thrashing around to keep the boys secure in their abilities.

OK, plan ditched.

'Terry, I am not, nor have ever been, a lesbian.'

'Thank heavens for that! I just knew you couldn't be. You were always so passionate.' (See what I mean?) 'So you'll think about it.'

'No.'

'You don't have to decide now.'

'The answer's still no.'

'But I might go away. You might never see me again.'

Yes? Your point being?

I waited in hope for signs of huff being taken and bags packed. Ah, well, life in possession of a nice warm castle has to have its downsides. This, I could see, was going to take some working on.

'Toast.'

'Pardon?'

'Your toast is cold. Make yourself some fresh. Excuse me, I've work to do.'

'Ah, yes: that meeting with Robin.'

I waited for him to grab his coat. Not to do a nose in air job and stalk out of my life forever, but to offer himself as chaperone. Just in case.

In your dreams, mate.

I was out of that castle door before you could say 'pink tutus'.

'And don't wait up!' I called, as I fled.

CHAPTER 23

DAMN. DAMN, DAMN, DAMN, DAMN, DAMN.

Why do husbands leave when you are desperately in need of them (or their wallets) to feed your children? And why, when you just can't wait to steer them firmly in the direction of the next seriously-in-need-of-a-brain-transplant bimbo, do they dig their heels in and get all comfortable?

I'd stormed all the way along the dual carriageway to Conwy without finding an answer to this one, let alone a solution to the little rat firmly ensconced in my castle.

Here I am, all my life looking for Mr Darcy, and what do I get?

Mr Collins.

Mr Collins, who won't even hear 'no' for an answer, let alone take it. And, in this day and age, with female careers and property rights, I'm not likely to find a friend desperate enough to take him off my hands. And, given a certain lack in the worldly goods department, I can't honestly think of a bimbo that dim, either.

Bugger.

The town walls of Conwy loomed up before me, as they always do, dark and solid, and decidedly ancient. I drove my way beneath the arch, through the narrow streets, and parked beneath the castle walls. Seagulls wheeled overhead and there was a smell of the sea in the air as I paid the ticket machine and made my way to the restaurant.

Robin was there first, punctual as ever. It was his companion, coolly sitting next to him with a half-drunk cappuccino, that had me pausing in the doorway. She was leaning slightly towards him, head on one side, listening intently to every word he said.

What the –

Suddenly, she nodded, briskly. 'Oh, I agree: you just *can't* throw people on the scrapheap the moment they reach sixty-five. All I'm saying is that I do feel there has to remain an element of choice, or you could be just driving older people into another kind of poverty trap.'

Blimey. When Cadi strips to her brain cells – even the most decorous of them – it usually means she's in serious pursuit. That, or any halfway passable male within reasonable hearing distance is gay.

But Robin isn't –

'Ah, there you are, Lissa, I knew you wouldn't be long.'

'Hi, Lissa.' Cadi was on her feet, all smiles and kisses. I smiled and kissed back. 'I'm running late, so I was passing through at lunch-time, after all.'

'Oh, right,' said I. 'Great. Can you stay for lunch?'

'No, no. I'll leave you two to it. I know you've got lots to talk about, with Bryn Glas all up and ready to roll, and all that. I'll be off once I've finished my coffee: don't want to risk missing my flight. I really just stopped to say hello, Lissa.'

'Brilliant.' I smiled. 'Well, that was good timing, then.' I sat down and poured myself a glass of water. 'So, when do you touch down in New York?'

We chatted about the usual things, as you do, for a decent interval, before Cadi was on her way once more to Manchester and the flight to the delights of Bloomingdales.

'And I'll be drumming up plenty of clientele for you over there,' she said, as she left. 'I'm using Bryn Glas's website as a demonstration of my talents, so expect the bookings to come rolling in.'

'But not until after Christmas.'

'Spoilsport. What about the traditional Winter Wonderland to draw your guests in?'

'What about global warming?' She laughed at that, and with a quick kiss for me and a casual wave for Robin, was out of there as fast as her clickety high heels could take her.

When I sat down again at the table, Robin was already pouring me a glass of white wine.

'To the successful completion of Bryn Glas,' he said, smiling.

'To the very successful completion.'

'I shall rather miss it, you know, Lissa. We make a good team, don't you think? I don't suppose you'll be requiring my services so much, now.' He was sounding rather thoughtful. I swallowed.

'Oh, I don't know. Castle today, tomorrow the world. And once this garden is up and going, who knows?' He was still looking thoughtful. Double swallow. 'And I've been thinking about the stables and the cottage.'

'Oh, yes?' He perked up at that, so I rushed on recklessly forward.

'Mmm. I'm not sure about the self-contained holiday lets. Why should just holidaymakers enjoy Bryn Glas? So many people from Llanestyn have been helping with the garden, I'd like to have something people round about might like to use, as well as my guests.'

'Wedding parties, you mean?' The shudder was barely repressed. I grinned. I could just imagine Robin's reaction to *The Birdie Song* drifting its way around my castle walls. Heaven knows what the peacocks would make of such shenanigans, as well. But this was no time to be sentimental.

'Well, I suppose a castle really is a great setting for wedding photos, and I expect doing receptions could be rather fun. It's the logical thing, I suppose.'

'Mm.'

'Although, personally speaking, I'd really prefer something a little more on the quiet side. I'm open to suggestions. So if you come across anything' He smiled at that, his brow clearing a little. 'And of course I'll want you as my project manager. If you're free, that is.'

'Of course I will be, Lissa. And I'll be there when the inspector from the tourist board arrives, if you like. Informally, of course.'

'Thanks. I think I'll need somebody to hold my hand.' I saw the perk arrive to his eyebrows. 'Psychologically speaking, of course,' I added, hastily, from sheer habit. He looked slightly crestfallen. Ah, *bechod*, he is such a sweetie. One of the best. And if I was on the look-out for a nice, rich attentive husband he'd be number one on my list. But as I'm not –

'Of course, Lissa, before he comes you'll need to ah – ' Robin was clearing his throat. 'State bedroom,' he muttered under his breath.

'Oh, no worries in that department. No worries at all.'

Yes, I needed to sort out that little problem, and pronto. Heaven knows how, but I wasn't going to be fobbed off and outmanoeuvred a second time. No way. The moment I got back to Bryn Glas –

'Ready to order?' My companion was all smiles again.

The lunch was delicious. Plenty of salad, of course, and small portions of the serious consumables, but I defied my companion's disapproval and opted for a large slice of chocolate cake, plus cream, to make up for it.

'If all goes well, I should have my first paying guest in by February half-term holidays,' I remarked, sinking into choco-late-fuelled contentment and sipping my espresso. 'I can hardly believe it.' I discovered Robin was eyeing me in a serious manner.

'You've taken on a lot, Lissa, running a Bed and Breakfast, and undertaking the restoration of that garden. Just don't overdo things. Your family need you, you know.'

'I'll be fine. Nothing like a new challenge to get the adrenalin going.'

'Although I must say I can't picture you slaving over a hot stove serving up full British breakfasts by the dozen, each morning.'

'No slaving over hot stoves for me, Robin, at least, not once I get seriously busy. Didn't I mention I'd be bringing in a cook?'

'A cook?' I could see alarm spread over his features. 'Won't that be rather expensive? At first, at least. I mean, you'll have cleaning staff – '

'Cleaning I can do.'

'Lissa!'

'Well, why not?'

'Lissa, you'll wear yourself out.'

'Nonsense. Other people do it. Best thing to keep me fit. And it *will* only be until I'm booked solid and can afford to bring in the hired help. Look, Robin, if it's a choice between cooking and cleaning, I'll take the place of the lower orders any day. Anyhow, it'll be early in the morning, or when they've gone, so who's to know?' I saw him shake his head in disapproval, but, not being my husband, lover, or acknowledged follower (except in rumour), there was nothing he could do.

'Lissa' He took my hand and eyed it for a few moments. 'Lissa, you do need to be careful. You know how much I think of you.'

'Robin – '

'I mean it, Lissa. I couldn't bear to see you hurt in any way.'

'I know. And I'm really grateful. Honest.' Hell and high water, what on earth had brought this on?

'I know you cope wonderfully, Lissa. You always have.' He was inspecting my fingers, carefully, one by one. 'I just sometimes wonder if you wouldn't wish to share it with someone.'

'Oh.'

'Obviously, if you feel that Terrence – '

'Definitely not.'

'Right,' he murmured, meeting my eyes again.

And what had brought this on, all of a sudden? Terry invading the territory that had been his own and installing himself in my best state bedroom making him realise his own feelings for me? Or an intimation that –

I swallowed. This is it, Lissa. Now or never. Get in there, quick, and have the ring on his finger before Cadi can wing her way back from New York wearing desire on her sleeve in a manner no decent male could ever resist. And no feeble hangovers of guilt and self-sacrifice. After all, didn't she do her damnest to filch the stud-of-the-century Raphael from under my nose? Come on, Lissa! This is the payback time you dreamed of!

Except that dream never was for long.

Did me a favour, really, did Cadi that time. Not that she meant to, of course. She just couldn't resist a new challenge. She was young, head-turningly perfect, and on a youthful mission to have every man that crossed her path, just to prove she could.

Not that she succeeded with Raph – at least, I don't think she did. I just saw the way his eyes watched her every move, and the cold wind of reality went whistling down through my cosy little dream of eternal passion under the stars and an olive grove in Tuscany.

That was where Raph was planning to take me. And the kids, of course. Sweep us away from the chill damp of the Thames valley and away to the family villa in the sun, amidst terracotta villages and orderly rows of vineyards. Sounded wonderful. A year before I'd have had no doubts whatsoever.

Trouble was, I'd just got the bailiffs off my back, and had my first bit of proper money coming in. For the first time in my life, I had a room (as in, an entire house) of my own, and enough to keep me and Merion and Katie fed, shod and clothed. We'd just acquired a secondhand TV, to replace the one Terry had somehow forgotten to finish paying for (along with the sofa and the kitchen table and chairs), and had even managed the odd night out at the cinema, with pizza as afters.

'My family will love you, Lissa,' Raph murmured one night, as we were curled up together, soft and relaxed after a rare night of child-free, no-holds-barred, complete and utter ruination of my bedsprings.

'Mm,' I said.

Look, I know women do it all the time, and always have done: leave family and friends, and even the land of their birth, to create a new world for themselves amongst strangers. But I'd just got back on my feet after my creation of a new life in England went down the pan, and, young as I was, I just knew I couldn't risk going through that again. Not yet. Not with two kids under ten to consider.

At least in London I was on home territory, of sorts. It might be a foreign country, but I spoke the language; knew the rules, more or less: could find my way about. Plus, if things got really desperate, a tank-full of petrol could get Merion and Katie to the safety of Llanestyn and Mam and Dad.

Besides, I was rather enjoying being in sole possession of a house and income, and already the illicit thrill of seeking out of my next bargain had me well and truly hooked: the heady scent of freedom had gone blasting though my nostrils and straight into my head.

'We can get married from my grandfather's house, and have tables outside in the olive grove. There hasn't been a family wedding there for years. It will be perfect, just perfect.'

I watched Raphael as he slept, that night, part of me wanting to hold on to him, and melt into him for ever, and never step out into the raw and windswept place that would be the world without him. It was an opportunity. A lifestyle to die for. And wasn't I being selfish, putting the chasing up of houses before the love of my life? Isn't that what love is all about?

But I, with my fear of the cardboard box beneath the arches, was not that brave. Not even for love. Not when I'd just had my nose well and truly rubbed in the ways love can go. Not when I had seen Raph's eyes follow Cadi's neat little behind sway itself invitingly across the room with more than a flicker of interest.

So Raphael had taken himself off to work in the family olive groves until time came for him to inherit the business and the terracotta villa in the sun. He wrote, sent postcards, even faxes, now and again. But they had slowly faded over the years to a standstill.

I looked at Robin, and sighed.

'Robin – '

'It's all right, Lissa.' He touched my face. And in public, too, where all sorts of people could spy him getting cosy with a middle-aged woman. Who needs Sir Lancelot when you've got that? I could have fallen into his arms, there and then.

Except, I bet Genevieve didn't fall into a man's arms just because he was *there*.

I took Robin's hand from my cheek and held it in mine. I couldn't utter a word. How on earth do you say: look, I'm fond of you, respect you, would fight to the death for you. I'd love for things to stay the same for ever. You thinking you might, me knowing you won't. But I'm happy as I am, and I don't want you in my bed, or in my castle. And I certainly don't want you taking possession of us both, however nicely.

It's just not the done thing. And I'm not sure he'd see the point, anyhow.

'It's been good,' I said, at last. 'Working together.' I released his hand, gently. 'And I hope we'll still work together in the future, and that we'll always stay the best of friends.'

A faint frown passed across his face, but he was too much of a gentleman to pursue it further. Perhaps he thought now was not the time. The thought was crossing my mind that there never would be another time. Not now. And that I might just be making the biggest mistake of my life.

Or maybe the second biggest one to turning down a Tuscan olive grove while I was still young enough to catch the eye of an olive grove prince.

'Of course.' Robin smiled at me, without any resentment in sight. Dear, sweet, impossible Robin. 'Coffee?'

I stopped in Llanestyn on the way back for a quick replenishment in the whisky stakes. For medicinal purposes, of course. I was feeling just a little bit fragile.

'Nice piece of work, Mrs Hamilton. Very nice.' I nearly jumped out of my skin and sent the whisky bottle on a terminal journey floorwards. The voice was so close I could feel the warm skim of breath across the back of my neck.

Great. Just what I need.

'Good evening, Mr Tudur.'

'Good job you've done on that castle of mine.'

'Which you've now sold on to me, Mr Tudur,' smiled I, nice as pie. 'And I've no intention of giving it up. Not for a long while.'

'Hrmph.' Griffin sounded like an unused motor about to get going. Oops! Time I was out of there before the bristling eyebrows and the suggestions of concrete boots made their reappearance.

'Now, if you'll excuse me, Mr Tudur...'

'Nice piece of work.' The motor appeared to be stuck. His eyes were watching me with an expression I'd never seen in them before. He couldn't be – No, surely not. Not after all those suggestive threats? *Surely.*

'Pardon?'

'Uncovering the garden. Getting the media involved. Nice piece of work.'

'Thank you.' It couldn't be a compliment. Just couldn't. Possibly. Probably more like a working up to accusing me of robbing the family vaults in search of information. But I was going to make my escape, pronto, just in case.

'You really are a very clever woman, Mrs Hamilton.'

'Miss.' Mmm. Is this my febrile imagination, or is that a wolfish grin I see before me?

'Miss. Elissa. I may call you Elissa, may I not?'

Bugger.

There was just no escaping it: the old devil was being quite scarily civilised. And that really *was* an attempt at a smile. Even a glimpse of greying teeth. Bad sign.

Very bad sign, if you ask me.

'Er – If you want to.'

'Good, good. Good, good.' He smiled again. I began to feel distinctly queasy. 'They're coming to see me, you know.' I blinked. 'The media people. Phoned this morning.'

'Really.' Look couldn't we just go back to the concrete boots treatment? At this moment, it felt one hell of a lot safer. 'Um, great.'

'So I'll see you at Bryn Glas, then,' he said, tipping his hat and stepping on his way.

He couldn't possibly – He wouldn't – He couldn't. I mean, just how daft, desperate, or just plain stupid does he think I am?

OK, don't answer that one.

'Are you all right?' Ah, my handsome prince, at last, shield at the ready, sword drawn, ready to battle to the death –

'Oh!' I opened my eyes. Well, perhaps not, then. 'Hello Gareth.'

'Hello Elissa. I was wondering when I would bump into you, ever since Aled told me who had taken on Bryn Glas. Quite a lucky buy, I hear.'

Diawl uffern dân! Not another one.

'It is?' I sounded feeble in my own ears.

'Media attention. National treasure, and all that. The selling price must have gone up quite a bit, even in this short time.'

'And there I was, thinking I was just spending money on it.'

'Your investment will help, naturally. It's that garden, if you can pull it off. Now that will make the place unique. National Trust potential, if nothing else. Films, celebrity visitors. The sky's the limit.' His beady little eyes – never slow on the uptake where property potential was concerned – sharpened. 'Are you sure you're all right?'

'Oh, fine.'

'You look quite pale, Elissa. Would you like to sit down? A brandy in the Tryfan Arms, perhaps?'

'No!' That brought me to my senses in a moment, I can tell you. 'Thank you. Nice thought. But I'm feeling great. Well, must get on, Christmas round the corner and all that.'

'Ah, well, I won't stop you, then. But you must come and have a drink sometime. When you're not so busy. We always got on well, didn't we, Elissa.' And yes, that was a statement, not a question. And no, it did not tally with my memory of past events. Which was why I declined to be Mrs Gareth Jones all those years ago. Yep, a decided case of:

1. A serious senior moment.

2. Coming to his senses as far as the leather-sofa obsessed bimbos were concerned.

3. Desperation.

4. My assets having grown considerably in proportion since last we met.

Or possibly all four. I did not, I hasten to add, stay to tick the boxes.

'Yes. Of course. Whatever. See you, Gareth,' I mumbled, scurrying off on my way back to the (relative) safety of my castle.

CHAPTER 24

THERE'S NOTHING LIKE AN EX-HUSBAND who has outstayed his welcome to enable a lady of the castle to let off no end of steam.

I strode straight in, whisky bottle (encased in plastic Spar carrier, naturally) to hand and –

'Oh!' I said, meeting Terry coming out with his rucksack over one shoulder.

'Good meeting?'

'I – er – um. Yes. I suppose.' I took a deep breath and tried not to sound too eager. 'You off then?'

'Yes.' He didn't half sound cheerful: poor Findhorn, is all I can say. From what Tilly told me during her earth mother phase, they sounded like a decent, hardworking lot, and doing quite nicely without the lord incarnate descending upon, thank you. 'See you then.'

'Yeah, sure,' said I. Just not too soon, eh?

He set off down the steps and towards the driveway. I was just pulling the door closed when he turned.

'And if you could just look out that bed for me,' he said.

What?

'Bed?'

He gave me the patient smile best aimed at the none-too-bright dog after a first (not entirely productive) time at puppy class.

'The blow-up one Katie used, first time she stayed. You're not going to be using it, and it will do me fine until I've got myself sorted out. I'll be back for the mugs in a bit, I'll pick it up then.'

Look, am I missing something here? I didn't like to ask, it would mean entering into a conversation where he was the tutor and I the pupil, and that could end in serious bloodshed (his, not mine), so I took the time to peer around me for clues. Sure enough, next to the door was a neatly packed cardboard box with a selection of plates, saucepans and assorted cutlery. Not my best, or he'd have found them sailing past his ears at a hundred miles an hour, no worries; but not the kind of articles you lug around the country, either – at least not up to the far north of Scotland. Very lucky Findhorn, so it seemed.

'Terry – '

'I know.' He beamed tolerance and understanding towards me. 'You need your space: we all do, at times.'

'Erm, yes.'

'And you're right, Elissa, it's been a long time.'

'Mmmm.'

'I was impetuous. I tried to rush you.'

'Oh, yes?' I wasn't committing myself: it might be misread. I mean, he couldn't really be in First Date with Timid Young Thing mode, could he? Could he? Look, I ain't young, I ain't timid, and, with two children to our mutual names, he could hardly find me virginal. Could he?

Could he? My very nice lunch squirmed nastily in my stomach.

Bugger.

'The stables will do me fine, for now.'

'For now?'

'Until Hugh has brought over his brother's old cooker. It was so very obliging of him to offer, and we'll have that old cottage fixed up in no time. It's not too bad, you know. The housekeeper stayed there for a while when the old lady was here. Lick of paint and a bit of airing, and it will do in no time. And I've lived in far worse in my time.'

'Look, Terry...'

'And now that Hugh needs workers on the garden, I'll have a bit of cash to do it up for you.'

'Terry – '

'And you can take as long as you need, Elissa. Just as long as you need.'

With that, he sauntered cheerily down the drive, leaving me on my doorstep with the whisky and the blood pressure.

Well, I suppose at least I had my castle back.

Technically, at least. I sat on my balcony that evening, wrapped up to the nose in all my thermals, sipping whisky and enjoying the quiet company of stars.

I'd either been a fool today, I contemplated, just a little gloomily – or made the wisest decision of my life. And we weren't talking Terry croaking softly in my stables (in lieu of a convenient well) waiting for me to come to my senses and get on with all that kissing business, so he could turn into the King of the Castle in the bat of an eyelid.

I sighed a silvery breath into the night air. OK, come on Lissa, just what *is* it you want? Love? Security? Good old-fashioned sex? Or just happily ever after? Surely it can't be just you and the castle, for ever and ever. Can it?

This was new territory. I wasn't an eager young thing with raging hormones eager for rampant sex and lots of babies and setting up a nest of my own. I wasn't even waiting for my Prince Charming to arrive: he'd been and gone. Several of them, in fact. It's not quite the same.

They don't make fairy-tales for the over thirty-fives. By the time you get to my age, you're supposed to be doing deals with fairy godmothers and shedding a tear as Sleeping Beauty makes her way home at last, and then set about arranging weddings. Not setting out anew. Not with a whole life ahead of you, and all clued up and ready to go. And in no self-respecting fairy-tale does the princess end up happily in a castle on her own, pulling up the drawbridge as the knights wave their lances invitingly outside.

I peered down into the star-shine darkness of my garden. Well, OK, it isn't the man thing, *per se*, I object to: it's the marriage thing. A bit of sex would be nice, every now and again, but I've grown fussy in my old age, and not any old thing will do. And I can definitely do without all that domestic stuff.

And fine, having someone around to sort out blocked sinks, telling double-glazing salesman to sod off, under-standing the logic of the banking system, and ensuring Griffin Tudur keeps going limp in all the particulars – OK, this might be useful.

But any plumbing I can't manage myself I can pay for; attempts to double-glaze me can't half get the pent up frustrations of the day a good airing, and even the banking system is understandable, once you give it a go. I mean, I am the proud owner of one human brain, only slightly dented and

252

rusted by the effects of time, alcohol and, er, other recreational substances – and a human brain thought of it, so, once you get past the jargon and the slightly dodgy logic, just how complicated can it be?

And as for Griffin Tudur – fine, I was weak once, in that regard, and it led me from the frying pan into the Terry-fuelled fire. Never again. I'll get a hound of the Baskervilles, if necessary (although I'd much prefer some half dopey Labrador, all soft eyes and slobber) and keep a pepper spray stuffed down my sagging cleavage in case Mr G. Tudur, Esquire ever threatens to waft his particulars near me again.

The peace of my castle settled back around me. OK, I was definitely giving up men for good. Absolutely. Once and for all. Never again. Never. There was just the little matter of sending Terry on his way, and then this was it: my purple-wearing, gin swilling, don't-give-a-damn old age beckoning gently across the begonias.

I mean, it wasn't as though there was a man on the horizon I'd even look at twice.

OK, well, maybe look. No harm in that, is there? And a bit of a wistful sigh, every now and again. But then, don't we all when Keanu Reeves turns in such delicious slow motion across our screens? Doesn't mean we seriously want to spin the lasso around him, land him across our white steed, and whisk him off to our castle until he gives in and says 'yes', do we?

And, anyhow, chance would be a fine thing.

I gave Terry until Christmas.

I didn't consult him on the matter, just settled upon it in my own mind. I was being fair: not throwing him out in the bleak midwinter, and giving him a chance to save enough cash to get himself out of here. Besides, Merion might be off to the south of Spain to spend Christmas climbing with friends, as he always did, but I still had to face Katie and Tim-the-resurrected for Christmas Day, and a heartless ejection of Terry before the festive season might lead to a very unhappy Christmas all round.

Fortunately, Terry seemed to have decided to play things cool, and left me well alone after absconding with half a dinner service and my blow-up mattress. Hugh good-humouredly brought along a cooker, as promised, and even helped to move the ancient fridge from Bryn Glas kitchens and trundled it down to the cottage. I listened to Terry chopping wood, and vowed that the first sign of him taking too many breaks from his digging duties, and I'd be after him like a shot. He wasn't to know that Hugh and I had come to a little agreement over the matter of certain wages.

Hugh had promised on pain of freelance dental extraction that Terry would never learn who was really footing the bill for his services, but I still had a vested interest in the matter: any flow of cash in that direction – in a good cause or no – still stuck in my gullet.

And it did prompt me to take time out from sorting leaflets and websites, the inspections to make me legal, and possible grants to aid the restoration of the garden, to sound out Tilly on the subject of any contacts she might still have in Findhorn. Tilly chuckled, and promised to look into it before she and Coral arrived for Christmas.

'There's still the matter of getting him there, Lissa.'

'Oh, don't you worry: I'll find someone going up in that direction. Or put him on the train. I'll drive him to the door myself, if needs be.'

'Atta girl! That's the spirit.'

Which left me with just the small matter of managing my Christmas shopping while dodging Gareth's attempts to lure me into the local pub, and sight of Griffin altogether. I was pretty well successful. In fact, so successful the only sign I had of either of them over the next few weeks was a bunch of red roses that appeared on my front doorstep one morning.

At least, I presumed it was a sign of one or other of them. Terry had never been one for flowers, and I couldn't think of anyone else, however hard I tried to dream away to myself.

I mean, just let's get real, here.

Well in time for Christmas, my castle was fully inspected, legal and with an approving nod for a probable four stars rating from the Tourist Board – five next year, or bust – and ready to receive my guests.

'Pleased?' asked Robin. He hadn't diminished any friend-ship, bless him, and seemed just as delighted at the end result of all our labours.

'Very pleased,' I replied, smiling. I could feel a flicker of excitement in my belly as I looked around. Personally, I couldn't wait until it was full, and I was greeting guests, cooking breakfasts, and being a real lady of the castle.

And, meanwhile, the work on the garden was taking shape. We were fortunate the weather was mild that year, right up until just before the last-minute panic shopping began. By the time I was putting up my tree and making the final preparations, the ground was cleared, leaving four rectangles ready for the knot gardens, with paths in-between, all ready for paths and planting.

So by Christmas Eve I was feeling calm, in control, and really quite pleased with myself. Hey, I could do this! Nothing to it. I was going to be the best, most organised B&B holder ever. Provisions were in the kitchen, the tree glittered in gaudy splendour in the conservatory, and a few icicles shimmered tastefully round the door. The kind driven by electricity, not ice.

And no, I did not have a rope of lights, Santa heading for the chimneys and demented snowmen singing 'Jingle Bells' every time I passed, like the rest of Llanestyn. Katie was arriving soon, but even motherly love for my Christmas-with-all-the-trimmings daughter couldn't get me to enter into the spirit of things quite so wholeheartedly. I mean, an old trout has old trout standards to maintain – especially with one or two asset hunters peering from the bushes (so to speak) looking for any sign of weakness. I was having her father for dinner: that was quite enough goodwill to all men for one year.

Arwen, along with Hugh and several other of the older volunteers without children to keep happy over the festive period, were finishing the last of the clearing. The weather had turned colder these past few days, leaving a dusting of snow on the mountains, and a hint of frost in the air.

'Are you sure you don't want to get home?' I said, as they came in for a warm and a cup of tea into the conservatory.

'Oh no,' said Arwen. 'Best place to be on Christmas Eve. We're the refugees from the shopping frenzy, can't you tell?'

I grinned. I'd made a show of inviting them all for Christmas dinner, but Arwen was spending it with her grandmother, while Hugh and the rest had the usual family commitments. And, anyhow, our party was going to be a garden party, when the planting was in and the knot garden had taken shape.

The phone rang.

'Excuse me,' I muttered. 'Finish off the mince pies, if you can. They're not homemade, and very delicious.'

I shot into the hallway, where the bunch of red roses had now been joined by an equally anonymous bunch of yellow (this was getting worrying) and grabbed the phone.

'Maaaam...' came Katie's wail down the line.

Oh-oh. I knew this had been too good to last.

'It's all right, *cariad*.'

'Oh, Mam, he said such *horrible* things.'

'I'm sure he didn't really mean them, sweetheart.'

'Yes he did. He *did*. He said he'd known for ages we weren't really suited. That he needed someone–' I winced at the quick choke at the other end of the line – 'someone more *serious*.'

Did he, now. Well, that was another one off my Christmas list for the next millennium or so.

'That was very silly thing for him to say.'

'Mam, I'm not really frivolous, am I?'

'Of course not, darling.'

'And I do have ambition. I *do*. I don't want to work in the bank forever. I just – '

'I know, I know,' I murmured, as soothingly as I knew how, to the sniffles on the other end. I knew all about the bank. The maternity benefits and positive attitude to part-time working had been the part Katie had gushed about the moment she saw the post advertised. I wondered if this fact had recently percolated its way through to Tim at last.

'And he wants us to stay friends,' she sobbed, as if this was the part where the world ended.

'Well, that does show he still thinks a lot of you. He probably isn't ready for a serious relationship, darling.' Just ripe for a spot of amateur neutering, instead. 'And it's better you found out now than – well a little further down the line.'

'Like you and Dad, you mean.'

'No, not at all like me and your dad. Nothing at all.'

She calmed down, after a bit and, after exacting a firm promise she hadn't been drinking, and she wouldn't drink, and wouldn't even think of starting off until she'd settled down and got herself together, I sent her off to do her last-minute present wrapping and packing, with a promise of her beloved Tilly and Coral installed by the fire and ready for her when she arrived.

Distractions. That's what my daughter needed this Christmas. Distractions, and plenty of them. Funny how one in particular sprang instantly to mind.

'More tea?' I smiled at my gardeners, who were, by now, steaming gently in front of the radiators in the conservatory. I couldn't offer a serious drink, Christmas Eve or no Christmas Eve, as most of them were driving. 'More mince pies? Christmas cake?'

'So you're all set for Christmas, then,' I remarked to Arwen, as she helped me distribute the next batch of steaming mugs.

'Yes, thanks. We don't do much. It's all very quiet.'

'Great stuff. I suppose Drystan has plenty of places to go. The Tudurs always made a great thing of Christmas, as I remember.'

I found Arwen eyeing me, thoughtfully. 'Oh, they never invite him, not since some big row he had with Griffin.'

'Oh, right.'

That row, I seem to remember, was over a certain matter of ownership of my castle. At least according to Griffin, and I couldn't see any reason for him to lie on this particular morsel of Tudur family life. Hmmm. Maybe this wasn't such a good idea, after all.

'Drys doesn't really do Christmas, nowadays. He was talking about starting work on his solar panels, if the weather holds. It's the only really quiet time he has these days: no one ever wants insulation and alternative heating installed during the party season.'

'Oh. Right.' The sensible thing to do was to say 'Happy Christmas' and walk away.

And just when did I ever do the sensible thing?

'So he might be free to join us all at Bryn Glas for Christmas Day. If he's on his own, with nothing else, that is.'

I discovered Arwen eyeing me with a very strange glance. She couldn't possibly think – I mean, the idea was preposterous, ridiculous, not even worth thinking about... Although perhaps I could have explained myself just a *teensy* bit better, just now.

'I'm sure he'd be delighted,' she said.

CHAPTER 25

KATIE ARRIVED JUST BEFORE MIDNIGHT. By that time, Tilly and Coral were fully unpacked into my best state bedroom and making inroads into mulled wine in Elinor's room, with a few huge logs crackling merrily away in the fireplace.

They had arrived just in time for the briefest of tours of my emerging knot garden before descending night and a cold wind had sent us scurrying back inside. The full works tour of my castle had been left, by mutual agreement, for Katie to do the honours. Nothing like showing her darling Tilly around a real castle to cheer up my daughter: especially one decked out in the full holly and ivy and mistletoe, with fairy lights in every room.

Hey, 'Christmas in the Castle' was going to be one of my selling points: I had to get some practice in, didn't I?

'Oh, Mam. The tree!' It had been worth all the hauling and shoving and pushing to get the monstrosity up to Elinor's room – something I'd never have managed without Hugh spotting me struggling the thing from the roof of my car and loping over to assist with the removals – just to see my daughter's face.

Tim? Pah! By the time he came crawling back, Katie would have well and truly forgotten him.

'So you approve, then?'

'I thought you said you were going to drag out the old artificial one?'

'Did I?'

'Don't look so innocent. You know you did. And you said Christmas was humbug and you didn't see why you should spend lots of time putting up decorations, just for a few weeks.'

'Did I say that?'

'You know you did. Oh, and you found all those old things we used to make!' I saw her touch a crumpled cardboard angel, slightly balding of her glitter, but with the shiny chocolate wrapper covered wings still in place. Katie and I had been in the middle of making that particular one the first Christmas in our house in Kingston when Tilly first knocked on the door with Christmas carols and mince pies. Katie was smiling as her eyes travelled up the tree with its necklace of white light twinkling in amongst the pine needles, interspersed with glass baubles, tiny parcels and wooden animals of every variety, right up to the very top, where it almost reached the ceiling. 'And the fairy!'

'It wouldn't be the same without the fairy,' I smiled indulgently at the Sindy doll with an age-tarnished crown of tinsel above those wide blue eyes of hers, with a piece of slightly grubby netting lovingly sewn into a tutu. 'And she doesn't look too bad from down here, poor old thing.'

'Mam, she's perfect.' You couldn't see Katie's eyes for the tears, but she had them blinked away in a moment. 'Can I put my presents underneath, with all the rest?'

'Of course you can, *cariad*.'

'I'll help you,' said Coral, quickly. Coral is only a few years older than my daughter, with long blonde hair, blue eyes, and as a rising TV reporter has always had a good excuse for sharing Katie's interest in the delights of retail therapy.

They've spent many a happy hour together over the years, blitzing Oxford Street and Camden Market, leaving Tilly and me to wander from one coffee shop to another, leisurely sampling the delights of cake, and people-watching.

'Oh, yes please, Cori. I've got lots.'

They were deep in comparisons of Monsoon's winter party dresses, and making arrangements for mutual rampaging round the January sales, before they were halfway down the stairs.

'She'll be fine, darling, just you see,' said Tilly quietly, as I gave the yuletide log a good kicking to remind it of its hearthwarming duties.

'She'd bloody better be.'

'It's going to be so busy, with everyone arriving tomorrow, she won't have time to think. The best thing for her.'

'Yes. Yes, of course.' I began to smile. After all, hadn't I laid on the very best of plans? Christmas, open fires, plenty of mulled wine and good company.

Yes, and the more fool Tim. He was the one going to have to live his life without Katie beside him, that's all I could say.

Below us, I could hear Katie and Coral unloading the car, giggling as they stashed an alarming number of loads in the hallway. I smiled at Tilly, who was eyeing me closely from her armchair by the fire.

'Well, and you're looking particularly blooming, Miss Deryn.'

'Thank you. It's the fairy lights. I put the red ones over the mantelpiece especially for the subtle glow.'

'Subtle glow, my foot. Castle life suits you, Lissa. I suppose it *could* be down to all that gardening I've been hearing about.'

'Bound to be.'

'Nothing else, eh?'

'Absolutely nothing.'

'I see.'

I could see that she wasn't about to finish there, which for some reason made me go all jumpy. I know Tilly is as sharp as they come, and has known me almost longer than anyone, but fine, she could question me. I had nothing to hide.

I could just see this was about to be tested to the limit, when sound of a third voice came drifting up the stairs. Tilly and I exchanged glances.

'Mam?'

'Yes, darling?'

'Can Dad come up and join us? We can see in Christmas Day together.'

'Of course, *cariad*.' I heard footsteps begin to make their way up towards us. 'Tilly, did you manage to...?'

'No problemo, darling. No problemo whatsoever.'

Phew. And Drystan had answered my phone call with the invitation to dinner with a definite yes, as if he couldn't think of anything better. Which was promising. My plans were falling into place, at last.

Yes, maybe life is about to get sorted, after all.

Well, apart from the red and yellow roses in my hall, now joined by an even larger bunch of white. Fragranced, this time. I'm going to be running out of vases, at this rate.

We didn't wake up to a covering of snow on Christmas morning, although, according to the radio, most of the rest of the country had had some flurry or other, if not a full covering.

But I had warned my guests that snow was unlikely this close to the sea, and nobody seemed too distraught. While I was too busy enjoying having my castle full of people at last, to mind at all.

I had wondered, beforehand, how I would feel about so many invading my space. But, thankfully, I loved it. I'd always suspected Bryn Glas needed voices in every room and footsteps up and down the stairs to make it come alive, and from the moment I woke up to the sounds of water gushing down pipes and the creak of footsteps on boards, I felt the old place breathe in and absorb the warm of human company into its old walls.

'Christmas in a real castle,' smiled Tilly, sending toast popping from the toaster as I rustled up mountains of eggs and bacon (no one was escaping my practice run at serious breakfasts). 'I don't know anyone having Christmas in a real castle – '

'Apart from the Queen, of course.'

'Apart from the Queen, darling. They'll be *so* jealous back in Richmond. I've told Coral to take as many photos as she can, and I'm taking as many leaflets as you can spare. Some of my clients are seriously rich, you know, and I'm sure this is just their kind of thing. And, good lord, Lissa – '

I looked up to find her peering at me, severely.

'What?'

'Are you quite sure you've not succumbed to botox?'

'Bugger off! Does my face look frozen?'

'Not in the least, darling. Not in the least.' She was looking thoughtful. 'And you still haven't changed your mind about – '

She gave a quick glance up the stairs towards the dining room, where my never-to-be-touched-with-a-bargepole ex was downing coffee and my best organic muesli from his vantage point at the head of the table.

'Oh, definitely not. Absolutely, totally and definitely not.'

'I see.'

Christmas Day went with a swing. I was doing the full works Christmas dinner, just as I'd promised Katie, but with no more of the slaving over the stove bit than I could help. I'd prepared as much as I could, and Cadi came over early, with her party clothes on a hanger, ready to attack any mountain of vegetables and stir cauldrons of brandy sauce into the right alcoholic smoothness. With the turkey browning nicely, the Christmas pudding in position next to the microwave, potatoes all ready for roasting and the Brussels sprouts and chestnuts peeled and set to go, I settled down to enjoy myself.

By the time we'd done the mulled wine and mince pies, and opened the presents under the tree, even Katie was beaming as if she didn't have a care in the world. I could see her, every now and again, glancing towards me and her dad and smiling to herself.

Ouch.

I tried not to look in the direction of Tilly, who had glued herself to Terry's side and was listening with the most convincing appreciation I'd ever seen to his every pronouncement. While her 'young friend' (as I heard her refer tactfully to Coral) busied herself with taking photos, somehow seeming to always be catching Terry in the middle of the picture, sending him a most bewitchingly apologetic smile each time he blinked at the flash. Yep, it was a picture of a Terrence in clover.

Enough to put you off your dinner, really.

Funny, I enjoyed mine, right down to the last chipolata.

'Piece of cake, darling,' murmured Tilly, afterwards, as she braved the mysteries of my industrial strength dishwasher, while steering me firmly in the direction of the log fire in Elinor's room, coffee in one hand, best brandy in the other. 'Piece of cake.'

The afternoon was nice and relaxed in the usual festive blur of being weighed down by just too much good food, and just enough alcohol to render everyone mellow. After a short recovery time for the mild excesses, we all donned wellies (I'd made sure I'd plenty in all different sizes waiting in the hallway) and took a muddy tour of inspection of my sleeping garden, waiting patiently for knots to be planted, and lavender to settle into bloom, and really not looking anything much at the moment.

The walled garden dripped in winter decay, with frostbitten weeds spread limply across the earth and the branches of the fruit-trees spidering against a darkening sky. I breathed in damp air, and smiled to myself. Yes, Bryn Glas was definitely home: and I had plans for this place, and the stables dripping the morning's ice slowly, drop by drop, from its eaves into the still afternoon. I wasn't entirely clear in my mind what my plans were, exactly: but I had plans.

Evening came, and with it first Robin, then Drystan, to complete our little party.

I was still in my comfortable expanding-waist dress and woolly cardigan, making sure the last of the evening's offerings were all set up and ready, buffet style, in the dining room, so I could forget about them and concentrate on partying.

'Hi Robin!' Cadi was right behind me as I took charge of very expensive-looking pâté and champagne. 'You look freezing. What you need is a real fire. Tilly's just been building it up, come and feel the heat.' The next minute, he was following her upstairs.

As I went out to shut the door, the security light came on again, sending a beam of white light into the blackness as Drystan's battered old Land Rover drew up and parked behind the rest. So he was driving: not planning to make a night of it, then. As he swung down there was soft cold settling on my cheek.

'Happy Christmas, Lissa.' He came into the warmth looking beautiful as ever, the tan of his skin scarcely faded by winter at all. Some people have all the luck. I turned my face up into the tunnel of white spiralling down towards me.

'It's snowing.'

'Well, so it is. It might be a white Christmas, after all.'

Six foot high drifts in two hours, Santa, baby? And no snow ploughs. Please.

'Oh!' I looked down at the lightly wrapped gift placed in my hands. 'Hyacinths.' There were three of them, in a basket, one blue, one pink, and one white, and all of them just opening their tight glossy flowers to release their smell of spring. 'Thank you, Drys. They're beautiful.'

'A little bird told me they were your favourite indoor flowers.'

'Did they, now?'

'I hope they're right.'

'They could be.' I replied, warily. He wasn't my son-in-law yet, so no need to get quite so cosy. Mind you, he was smiling at me: rather a nice smile, as it happens. I found myself smiling back. Must be the wine still in my system from dinner. 'And thank heaven they're not roses.' He frowned. 'Joke, Drys. Joke. I'll tell you all about it later.' He was still frowning. Oh, for heaven's sake. What on earth had got into the man, now? Couldn't we ever have just one civilised conversation? I might be planning to capture him for my daughter, but I wasn't going to play the mother-in-law from hell. No way.

'Lissa – '

'Hey, Drys.' Katie was down the stairs in an instant, smiling as if she had never heard the name 'Tim' in her life. 'Mam said you were coming. You have to see the tree, it's *so* beautiful. Coral's making coffee, it'll be ready in a minute.' And there she was, vanishing up the stairs, practically dragging her captive behind her.

I stood in the hall for a moment, setting the hyacinths onto a table, listening to the sounds of jollity upstairs.

Right. Fine. Things were going swimmingly. Just as I'd planned. It was going to be a great evening. The best.

So I twitched my shoulders, and went down to the kitchens to help Coral.

268

'**M**AM!' THE MOMENT I HAD CLEARED the kitchen door with mince pies, in the wake of Coral's steaming tray of coffee, I walked straight into an ambush.

'Yes, darling?'

'Mam, you're not going to go up there like that, are you?' Katie was pink and glittery-eyed and just buzzing with – oh, an overdose of pheromones, I expect.

'Well, *cariad*, everyone up there has already seen me like this, and no one has passed out, yet.'

'Oh, Mam! Don't just turn it into one of your jokes. Your analyst would tell you they're just a defence mechanism.'

'Good job I don't have an analyst, then.'

'Mam!'

I sighed. *Duw*, the young don't half take themselves seriously. 'Look, I am going to change. In a minute. When I've taken these upstairs.'

'Into what?'

'Wait and see. Don't spoil the surprise.'

'Not those trousers and top on your bed?'

'Aha! So you've been spying.'

'Investigating. For your own good, Mam.'

'Darling, they're smart enough, they're comfortable, and if you think I'm getting the iron out again at this time of day – '

'You don't need to.'

Oh-oh.

'Really?'

'Yes, really. Now give me those and go upstairs to your room.'

'Yes, dear,' I said, meekly.

No way! Absolutely and totally, no way.

I stared at the emerald velvet dress that had magically replaced my party clothes, and made a note to throttle my daughter, forthwith. Emergency purposes only: that was what we agreed that day in Chester. And even without my curves anywhere near it, the cut of the neck was quite horrifyingly low.

'Oh no you don't.' Katie had caught up with me just as I was opening the wardrobe. 'This will be perfect, Mam.'

'Don't be silly. I'll look ridiculous. Mutton dressed as lamb. And I'm not showing my arms.'

'So wear the jacket, then.' She slipped a suspiciously newly-ironed-looking velvet jacket from a hanger behind the door. 'I'll do your hair. It won't take a moment. And look, these earrings go perfectly...'

'They're old ones, Katie. Your dad gave them to me.' In the days when we actually liked each other. Positively ancient.

'So?'

'Katie – '

'He probably won't remember them anyhow. And they're just right with the dress.'

I blinked. This was an odd choice of sentiment, so far as Katie and happy families were concerned.

'I – erm...' Just what was she up to?

'Oh, come on, Mam. You're the lady of Bryn Glas. You're going to have to look the part at some time, so why not now?'

No arguing with that, I suppose. Clearly sensing victory, Katie began rustling amongst the clutter on my dressing table. Now that was going *too* far!

'No make-up.'

'Oh, Mam!'

'Make-up, or dress. I'm not doing both.'

'Just mascara, then. Just a little bit. A little, *little* bit. You'll hardly notice. Go on, Mam. *Please.*'

Well, I'd run out of energy to argue, and, anyhow, what else can a mother do for a daughter in possession of a broken heart?

'Just no lipstick,' I muttered, gruffly.

We created quite a stir when we finally re-emerged. Even a short burst of applause, and a request for a twirl from Tilly, to which I obliged, but only because she's my oldest friend and I love her.

Although, actually, I could quite get into this lady of the castle bit. After months and months of building dust in my hair and earth beneath my fingers, and paint and general dirt etched into every piece of clothing I'd worn since arriving at Bryn Glas, I'd forgotten just what nicely-brushed hair and a close-fitting, well-cut dress can do for the spirits.

I found myself almost gliding from one guest to another, brushing my cheek against the soft pile of my jacket every now and again, just to remind myself of my sudden elevation to elegance. Now *this* was the life.

My duties done for the day, I could sit back and relax. I had stocked up with plenty of games in preparation for my new career, and Robin had brought along a jigsaw, which he declared would also be perfect for my paying guests.

So by the time we'd tested the Monopoly, *Who Wants to Be a Millionaire,* and a *Lord of the Rings* board game, and settled down to completing Robin's jigsaw of a slightly overblown Pre-Raphaelite version of Lancelot and Genevieve in deep clinch in the middle of a forest (oh, well: Londoners and Americans would no doubt love it), it only took the phone call from Merion to complete my day.

I retreated down to the radiator in the hallway to have Merion all to myself for a few minutes, once he and his sister had exchanged Christmas greetings.

I couldn't help sitting for a moment, after I'd put the phone down, remembering all the Christmases when the children were little. It all seemed so long ago now, and maybe we would never have another one, all together as a family like that, ever again.

OK Lissa, just snap out it! Now. At least with guests flocking in, you'll never have to spend a Christmas on your own.

I made my way slowly up the stairs, and slipped back into Elinor's room. A peaceful scene greeted me. The games had been packed away, and Tilly was installed once more on the sofa, an enraptured Terrence at her side. I suppressed a grin. Tilly on top form was mesmerising: she'd left both my children star-struck ever since they were babies, and even passing friends – both child and adult – had tended to succumb and take on the glazed 'let me sit at your feet and be your slave' look within minutes.

'Oh no,' she was saying. 'The wind was bitter. Really bitter. You could never get away from it, even in summer. I've still a touch of rheumatism in my fingers from all that work they insist you do outside.'

Hang on! That was not what she'd ever told me, and wasn't she my last hope of –

'Oh, I'd never have thought of putting that piece there, not in a million years! How on earth did you work it out?' Cadi was still lingering beside the last pieces of the jigsaw, her long legs tucked neatly to one side as they emerged from her very little black dress.

'It's the pattern, see,' Robin replied. I couldn't help noticing he was trying his utmost to keep his eyes from straying to the low curve of the neckline to that aforementioned excuse for a party frock.

By the fire, Coral was contentedly melting marshmallows, passing them on to Katie and Drystan, who were sharing a large cushion next to the Christmas tree, along with what looked like an extremely animated conversation.

It had been a long day. A long year, come to that. So no wonder I was tired and the party mood had gone. I left them to it, and wandered downstairs again to see how the snow was progressing.

It was cold outside. Not the freezing kind, but the still, quiet cold of snowfall, when everything is muffled and even the air seems wrapped up in a blanket. Snow was still falling, just enough to give my garden a covering of white, but not enough to resist the warmth of my chimney, and of the driveway, where flakes were still vanishing the moment they landed. My castle rose above me, as a half-moon emerged ghost-like into a lighter patch of cloud, the snow-covered turrets at last the fairy-tale version its creators had so unsubtly wished for.

I sighed.

'A penny for them?'

'Oh!' I was nearly out of my skin, I can tell you. Not good on a night like this. 'Hi, Drystan. You off, then?'

'I think I'd better. This snow doesn't look like stopping.'

'No,' I said. There was a moment's pause.

'You OK?'

'Yeah, fine. Great. The best.'

'If you're sure.'

'Yes, of course I'm sure.'

'Well, thanks, Lissa. It's been a great evening. I never thought I'd have a Christmas Day at Bryn Glas again: it's been good.'

'Great. Glad you enjoyed it. And thanks for looking after Katie.'

'I enjoyed it. She's a nice girl. That boyfriend of hers sounded a proper – '

'Wanker?' I supplied, as he searched.

'Sounds about right.' I caught his grin in the security light. 'Funny how great minds think alike.' Despite myself, I giggled. 'Anyhow, it's been great, Lissa. Thanks.'

'You're welcome,' I replied, nicely. He was hovering, moving from one foot to the other in the snow, almost as if he needed to unburden himself –

Good heavens! He wasn't actually going to ask my permission to court my daughter, was he? I thought that had gone out with the Victorians. I just knew I hadn't kept up enough with modern youth culture.

'Lissa?'

'Yes?' I heard him take a deep breath. He *was* going to ask my permission. 'Look, can we do this another day?' I said, hastily. 'I'm really tired, and it's freezing out here.'

'Yeah, sure.' He almost sounded disappointed. Oh, well. Tough. I just wasn't in the mood, right?

'Good night, then.'

'Good night. And Lissa – '

'Yes?'

'Happy Christmas.' He was leaning towards me. Yes, really leaning towards me. Almost as if he was going to –

It was a very chaste kiss, of course.

Er, well, OK – it was for two seconds, at least. After that – all I'm saying is I'm not sure what happened after that. It could have been him, it could have been me. And once it had started – well, he was a damn good kisser, OK? A damn good kisser. Not one of these quick fumble round the tonsils and let's-get-to-the-main-course, jobs, but one real slow and savour it variety, that could lead to all kinds of trouble.

And what's a girl to do? I mean, just how many serious snogging sessions d'you think I've got left in me? And it would have been most ungrateful – and just a teensy bit less than convincing, given my present activity – to start squealing 'unhand me, sir'. I just couldn't, now, could I?

Hey, I was making the most of it, while it lasted.

I had a feeling there would be all hell to pay when it did end. So, like a child who just knows it's in trouble when they get back home, and goes for broke for as long as possible, I hung right on in there.

'Blimey,' I muttered, when the need for oxygen released me into the night air once more.

'That doesn't sound much of a vote of confidence,' he breathed into my ear.

'Oh, I don't know. Hard to tell, really, on such a short – oooh.'

This time I was need of serious resuscitation when we came up for air. And I'd gone all wobbly round the knees. So I thought I'd better lean against him. Just in case.

'Well, well.'

'Mm?'

'I never thought I'd see the day you'd be lost for words, Elissa Deryn.'

'I'm not: I'm thinking.'

'That's OK by me. You keep thinking, and I'll – '

'Just a moment.' Well, I had to come to my senses some time. I pushed him away to arm's length. 'Just what the hell d'you think you're playing at?'

'For heaven's sake, Lissa! I'd have thought that was obvious. We've been getting on so well lately, and you inviting me here with your family... I thought you must have some idea how I feel about you.'

'Really?' You mean, my prince has arrived at last, and no slimy frog-lips to overcome? Wow. It must be Christmas.

'Really. This is something I should have done ages ago, if I'd thought I'd have half a chance – '

'Half a chance?' I squeaked. I mean, was he blind, or something?

'The born-again hippy amongst the solar panels? I'm not exactly the catch of the century.'

'Oh, I don't know. I'm sure I could find some compensations, given time.'

He laughed, his breath warm and soft against my lips. OK, I just never want to wake up from this one: then I'll die happy.

'Lissa, Lissa, Lissa. Life just wouldn't be the same without you. And with Katie telling me about all these secret admirers and all those roses appearing every day – well I had to take the chance: it was now, or never.'

Roses.

Diawl! Well, that had me awake all right.

'Oh shit. Not another one!'

He blinked at me. 'Another one what?'

'Oh, you know all right, you bastard: just how gullible d'you think I am?'

'I *beg* your pardon?'

'Oh, don't tell, me: you fell madly in love with me the moment you laid eyes on me.'

'Well, actually, no.'

'There, you see – what did you just say?'

'I said no, I did not fall in love with you the moment I saw you.' There was a dangerous glint to his eye. I swallowed.

'Right. Fine. That's cleared that one up. Too much mulled wine. Happens all the time. Go on: you can bugger off, then.'

'Lissa, I'd always assumed that you and Robin – '

'Well, we weren't. Never have been, never will. He's my employee, for heaven's sake!'

'OK, OK. How was I to know? And by the time I'd begun to work that one out, there was your husband back on the scene.'

'Ex-husband,' I snarled.

'Ex-husband.' Ooops! He was pulling me back towards him. I know I should have struggled, but –

'So? Go on: I'm all ears.'

'You grew on me. Bit by bit, so that I hardly noticed at the time. Not until it was far, far too late, and I was a total goner, Elissa Deryn.' It was nice and warm inside his coat. I could have stayed there for hours.

'Really?'

'Mmm.' And who told him that nibbling my ears had me at anybody's mercy in no time flat?

'Not exactly the romantic statement of the year,' I remarked, softening a little.

'Who needs overblown romantic words when you're the lady of the castle?' he murmured against my lips. 'And, anyhow, I've got some far better ideas.'

Wow. Promises, promises!

Just for a moment I hesitated. OK, just go for it, Lissa: throw caution to the winds, drag him off to a convenient haystack and have your wicked way with him before he has a chance to change his mind.

But I was the lady of the castle, and I wasn't having the wool pulled over my eyes that easily. Oh no: never, *ever* again.

'My assets, you mean,' I said, shaking myself free.

'Your assets?'

'My castle. My castle, Drys. The one you and the rest of your bloody family just couldn't bear to get rid of. So tell me, what better way to work yourself back into possession?'

'Don't be ridiculous. Just what do you think I am?'

'A Tudur? Just the lot who've been looking down on me and my family ever since I can remember. Why do you think I couldn't wait to get out of this village in the first place?'

'Lissa – '

'Look, I've had enough. I've a whole queue waiting for me to just hand over Bryn Glas on a plate. Or should I say a wedding ring? And you're as bad as the rest of them. Well, you're not worming your way into my castle, whatever your intentions might be. So piss off pronto before I start yelling "rape".'

'Right, that's it.' He grabbed my hand. I don't go for masterful in general, but this was, well, just a little bit thrilling, for all my bravado just now. And he was *very* beautiful. Every single last bit of him, as far as I could see. And my little weakness was going straight to my knees.

'You can't drag me off by my hair!'

'Oh yes I can. You were the one who just implied I was some sort of retro-caveman, so what else do you expect? Anyhow, if you want to get technical, I'm not touching your hair.' He tucked my arm firmly into his. 'You won't listen, so there's only one thing for it.'

'Oooh,' I said. Yes, I know I should have kneed him in the whatsits, but I have led a prudent life and never risked damaged goods coming my way.

'Don't get your hopes up,' he said, grimly. 'I wouldn't touch you with a bargepole in this mood.'

Charming.

'So where are we going, then?'

'Oh, you'll see, Ms Deryn. You might not like it, but you'll see.'

So there I was, frogmarched, yes, practically frogmarched in my beautiful velvet dress, through the gathering snow, away from my castle walls, and into his battered Land Rover.

'Seatbelt,' he said, tersely.

'Yes, I know what they are.' I fastened the thing, quite meekly for me, and awaited my fate, curiosity beginning to overcome my temper. I even waited until we were down the drive and safely onto the road before I opened my mouth again. 'Come on Drys, where *are* we going?'

'You'll see. I should have done this a long time ago.'

'Well, you're not going to do it at all if you drive like a maniac.'

'Are you telling me how to drive?'

'No. I was just mentioning I would like to live a little longer, and so would the sheep, I suspect.' We came to a squealing halt, as a mother and last year's lamb (twice her size, having not been shorn) left the verge to saunter across the road in front of us. Never argue with a sheep. Solid buggers, and not half so daft as they look, and can total a car, no worries. Not even a Land Rover can count itself entirely safe from their attentions.

'Aherm,' grunted Drys. He didn't look at me, but at least when we set off again he was looking at the road, and driving in a reasonable manner. We followed mother and child for a good while, as you do with sheep. They ran along the middle of the road, as sheep do, in the snow-storm beam of the headlights, threatening to veer into this verge, and then that, but not quite making up their minds, until they finally dodged into the black hole of a neighbouring farm, leaving us to speed on our way.

We drove down Llanestyn High Street, past fairy lights twinkling happily beneath rapidly whitening roofs; past children out in the last minute miracle, doing their best to form snowballs from the meagre offering on the ground. A sharp turn, and we were travelling up a network of little lanes to the hillside above. Right on the very edge of the village, we pulled into a drive, and came to a halt in front of a stone cottage, now almost completely encased in white.

'Where's this?' I demanded, warily. Supposing he was a serial killer, after all? 'And isn't that Arwen's car?' I added, in a squeak. Serial killer and accomplice lure unsuspecting middle-aged woman into their lair? I could just see the headlines now.

'Yes, it is Arwen's car. This is her grandmother's house.'

'Mrs Jenkins?'

'Yes, Lissa. Mrs Jenkins does happen to be Arwen's grandmother.'

'No need to be sarcastic.'

'No need to be defensive.'

'I am not being – '

'Oh, for heaven's sake! Do you always have to argue over everything?

'Not everything – '

'Lissa! D'you seriously want to freeze out here?'

'All right, all right,' I muttered, clambering out of the Land Rover with as much dignity as I could, given the restrictions of ridiculously inappropriate attire.

The cottage was dark. We stepped through a dimly-lit hall and into a room at the back of the house. Night-lights flickered around us, supplemented by fat, round candles resting on old-fashioned furniture rising out of the gloom, and a fire roaring away in a large grate. It smelt of apples, and Christmas cake: warm and spicy, and strangely timeless.

I blinked, my eyes adjusting. On the mantelpiece above the fire, a large white candle, its glowing sides picked out delicately in pressed flowers and the etched skeletons of leaves, swirled its flame in a sudden draft, sending beams dancing over the elongated features of an African mask, on a photograph in an old-fashioned frame, and on the glass case on its wooden base, right through to the curled darkness of the stone shell within.

'Drys?' Arwen's voice rose in astonishment from the shadow of a sofa in front of the fire. I could just make her out as she uncurled herself quickly from a very cosy entanglement with –

'Hi, Drys. Hi, Lissa.'

Hugh?

Hugh!

'You OK, Lissa?' Arwen was looking anxious.

'Fine,' I managed, without hyperventilating overmuch.

'Drys, just what the *hell* d'you think you're doing?' Arwen had by now fully disentangled herself, and joined us by the fire.

'Lissa thought, Lissa said – ' The temper seemed to have gone out of my captor, all of a sudden. 'Lissa appears to be under the impression that you and I – well, particularly *I* – am after Bryn Glas.'

'Oh.' I saw Arwen swallow, hard. Hugh was sitting on the edge of the sofa, as if ready to spring into action to throttle someone. I was too bewildered to worry if that person might be me. 'I'm sorry, Lissa, I – ' She came to a halt.

'She seems to think it's all a plot. I thought your grandmother was the best one to explain.'

'Oh.' I saw her eyes rise instinctively to the sway of a long curtain at the far end of the room. 'Lissa – '

But I was already there, pushing back the heavy material, and stepping through the half-open door into the frosty whiteness of a security light. I had already seen the figure walking through the garden in the snow, slowly, like a shadow between the shrubs, face skywards towards the falling flakes, then bending to catch the scent of a little pink viburnum.

I was already moving down the little path towards her, as if a dream had caught hold of me, the voices from the house calling me back fading to nothing behind me.

I knew who she was, of course. The moment I saw her, I knew who she was: just as I should have guessed, that first morning in Bryn Glas when I watched her move through my garden, the ghost making its final farewells.

But it still came as a shock when she did finally hear the crunch of footsteps on gravel, and turned.

'Oh my God,' I heard myself whisper. 'Elinor!'

CHAPTER 27

'ARE YOU ALL RIGHT, LISSA?' Drys sounded suitably anxious. Guilty conscience, I suppose, and serve him right too, the sod. Arwen handed me a second large whisky.

'Thanks. Fine,' I muttered, taking a large swig with a loud sniff. Shock, you know. I was allowed.

I was sitting in an armchair next to the fire. The lights had been switched on, leaving the candles and night-lights flickering in pale echoes of their former brightness. I blinked once again at the small, upright figure sitting opposite me.

'I didn't mean to startle you, my dear.'

'I know. And it wasn't you, it was me, barging in like that, bull at a gate, as ever.'

She smiled, faintly. Oh, that smile was all Elinor, all right. It went through me, like wind through muslin. Right to the very core. The world turned all wavery again, and I reached for the box of tissues, thoughtfully placed at my side.

'*Mochyn*,' said Arwen. 'Pig.' She did not mean me or Hugh, or her grandmother.

'Sorry,' I heard Drys mutter. Well, that temper of his seemed to have evaporated into thin air. Good job too: mine was nowhere to be seen, which would have made any ensuing fight very one-sided. I shot a look at Arwen, sitting hunched up and taut next to Hugh on the sofa. She was white as a sheet.

Hell and high water! Was I the only one in the whole of Snowdonia who didn't know? All this time, had the entire population of Llanestyn been sniggering quietly behind their hands as I strode by in my lady of the castle confidence?

Could I ever lift my head high outside my castle walls again?

Or inside them, come to that.

How on earth had I reached the age of fifty-two and still be so blindingly stupid?

I blinked, and my eyes cleared once more. On the mantelpiece the airman stood in sepia tones, just as I remembered him, next to his little biplane; the collar of his leather flying jacket turned up, eyes gazing out into some far distance.

'Is that your father?' I asked. Mrs Jenkins nodded.

'Yes.' She took down the picture and handed it to me. 'I never knew him, of course. His plane came down in the Mediterranean before I was born.'

I looked down at the face before me. A daredevil, I thought: as you would need to be to take that fragile craft high into the air, come wind and all weathers. But not a heartless one: not with that wide sweep of a smile on him. The kind of man who might have a conscience, and in those days a single mother –

Well, I'd had it soft, in comparison.

'Was that why they never married?'

'I should imagine so. They were idealists, that's what my mother always said: in revolt against the whole Victorian idea of marriage as arranged by parents in their own best interests, and simply an exchange of property.' The smile appeared again. 'Free love was invented long before the Sixties, you know.'

I smiled back. Trust Elinor.

'Mrs Jenkins – '

'Elsa.'

'Elsa,' I said, voice all over the place again. 'Why didn't anyone tell me about you?'

'You can't imagine the Tudurs even acknowledging my existence, can you? They had a husband all lined up for my mother, at the time: it was a marriage that would have brought in enough money to keep them in Bryn Glas for centuries – but not with an illegitimate child in tow. Elinor wouldn't play the game and give me up, so neither of us existed as far as the family were concerned. My grandfather may have relented in his old age, and insisted Elinor should have Bryn Glas, but the rest of us – well, we still don't exist, I'm afraid.'

'Pigs,' I muttered, with a pointed glance towards Drystan.

'Hey, not even you can pin this one on me, Lissa: I wasn't even born when this all started.'

I didn't see this as a valid excuse, myself, but now was not exactly the time to argue. And besides –

I swallowed.

'But Mrs Jenkins – Elsa – Bryn Glas should be *yours*. I shouldn't be living there at all.'

Of course, I still had my bolthole in Kingston-upon-Thames, and there are still tenants to be had, and I'd done it before and knew all the ropes by now...

I discovered Elsa chuckling away merrily. It was so much an echo of Elinor, amused at one of my childish stories, I could feel the crackles going up and down my spine again.

'Nonsense, my dear. What on earth would I be doing with a castle at my time of life? My mother loved Bryn Glas, but I'd never even seen inside the place until she moved back here. This cottage is enough for me to cope with. I'm lucky I have Arwen so close by, popping in so often. I'd be lost with seven bedrooms and acres of land to keep up. I don't have the money, and I certainly don't have your energy to make that great old thing work for me.'

'But Arwen – ' I glanced at her. No wonder she'd been wary of me, all that time. Rushing in to take over her great-grandmother's home and ripping it all out without so much as a by your leave. 'Arwen, you love that garden. You wanted to see it restored as much as I did. *Anyone* could have taken over Bryn Glas. It could have been turned into a golf course, anything.'

'And where do you think gardeners get that kind of cash?' demanded Drystan. Jumping right in to her defence, of course, the –

Oops! I hadn't quite caught up with that side of things. So there never had been any gyrating in the attics, after all.

OK, so the two of them may not be exactly brother and sister, and cousins might have married cousins in Victorian times, to keep it in the family, but there's a reason that died out, and nowadays it's positively –

Is there anything I didn't miss, here?

'And I don't want a castle to run,' Arwen put in quickly. 'Drys did his best. He even got Iestin Lloyd Jones interested, at one point.' Oh, great: so Robin is in on this, too. Humiliation complete, Lissa. 'And he offered to try to buy Griffin and the others out.'

'I thought you crashed?'

'We did. Just because I didn't get out in time to be worth millions doesn't mean I didn't sell in time to have *something*. How else do you think I found the capital to start my business?'

'Oh.' Fine; I'll just go and crawl away under a stone, then. Now. This moment.

'But there wouldn't have been enough left over to do anything with the castle, let alone the garden,' added Arwen, quickly. 'And, anyhow, Griffin turned pretty nasty. If we'd carried on, he wasn't going to let Nain carry on looking after Elinor, even as her housekeeper. He was talking about putting Elinor into a home. And he'd have made sure she had no other choice, too.'

'You really mustn't feel badly about this, Lissa.' Elsa took my free hand in hers. 'You've turned Bryn Glas into a real living place again. And you're restoring the gardens. None of us would have had the time, the energy, or the resources to achieve everything you've done. And Drystan always made sure Griffin didn't throw me out, not for as long as my mother was alive.'

'But it's not fair! That means Griffin got away with it. Just because he's got money and knows people, and doesn't care.'

I found my hand being squeezed. 'Don't get upset, Lissa. I was able to look after my mother as she grew frail, and make sure she could live her life to its end at Bryn Glas. That was all she or I, or any of us ever wanted.'

'But the garden. Elinor always loved the garden. And she never restored it. She told me she wanted to restore it to the way it had been. But she never did.'

I looked round the faces watching me, all ready to reach for the tissues again.

There was something about their look. Something I wasn't quite getting.

'Lissa – ' began Elsa, gently. And all of a sudden the penny dropped.

'El-in-or!' I exclaimed, beginning to giggle. 'You crafty little devil! So that was why she had the false wall built in her bedroom. No garden, no interest in the place: no grants, no nothing. She was making damn sure Griffin hadn't a hope in hell of keeping Bryn Glas. Nice one.' I looked round at them all in sudden hope. 'I don't suppose she left any plans for the knot garden, after all?'

Arwen shook her head. 'I'm afraid not.'

'Pity.'

'She never even said anything about the frieze under the mirror and the tapestries,' said Elsa. 'We all assumed, just like Griffin, that she'd just blocked off the fireplace when the radiators went in, and the room was redecorated. It was her bedroom. She never let anyone in there. Not until she became too frail to look after it herself.'

'If only she'd left something,' I sighed, as Elsa took the photograph from my hands and replaced it on the mantel-piece.

'Elinor always said everything was burnt, Lissa,' said Arwen.

'But there *were* plans of the garden. Griffin said there were papers. And Elinor was going to restore the garden. She *must* have had some kind of plan, or description. Or something. And she might have made sure Griffin never found them, but I don't believe she didn't *ever* want them to be found.'

'But we've all searched, Lissa,' said Drystan. 'Over and over again. There's nothing in Bryn Glas. And where else could they be?'

'The stables?' I was watching Elsa placing the photograph back into its place on the mantelpiece

'Those have been searched, too, I'm afraid.'

I wasn't listening. It made my spine go all quivery to see the photograph just as it had been in Elinor's room, standing between the African mask and –

'The ammonites.' My heart was racing so fast I could scarcely breath. 'I have one, Cadi has one, and Elsa has one. I bet those bases are hollow.'

'But wouldn't she have left at least one to Arwen, in that case,' objected Drys.

'Too obvious. The same if she'd left them to you. Elinor knew Cadi and I loved the place. She couldn't know that I'd buy Bryn Glas, but she'd know we'd never let go of the ammonites and they'd always be safe, and that maybe one day – '

290

Drys looked at Elsa. She nodded. The next minute the ammonite box was on the table between us.

It was light as could be: far too light for diamonds. And I bet Griffin never went near them in his life. Bits of stone? Fossils, two a penny kind, with not even a market value for a museum? Why would he waste his time on that kind of tat?

Drys fiddled around. Arwen brought a toolbox, ready for action. But in the end we didn't need it. There was a tiny catch, just inside the legs of the base. Drys released it, and the entire side swung open.

The papers were old, and carefully wrapped. Hugh fetched a pair of those sterilised gloves doctors use, from the kitchen, and unfolded the package gently onto the table. The paper was large, and very fragile. One corner had been burnt almost completely away, and water stains obscured much of the rest. But in between, I could just make out neat swirls of writing. As the pages moved apart a little, drawings appeared.

'That looks like the walled garden.' Arwen was bending closely over the page. 'Look, that looks like a cherry tree. And those must be vegetable beds.'

'So the plans for the knot garden must be in mine or Cadi's.' I was up in a moment, reaching for my coat. Before I could shuffle it back on, Drystan was on his feet.

'Where do you think you're going?'

'Home to Bryn Glas, of course. I want to see what's in my ammonite box, and anyhow, Drys, don't you think my guests might be wondering where I am?'

'I'll drive you.'

'No!' It had been a long evening, and my brain was whirring. I wasn't ready to be confined at close quarters with Drystan Tudur. Not yet, at least. 'Thank you. I'll walk.'

'Don't be daft. It's miles, and it's still snowing.'

'I'll drive you, Lissa.' It was Arwen, standing up and reaching for a bunch of keys on the Welsh dresser. 'I can't wait to see what you find, either.'

When we got back, the party was still in full swing. I let Arwen in through the kitchen and up the servants' stairs where she wouldn't be spotted and awkward questions asked.

I don't think either of us was ready for any questions. Not yet.

'Oh, hi, Mam.' I met Katie at the door of Elinor's room, as I slipped discreetly back inside. She gave me a knowing smile. Oh-oh. And just what had she been saying in that animated *tête-à-tête* with Drystan, earlier? 'I was just coming to see if you'd eloped, you know.'

'Of course not, darling. I went for a bit of a lie down, that's all. I must have drifted off to sleep.'

'Mam, you're all wet! You're dripping!'

'Oh, yes. So I am. I just popped outside to clear my head. The snow's stopped,' I added hastily, and not altogether truthfully, as heads were raised with interest. I didn't want anyone wandering outside and spotting Arwen's van parked just outside the range of the security lights. 'I'd better go up and get changed.' I beamed at them all. 'And I thought you wanted us all to watch *Gone with the Wind, cariad*?' Why else do you think I got you that DVD? It's a family tradition,' I added to Terry, who was beginning a look of disdain. 'We've worn out the video, so that DVD was bought especially. Well, Katie, you'd better get it up and running, if you don't want us to be still here at dawn. Don't wait for me, I'll be down in a minute.'

Fortunately, Katie took me at my word: as I made my way up the stairs, I could hear chairs being moved, and then the sweep of the familiar music start. But not before I heard Tilly, apparently too far gone in full flow to be distracted.

'It is such a worthwhile cause. Immensely satisfying. The pay is not much, of course: we are a charity. But I can offer rooms in my house for those who give us their time. And we have had some quite famous people joining us, especially just before Christmas, don't we, Coral? And they all muck in, serving soup and handing out blankets, just like the rest of us.'

'Oh, yes. You should see them, Terry: pop stars. Movie stars. Loads of people from Coronation Street and EastEnders, of course. We had Ant and Dec last Christmas. Princess Diana came one year, poor thing.'

'Quite. I'm really rather sad I'm missing it this year. But then I definitely need to be there next Christmas.' Tilly's voice lowered into a loud conspiratorial whisper. 'This is strictly hush-hush, of course, but we do believe it could be – ' the whisper deepened, but grew even louder: 'Prince William.'

I shot back up the stairs before I exploded.

'Lissa?' Arwen clearly thought I'd been at the whisky again.

'Oh, nothing. My friend Tilly is just persuading my ex-husband to go and work for her charity in London, that's all.'

'That's good, isn't it?'

293

'Oh, yes, wonderful.' My sides were quite painful from keeping the round-the-cauldron cackles suppressed, just in case Terry heard me, even from here. I smiled at Arwen's puzzled face. 'They do really good work with the homeless. All year round, too, not just at Christmas. Tilly's always looking for helpers for her hostels.'

'So that really is good.'

'Oh, yes.' I hugged my aching ribs. 'She just hasn't mentioned the bit about where she starts off all her new recruits.'

'Which is?'

'Cleaning the loos,' I croaked, stifling a hiccup. Arwen was frowning at me, clearly considering I really did have a bottle stashed in my back pocket. I coughed, and smiled, and did my best to focus on the ammonite box sitting in front of her on my coffee table.

'There could be nothing.'

'It doesn't have to be plans. It could just be a copy of the book Elinor's father was supposed to have written. But that could have the knot garden it in. That's all that counts.'

'I hope it isn't, Lissa. I've seen it, Nain has a copy. It's horribly boring. It just proves that Elizabeth the First secretly married her cousin, the knot garden was a secret message. He said it showed clearly the letters 'E' and 'T' intertwined as part of the pattern.'

'Trust the Tudors. Oh, well, I suppose even that story will bring in visitors, even if it is completely loopy. Go on.'

Arwen found the catch, and opened the door. She rolled on a set of gloves, and lifted the papers out, opening them carefully. From the burnt edges, it was another section of Beth

Tudur's book. The swirling writing marched its way between the staining, interspersed with plans and drawings: the proud description of a proud creator putting it down for the whole world to see. I could see why Elinor did her damnedest to make sure Griffin wouldn't get his hands on these.

'They're beautiful.' Arwen was sounding a little wistful. 'You'll need to get them to a museum as soon as you can, and anything you find in your sister's ammonite box. You'll really be able to restore the garden, now.'

'We will, Arwen,' I frowned. 'Oh, come on, you don't think I'm going to let you get away from this, do you?'

'You mustn't feel you have to, Lissa. None of this is any of your fault.' She was back to frowning at me seriously, lips chewed once more.

'Don't be daft. I might have the energy and the resources for the castle, but there's no way I've the energy or the expertise to restore the garden. And if you won't let me hand back the castle, well then you're going to damn well let me hand back responsibility for the garden.' She was still hesitating. 'And if you're worried about being an employee of the upstart in your family pad, then may I remind you I'm a humble employee of Bryn Glas from now on: cook, cleaner and general bottlewasher. My destiny.' She began to smile at that. 'And don't forget Griffin himself has been trying to be paid by grants for years.'

Her smile faded. 'Griffin will be furious, Lissa. Now he'll really think you made friends with Elinor just to get a piece of her castle.'

I looked at her. 'Is that what you thought, too?'

She reddened. 'Maybe.'

'And Drystan as well, I suppose.'

'Only at first, Lissa. Just until we got to know you.'

'Mmm. And found what a bad-tempered, suspicious old trout I really am.'

'Oh, I don't know.' Arwen was smiling. It was a warm, open smile, with just a touch of mischief. It brought with it the faintest echo of Elinor, when you knew how to look. 'I like you, Lissa, and Drys – '

'Oh, my goodness.'

'What?'

'Look, Arwen. Look, there in the corner.' There was no mistaking the four rectangles, divided by paths, with a sundial in the very centre.

Let Griffin do his worst. There are some things worth dying for, and I'd just found one.

The marks were tiny, but they were clear.

'The pattern for the knot garden,' breathed Arwen.

CHAPTER 28

BY THE TIME EASTER ARRIVED, my knot garden was marked out, planted up, and causing more of a stir than ever. Cadi's ammonite had also given up treasure, in the form of the rest of Beth Tudor's description of her garden, and it had taken all my powers of persuasion not to have her opening up every single page before we handed over the precious paper to the museum.

The book might not exactly be in pristine condition, but it was still an exciting discovery. I had the experts, the media, and the simply curious fairly battering down my door the moment word got out. Suddenly I was unique, a national treasure. Well, at least my garden was, or about to be.

Meanwhile, I was leaving the experts to do the deciphering, and to come up with their conclusions about the planting of the walled garden. Arwen and I had our knot pattern, and that was all I could deal with at the moment with a B&B to get up and running.

It had been a great day when we finally laid out the intricate twists and curves of the knot garden. Arwen had copied the pattern in the book onto squared paper, while Hugh and his willing helpers had marked out each square of the garden into a grid with string. Then it was a matter of transferring the pattern onto the ground, with different coloured sands in old drinks bottles. And there it was: the pattern of the knot garden, ready for planting.

It wasn't exactly a private occasion. The cameras rolled, while Drystan stood at one end, Griffin and the rest of the Tudurs at the other: not one of them managing to look over-friendly, not even for the BBC.

'Remarkable,' said Griffin, as he and I accompanied the Tudurs to their smart new Range Rovers. Not that I was seeing them off the premises with dogs and shotguns and laying down the mantraps on the way back, of course. At least, not while the cameras were still rolling. 'Quite a turn of events, Elissa.'

Roses were still arriving on my doorstep at regular intervals, so I gave him my blandest smile. I discovered one eyebrow bristling in my direction. 'The television company seems most interested in our family history. Most interested. I've journalists knocking on my door every day.'

'You don't say.'

A gleam had appeared in the orange eye nearest me: 'They've been asking questions. Absolutely impertinent questions, at that. '

'Ah, well, Mr Tudur, you know the media. Always looking for a scandal to fill their pages. Sex, money, that sort of thing. And then there's the TV: full of liberal types. No respect, especially, when it comes to old families with castles knocking around in their past.'

'Not that there is anything to interest them here, of course. Apart from the garden.'

'Nooo...' I kept a slight uncertainty to my tone. Always play it cool when playing with fire, that's my motto. Griffin stopped, both eyebrows bristling this time in an undisguised fashion. Interflora was about to lose a customer, then, and my hallway was about to be clean out of roses. Diddums. 'Oh, look. They're interviewing Arwen now. *She'll* be able to keep their minds on the garden, I should think.'

'Arrrmph.' Less a motor than a rocket starting up, ready to shoot itself into the stratosphere. Poor old Mars, that's all I can say. One sight of Griffin floating down through the ether and the little green men will be heading to their spaceships and speeding away to Pluto before you can bleep 'Uranus'.

'And I'm sure we can keep the media at bay.' I smiled at Griffin. Innocent, but not quite sweet. Almost; not quite. 'Just so long as we are all left in peace and quiet.'

'Hrrrrmph.'

'Wouldn't you say so, Mr Tudur?'

'Undoubtedly, Ms Deryn,' he growled. His teeth appeared to have been superglued together, all of a sudden. Brilliant invention, superglue. Got me out of no end of sticky situations in my time.

'Good-bye, Mr Tudur. I'm quite sure you know your way out.'

'Trouble?' Arwen joined me as I returned from watching Griffin's black Range Rover roar down the drive after the rest.

'Oh no, not at all.' I had a quick glance back to where the camera crew were packing up for the day, but Drystan had vanished.

Great. Fine. I didn't want to talk things over, either. In fact, the further he kept away from me and Bryn Glas the better. He might have turned out to be on the level, hero and general good guy in all this, but that didn't mean I had to like him. And as for anything else –

'I'm sure he had a client to see,' said Arwen. 'He's rushed off his feet, these days. He'll have half of North Wales covered in solar panels at this rate.'

'I expect those cameramen could do with a *panad*,' I replied, quickly.

The garden was certainly doing my B&B ambitions no harm. No harm at all. I'd only expected one or two visitors before the season really got going at Easter, but after the hour-long special on the local network, and several more mentions in the national press, I had rapidly found myself with at least one set of guests every weekend, with bookings starting in the week, as well.

After we hit Sky news, and the Sunday supplements descended, I was no longer surprised – and only just a teensy bit nervous – when the summer began to fill up nicely. I'd even had several Internet bookings from America, thanks to Cadi's diligence with the leaflets, and a truly stunning website.

OK, Cadi: you can come out of hiding, all is forgiven. Robin hadn't entirely defected. At least, not yet. In fact, I suspected that he was far too much of a gentleman ever to change much towards me, whatever developments might ensue in his domestic arrangements. He was a truly nice man. One of the best. There were times when my brain started whirring at three o'clock in the morning and wouldn't stop, and I still considered dashing over there in my nightie, but, on the whole, this was fading.

I mean, what did I need with a man? I didn't have time for romance, let alone cooking dinners and washing socks and listening to the vagaries of my beloved's day. And I was so tired with greeting guests, and getting into the swing of bacon and eggs and shooting in and out with the hoover when no one was looking, that at night I just fell flat on my pillow and lay there, stunned, until dawn.

I'd even got into baking scones and muffins, like they said in the books. Well, it was part of the business, so it couldn't really count as being domestic, really, whatever Katie might say between rundowns of her interior design course, and the delights of speed dating.

Elsa came down regularly to inspect progress, in the guise of Arwen's grandmother, and my friend. And if it kept Griffin awake at nights, waiting for the knock at the door from the *News of the World,* so much the better. He'd taken to diving into doorways and peering intently into shop windows on the rare occasions we passed in the street.

Suited me fine. If I never had to see another Tudur in my life again, I'd be happy. Bad news, the lot of them. Elsa and Arwen excepted, of course, and they were all Elinor's, and not real Tudurs at all.

On a cold, bright sunny day just before the Easter rush began, Elsa came down for lunch in the conservatory and an inspection of the knot garden in its first full bloom.

'No Arwen?' I said in surprise, as I opened the door. A battered Land Rover was making its way down the drive.

'Hugh's taken her to Greece for Easter. They left last night. A surprise, apparently. Best time to see the spring flowers.'

I eyed her with suspicion, but she was busy admiring the daffodils within the pattern of the knot, and didn't seem to notice.

It was one of my between-guests days, so we were able to eat our meal amongst my growing collection of ferns and palms, before taking a leisurely walk around the knot garden, pausing at every bench placed at vantage points along the way. We sat for a long time by the pool, watching the flow of the water and the black wriggle of tadpoles around the edges, soaking in the warmth of the sun.

'I always meant to ask you,' I said. 'What was it you placed in here that morning?'

'I didn't realise you'd seen me. I didn't intend to give you a fright.'

'I know. So? What was it?'

'Oh, nothing mysterious. Just a stone my mother had brought back from the beach near Venice where my father's plane was last seen. She always said she felt it was a part of him, and wanted it to remain with her. I didn't have any say once she had died and the Tudurs took over, so it seemed the best way. She always loved this garden so much, I felt that if she was anywhere, then it must be here.'

'I hope so. I really hope so. I'd like to think Elinor could see that we really did restore the knot garden.'

'And that Arwen and I are still part of the place, thanks to you, Lissa.'

'Well, it was you or Griffin, you know. Hard choice, that one. When you're ready, we can have a look at the walled garden before the rotavator moves in.'

We were still inspecting the walled garden when Drystan returned to take Elsa home. I looked up to see him standing in the arch of the doorway in the stables.

'You can come in, you know,' I said, taking a deep breath and making my way between the weeds to join him. 'I'm not exactly going to set the dogs on you.'

'I know.'

We stood for a few minutes in silence, watching Elsa, who seemed to want to take her time about her inspection. Almost, the thought briefly crossed my mind, as if someone – as in her granddaughter, no doubt – had thought this was a good idea. Well, nice try. Pointless, but a nice thought, none the less.

The silence was growing a trifle awkward.

'I still haven't decided what to do with the cottage and the stables,' I remarked. Safe subject, and all that.

'I expect you don't have much time, these days, with the garden, and the B&B taking off.'

'No, I don't. Not at the moment. I would like to make use of them, though.'

'Not for guests? I'm sure you'd be able to fill them.'

I eyed him sharply. 'Not for ex-husbands, certainly.'

'That's not what I meant, Lissa.'

'OK, OK.'

He turned to look back over the garden. 'I had a phone call from Terry last week, you know.'

'Not you as well!' I saw his eyebrows raise. 'You didn't lend him money, did you?'

'No, Lissa.' A grin appeared, creasing the corners of his mouth. 'I didn't think you'd appreciate the price of a train fare in his pocket.'

'Certainly not. I always remark how much our future king will appreciate his efforts. Oh, and that I'm quite sure Tilly and Coral couldn't possibly, and he must be imagining things.'

We managed a brief exchange of smiles at that. Hey, I didn't want any more enemies than I could help, and he was my neighbour. Sort of.

'So, what were your ideas for the stables?'

'I can't think of anything that might work. I wanted something people from the village could enjoy. Trouble is, I can't think what.'

'OK. Well, why don't you think about what you would like, most in the world, given the choice.'

'I've got my castle.'

'Besides the castle. And the garden. Something you could have easily.'

'Aha! Like chocolate, you mean?'

'Like chocolate.'

Hey, we were managing a civilised conversation here. It was rather nice. Soothing, even.

'Oh!' I said. For some reason, a memory of that day on the steps of the conservatory came into my mind, with Cadi massaging my shoulders. Bliss. I looked round: no, he wasn't anywhere near my shoulders, and the baby oil definitely had not made an appearance.

'That sounds promising.'

'Pampering,' I said, slowly. 'A place to go to where I could just relax and be looked after for a few hours. Without having to do anything in return. Except pay my money, of course.' I looked around me at the walled garden, and at the stables. 'Aromatherapy. Massage. Yoga. Reflexology,' I said, dreamily. 'All in a garden lost in time. Perfect.'

'There you are then. That sounds like a good enough idea to start with. Can I come along when it's finished?'

'Of course.' I smiled. 'But it might take a while.'

Elsa had turned, and was making her slow way back towards us.

'Lissa?'

'Yes?'

'I don't have any regrets, you know. Not the dragging you off in the snow bit and nearly scaring the life out of you. The other bit.'

'Neither do I.'

'Good.'

'Great.' I took a deep breath. 'And I'm sorry I was a tad hasty. About you and Bryn Glas I mean.'

'That's OK. Maybe I could have explained myself a little better.'

'Just a bit.'

There was a moment's silence.

OK, Lissa, your one chance, and you've well and truly blown it. I mean, a man does have his pride, and you weren't exactly –

'We could always go out for a drink, sometime,' he remarked, still gazing out into the garden. I winced at the note of caution in his voice. Waiting for daggers to arrive *en masse* in his back, no doubt.

'Drys – ' Time for another deep breath. 'Look, Drys, who are we kidding? I like you, I really do.' Right, stop there, Lissa. Just quit while you're ahead. 'In fact, I more than like you.' He turned towards me at that. One look from those eyes, and I was jelly. Come on, Lissa: it has to be said: no bottling out now.

'But, let's face it, I haven't exactly got a great track record when it comes to men. Besides, we'd be a laughing stock. I'm old enough to be your mother.'

He grinned. A very slow, quiet grin.

'Elissa Deryn! Just how much do think you can tell a failed dot-com retro-hippy who peddles windmills and compost toilets for a living about being a laughing stock?'

'True.'

'And let me tell you, that however long you live, you will never be old enough to be my mother.'

'Are you saying I'm immature?'

'No. I'm saying that I love you.'

'Oh.' I gulped. Perhaps I should run away *now*?

'In fact, Lissa, I just happen to love every impossible, opinionated, argumentative, warm and loving bit of you.'

'Oh.'

'So might you consider drinking a glass of wine with me in a public place, and with no expectations from me of coming in for coffee afterwards?'

Better say 'no', Lissa. We all know where that's going to end, and it's definitely a bad idea. A very bad idea.

'Yes,' I said.

'Tonight?'

'Sorry. I've guests arriving at seven.'

'Oh. Right. OK. Another time then.'

'Another time.' I'd have thought of loads of reasons why not by then.

Elsa had paused amongst a cluster of daffodils and was picking up the ones blown over in last night's wind.

'Right. I'd better go. See you, then, Lissa.'

Oh, come on, Lissa! Are you crazy? I mean, it's not as if he's offering marriage. Or even love eternal, most probably.

I gave him a sideways glance. On the other hand...

And what's so bad about love eternal? He's young, gorgeous, and is nice to his relatives. And he has his own pursuits, so he's hardly going to be under your feet all the time, now, is he? Just a good companion when you need one, and a bit of, or, indeed, rather a lot of –

We do make our own stories. And there never is any turning to the last page, or winding to the end, to see if it ends happily and it's OK to carry on. And I hate risks, but haven't I taken them all my life? And I've survived. Whatever life has thrown at me, I've survived.

And who said life was worth living in cotton wool? Personally, I can't imagine anything worse than a lifetime stuck in a castle with people dancing attendance on you hand and foot, and with nothing better to think about than the colour of my shoes for tonight's ball. Nice for a few days, a few weeks, even, but in the long run, just how tedious can you get?

I've well and truly had it with frogs, rats, and the rest of the fairytale menagerie. I got my castle all by myself, and I'm fine.

I took a deep breath.

'But I do have a couple of hours this afternoon,' I said.

'Oh?' He sounded wary. I could see his point: was this an invitation to a bit of wall-bashing, garden espionage, or just plain verbal pummelling?

OK. Deep breath number two. Look, I've not had much practice at this. Never would have dared, until I turned fifty-two. It's not something they exactly take a girl aside at school and tell her how to go about. Well, at least not when I was at school, they didn't.

'You could always come and see my etchings.'

'Your etchings.' He thought I'd lost the plot. He had that tone.

Bugger.

'Mmm. I've lots of them. Although they're not brilliant.' He was looking at me, and there was this gleam in his eye, and I was starting to gabble. 'In fact, some of them are downright ropey. Probably too worn out to be hung out anywhere.'

Oh, just crawl away and die of embarrassment, Lissa.

Mind you, he had somehow manoeuvred himself so close I could feel the warmth coming out through his jumper and in through mine. Which meant his lips were sort of resting on one cheek, just touching the edge of my mouth. Couldn't half make a girl go all –

'Lissa, there is nothing I would like more than to see your etchings.'

'You would?' Elsa was getting closer with her daffodils, which was probably a good thing, because my knees were beginning to shake, and I wasn't about to be responsible for my actions. 'Great.'

He stepped away from me as Elsa came towards us.

'Ready to go home then, Elsa?'

'Yes, thank you, Drys.' Elsa smiled at us, first one, then the other. 'And thank you Lissa, for a lovely day.'

'It's been lovely to have you. You'll have to come again soon.'

'I should love to, my dear. I'm sure Drystan won't mind driving me.'

'Not at all, Elsa. Any time.'

'Bye, Elsa.' I said. 'Bye Drys. See you.'

'See you,' he returned, with just the faintly wickedest of smiles.

Well, and I shot into my castle like nobody's business. Definitely no time for a bath, let alone a tummy-tuck and an extreme makeover.

So I made do with clean sheets and decent underwear. Then I put on the same clothes again. I mean, I wasn't going to show him I'd made an effort. Gives off entirely the wrong message. Might make me look desperate. Always start as you mean to go on: that's the hard lesson I've learnt in this life.

And, anyhow, just because he was coming back didn't mean we had to get up to anything, twenty-first century, or not. We could discuss solar panels. Gardening. Aromatherapy. And share a nice cup of tea until my guests were due to arrive.

In fact, perhaps better if we stuck to the cup of tea routine. I mean, isn't it best to get to know one another? Well, yes, I do know we know one another. Really rather well, when it comes down to it. But that's not the same. And anyhow –

The door bell rang. I'd been so busy wittering myself into a right old panic I hadn't heard the Land Rover.

'Coming!' I called, giving my hair a last brush, and sailing down the stairs. Oh, what the hell. Just who am I kidding? You don't think I'll be able to keep my hands off him for a moment, do you? And after that kissing session in the snow, with the steam rising above us, well I rather think that neither will –

It was the motorbike that caught my eye. A big, black, What-a-Man-am-I type motorbike, gleaming in the first rays of sun.

Drys?

Nice thought, *cariad*, but you've absolutely nothing to prove to me.

The rider, resplendent in black leather, removed his helmet, slowly, tantalisingly, shaking out his black locks – a little thin on top, maybe – so that they rippled down to his shoulders. He swung one leather-coated leg over his gleaming motorised stallion, landing firmly on his leather boots.

And there he stood, on my gravel drive, with the peacocks creating no end of fuss around him, smiling at me.

Eyes dark, I-have-come-for-you-to-sweep-you-away-to-eternal-bliss-(just not too far from your castle)-and-won't-take-no-for-an-answer type smile on his face.

Diawl uffern dân.

'Hello, Lissa. Long time, no see,' he said.

Yes, my castle had gone international, all right.

In the distance, I could just make out the roar of an engine as a Land Rover turned in at my gate and began to make its way up my drive.

Oh.

My.

God.

'Raphael?'